PICASSO'S ENVY

Pamiela Berenson

First published 2024 by Pamiela Berenson

Produced by Independent Ink
independentink.com.au

Cover design by Catucci Design
Edited by Victoria Steele
Internal design by Independent Ink
Typeset in 12/17 pt Garamond Premier Pro by Post Pre-press Group, Brisbane

ISBN 978-1-7637276-0-1 (paperback)
ISBN 978-1-7637276-1-8 (epub)
ISBN 978-1-7637276-2-5 (kindle)

To Alf

Vourkari — Kea

Korissia — Kea

Prologue

It's starting again. The thing I call my 'frozen moment.' I've not experienced it in years; now it's back. And it's driving me crazy. What does it mean?

This thing begins with a stillness, like the freezing of a movie frame. Nothing moves. Birds stop mid-flight. Sounds hush. Then a tingling hits my body. Pin pricks of electrical charges pulse through my fingers and feet. My skin burns.

Then, in a flash, it's gone.

Have minutes passed or just seconds?

As far as I can tell, it started when I was around five years old. I'd been playing with the toy motorboat my Uncle Terry gave me; his second of these gifts and much more elaborate than the first. To me it was like the Royal yacht, the one the Queen of England might sail on. I imagined dining on it, being waited on hand and foot.

One day I must have over-wound the toy's key. Where the boat usually bumped against the low plastic wall of the paddling pool in our garden, the over-winding sent it flipping, spinning crazily onto the grass, then bounced and crashed into the rock wall beyond. Upside down, it whizzed furiously, then abruptly stopped.

I was heartbroken.

PART ONE

One

1969

In dread I sat waiting. Prim, elegant, anxious, with my knees pressed tightly together. Not only for etiquette but to stop the trembling. Our beautiful lounge room was spacious and comfortable; its bay windows framing views that stretched across established trees to glimpses of the sea. I sat and waited for the return of my parents from their shopping trip.

My mother was on a mission for last-minute items for that evening's big event. My father was the carry-horse. He was always happy to help, in return for a chance to forage in the hardware store. The party was to announce my engagement to Clive. Apart from Clive and his family, only my parents knew. I suspect our friends guessed.

My fingers involuntarily tangled and untangled in my lap. At twenty-one, I was about to speak up for the first time in my life.

Annabelle Theodora Lagoudakis, you're quite pathetic sitting here waiting to be reprimanded.

The front door opened and I heard my parents walk to the kitchen to unpack the shopping. My mother made tea, then came through to the lounge room carrying the tray.

As always, she was immaculately dressed in a dusty pink, light wool twin set, pressed beige slacks and dark brown pumps. Her neat, hair-sprayed bob, flawlessly coloured honey-blond, framed her symmetrical face. You never knew who you would meet at the shops, she always said. It was best to be prepared. She was still a looker and caught the eye of many.

"Darling, there you are. I thought you were going to prepare the dessert for tonight? It's not done."

My father George filled the doorway. His thick, dishevelled, lightly grey-dusted hair, crowned a strong-jawed, bony face with a distinctive straight-bridged nose. A profile both my brother Peter and I had inherited.

In contrast to my mother, my father wore dungarees and an old green check shirt, washed pale. He had retrieved this shirt many times from the throw-out bag. His rolled sleeves exposed strong, muscular, brown arms and hard-worn hands. His impossibly tatty brown leather boots, with never a lick of polish, were my mother's continual headache. She had attempted to clean them once, only to have them snatched in the nick of time by my suspicious father when he smelt shoe polish.

"Lucy, you have free reign with most things, but not my boots."

I loved that about my father. My mother had long ago given up trying to dress him respectably, to match their standing in society. There was little my mother could say, as her husband was adored by everyone, despite his careless attitude. To put it mildly, he had buckets in the charisma department.

As I grew into my teens and understood such things, I was sure there could have been opportunities for him to stray. I doubted he ever did. By the time he married my mother, ten years his junior, after a whirlwind romance, he'd presumably sown his wild oats. She was a stunning woman and with all that considered, he loved her for who she was. More than that, he adored her. She was everything he was not. I'm sure for her, it was hard work keeping him under control for appearances' sake. He'd told me once that, through my mother, he'd discovered a different meaning to life. One of solid foundations and family. One of love and trust. He'd not understood that before.

"Come on dear," said my mother, "why are you sitting around like that, there's …"

"Mummy … daddy," I quickly interrupted, "I'm not getting engaged. I'm taking a year off to travel."

My rehearsed speech – tactful, respectful of their plans for me, and carefully introduced to ease my mother's pain – came completely unstuck. In a few words, my good intentions had fallen into a pit and I'd done the opposite.

Lucy Lagoudakis stopped in her tracks. Holding the tea tray, she began to wobble.

"What?"

My father took the tray.

"No … no … don't repeat it," my mother said hurriedly. Relieved of her burden, she sat opposite me.

"You're being impetuous again, Annabelle dear. Or has Clive called it off?"

Of course, it would be Clive who'd made the decision. My mother was good at diminishing me, albeit unintentionally. Life was mapped for me from day one. Why would I detour from that of my own accord? I was brought up to be a good girl, follow the protocols of society. Meaning, I must always listen to others, be respectful of their wishes, and therefore have no mind of my own.

"No mummy, he hasn't. I'm calling it off. No … I'm not calling it off, I'm delaying it. Now I must go and tell Clive." I moved to leave.

"He doesn't know? How could you do that to him?"

"Mummy, I wanted to tell you and daddy first." I sat. "I thought that would be the right thing to do. I ... I want to feel what it's like to know what I'm made of, good and bad. Just a year ... to explore myself."

"What rubbish is this? Such a ridiculous idea, I can barely fathom you're saying it. To throw away everything we've done for you, everything we've given you. All the sacrifices we've made. To just toss it away like ... like ... a bag of unwanted clothes."

"Mummy ... I'm coming back. I'll be the person you expect me to be. I'll do all the right things." I couldn't think for a minute what they were. "Um ... like I'll play tennis ... we'll get married, have children. I'll be a good wife, support Clive, do all the things expected of me."

"What about your job? You have an enviable position as an executive secretary in a law firm. Not something to scoff at. You're throwing that away too?"

"When I get married, mummy, I'd have to leave anyway."

"For a perfectly good reason. We'll not have it, Annabelle. Will we, George?"

She turned to eye him. He stood in the doorway, saying not a word.

She continued, "And risk losing Clive. Yes, tossing him away like old clothes too."

"I'm not. I'm not doing that." I slumped on the sofa.

My straight back, along with my courage, had wilted.

"As you've not told Clive of this ridiculous plan," my mother carried on, "there's no reason he should ever know. You'll dismiss this idea now and get on with helping with the party. Your party." She made to stand. "I expect your period's due," she muttered under her breath.

"I've booked and paid for my passage, on the ship, the *Canberra*."

"What?" she said and sat.

"It's docking at Southampton. Peter's meeting me. I'm going to stay with him for a bit."

"What? Your brother's in on this too? All my energy in bringing you up to be a caring, honourable young woman and you go behind my back ... you've turned into a deceitful girl, Annabelle. Deceitful!"

My mother stormed off upstairs, where she'd take a Bex and throw herself on the bed.

I turned to my father. "I really have to go and tell Clive."

My father remained silent, but I saw him smile as he took the tea tray into the kitchen. I had a friend.

Two

Outside Clive's house, the courage I thought I'd garnered wavered, paper thin as it was. I'd rehearsed the speech again, but judging by my performance for my parents, I didn't hold out much hope of sticking to the script. I knocked on the door.

"Oh, you're going out?" I said.

Clive stood at the door, immaculately casual in his pressed taupe slacks, un-scuffed, polished, brown leather shoes and short-sleeved, check sports shirt. I looked at him and realised I'd never really seen him before. About to make the biggest announcement of my life, and I'm looking at the man I'm to marry, as if for the first time. Did he always dress so perfectly? His sloping shoulders he usually disguised with a well-tailored jacket. The rest of him was slim, sport-strong and tallish. Not as tall as my father, but a respectable height for a man. His barber kept his fine, thin, light brown hair in the tidy style of the day. Yes, he was a man on the ladder to success. The reason my mother liked him so much.

"Yes ... but it's okay. I have a few minutes. Come in. What's up?"

We sat in his family's perfect, neat and comfortable lounge room, on a soft, squashy sofa with cushions to match.

My hands twisted in my lap again.

"Clive … I'd like to delay the engagement for a year. This time next year."

"Okay," Clive said, unruffled. His controlled composure uppermost. "And the reason?"

"I'd like to delay the engagement for a year."

"You said that. And?"

"I … um … need a year to … um … learn about myself. I need to go overseas, stay with my brother, see a bit of the world. Then I'll be okay to get on with my life, be your wife."

Clive smiled. "Been reading those women's magazines again, eh? What makes you think you'll be okay by then? And what makes you think I'll wait, Annabelle?"

"I'm hoping you will."

"So, I won't be announcing our engagement at the party?"

"No. I don't suppose so. But it won't make any difference. There will be a party. We don't always need a reason to have a party."

Privately I thought we could turn it into my farewell, but the moment wasn't right.

"Apart from finding out about yourself; any other reasons? Finding out how other men feel, could that be another? Do it away from home, so no one knows?"

Other men. I hadn't consciously thought of that.

"No, Clive. I need space to find out what I think."

"What's got into you? Last week you were talking about our wedding day, the house we'd buy, children we'd have. What happened between then and now?"

"No, Clive. Last week you were talking about the practice, how you hoped to become a partner before we married, earn a bigger salary to buy a good-sized house. How it would equal the Whites' or better. How I wouldn't need to work anymore, which would give me time to be a housewife and a mother."

"And all for you, our future, Annabelle. You have just walked in here and thrust this at me. No warning."

"I have hinted at wanting to see the world, or some of it, before settling down. I'm not sure you listened."

"I presumed it was a lavish honeymoon you were after. I'm capable of providing a good life for you Annabelle, but a year's honeymoon is beyond my means right now."

"Not a honeymoon, Clive. This is something I want to do for me. Perhaps I didn't express myself clearly enough. Just one year. You will then have the perfect wife for the rest of our lives."

"How selfish you are. I didn't know this side of you before.'

"I'm sorry it appears to be selfish and short notice. It's a shock, I know. I had to tell my parents first, my mother. To be honest, I was terrified."

"And how did she take it?"

"I came straight over here, so I'm not sure."

"So, it's not just me you don't care about."

"I do care. I care that I don't know who I am. What I think. Only what other people have told me to think. What's proper. I don't have a mind of my own."

"What is this rubbish? Mind of your own. Who else's do you think it is? You've been reading some self-help trash. Those stories are just someone you don't know, telling you how to live."

He had a point, but I hadn't read any story or self-help articles. Well maybe a little. But how I felt was all my own work. I knew that much. I knew that I wasn't sure how I felt about a lot of things.

"Clive, we talked about whether to get engaged this year or next, and if you waited, you would be in a better position at the law firm.

Well, now you will be. It was your thought, initially." Clive liked to make the decisions and I let him. Well, wasn't that what women were supposed to do? Support?

"You had no objections, if I remember."

"That's my point, Clive, I don't object, I don't express my wishes as I don't know them. You talked yourself out of the extra year, saying it wouldn't really make that much difference, financially."

"And you expect me to wait? What am I expected to tell our friends? How will that look?"

"Do they know we were to announce our engagement?"

"Not officially. But I expect they guessed."

Before I could say more, he said he had to go. We'd discuss it later.

"Clive ... I'm booked on the ship the *Canberra* which leaves in a month."

Clive glared at me. "I've been doing everything for you. Building a future for you. Do you love me, or have you been looking at the meal ticket?"

"Thank you, Clive. You've just made it easier for me. But I hope you'll wait."

He held the door open for me to leave and walked out behind me.

"See you later," he said.

He stormed off. I couldn't blame him. I'm sure I could have handled it differently. That's the thing. I could have asked my mother or my father, the best way to tell him, and I hadn't.

Two people I'd upset. How many more to go?

Three

If I was to go travelling, I had to start thinking for myself. Perhaps I was about to make many mistakes. It's said that's the only way to learn. I was sure I was in for a big learning curve. I had no guidelines on how to live my life, except within the confines of my small pond. Before I even needed to ask, my mother had always told me what to do. My father was there for a soft landing.

When I returned home from Clive's, I found my father sitting in the lounge room, reading the newspaper. He took one look at me, held out his hand and sat me down. He listened, while I burbled through my doubts and reasons for my decision.

"Daddy, you won't remember, as you would have been at work, but when I was a toddler, I used to help mummy with the washing. I remember my tiny, chubby hands trying to hold and pass her the pegs. I loved helping her with the washing. I loved to listen to her talking, telling me about myself. I didn't understand then, but she was mapping out my life, peg by peg." I stopped for a moment.

"I continued to help her, until I was at school. I've realised, as I've grown older, her words were instructions explaining what I would do each year. What a wonderful life I would have. The right school. The right job, to meet the right man. Have my own delightful children and live in a grand house. She used to say, 'You'll be the apple of my eye, my darling'. She told me how cute I looked with my big blue eyes. The cute way I had of turning my head up and smiling. 'Men will weaken. This is important to know. It will be a useful tool later in life,' she said.

My father listened, let me talk. He gave me a handkerchief to blow my nose.

"Daddy, I learnt to hate hanging out the washing."

"You might have to get over that if you're going travelling and intend to have clean clothes," he laughed.

My father never said a word against my mother. He loved her and would never be disloyal. He knew her melodramas and loved her all the same. He was also aware of her controlling attitude. He would call my mother over and give her a hug, diplomatically explaining she'd gone too far. As I grew older, I noticed the inter-action between the two, understood it more. My father had a large, generous personality, but only let her stretch the elastic of his life so far. My mother occasionally overstepped those boundaries. She felt his power underneath his joviality and easy-going demeanour. Another aspect I loved about him. When I had exhausted my self-indulgent whimpering, he spoke.

"I believe I know how you feel, Bellie. I support what you plan to do. There's nothing like seeing the world when you're young. There's a naive bravery in it. It's all new and exciting. Right now, the world has come out of its post-war gloom and is on the road to recovery. An exciting world, full of people like yourself and your brother, taking it on. I will worry about you, but I'll be there any time you need me, just a reverse-charge phone call away."

We both laughed, as my sniffles dried and I breathed. With my father on my side, I could handle anything.

"I'm so excited, daddy. The ship is sailing across the Indian Ocean and on through the Suez Canal, with several stops on the way. I've got my passport. It's all new and shiny. I've been saving for ages. You wouldn't let me pay rent, so I've saved a lot of money. I know mummy will be cross I didn't put my savings into a trousseau and towards a honeymoon, but ... well I had to do this. It's what I want."

"For a year, you say. You'll need to work. What will you do?"

"Pete says, there's plenty of temp secretarial work around in London. I can work there for a bit. Stay with him, help pay his rent. Once I've figured out what's going on, I'll go travelling in Europe. And, hopefully, make my way to Greece, to the Greek Islands. To your island, if you ever tell me what it's called."

My father smiled. "Good. You seem to have a focus. We just need to convince your mother that you'll be all right."

Getting a job had been easy in Sydney. Once I'd been to university and with my partly completed legal degree, I found a job in a law firm as a legal secretary for one of the partners. I wasn't particularly interested in law, my preference would have been an arts degree. Art history particularly interested me. But my mother had convinced me it was one of the degrees where I'd meet the right sort of man. She was right. That's where I met Clive shortly after I started at uni. I'd learnt to type for my assignments, so I was all ready to go as a secretary. Jobs were plentiful. I had my pick.

My brother Peter escaped my mother's clutches early. He left the country when he was nineteen and moved to London. Although it had been necessary for him to register for national service, he'd missed the birthday ballot callup to enlist in the war raging in Vietnam.

I looked at my father sitting there on the sofa next to me. He'd lived a life before he married my mother. He never talked about it, and I felt there was a story back there, somewhere. He was my adorable, mighty father, whatever he'd done. The big loving bear who could handle whatever life threw at him. Whatever he'd done, it couldn't be that bad, but I suspected a bit of naughtiness. He had a humorous twinkle in his eye.

"Why didn't you speak to me before, Bellie? When you were planning this?"

"I was worried you'd talk me out of it. I knew I had to do this for myself. I've been thinking about it for ages, but the final decision came upon me quickly. If I didn't act right away, I'd lose my courage. I may never have another chance, daddy. Once I'm married, that will be the end of my chance at free thought."

"That sounds a bit dramatic, but you might be right in the way you see it. But we could have planned this together, Bellie, just you and I."

"Daddy, that's exactly it. I want to do this myself."

"Yes of course. I'm doing the same as your mother, aren't I?

"Mmm ..." I nodded. "Besides ... it would have been disloyal to mummy. For you, I mean."

My father didn't answer, just chucked me under the chin.

"I'm twenty-one, daddy. You must have been out in the world at that age."

"Well, I'm a man and times were different. War had a big impact on everyone and everything."

"What pushed me into action, was when Clive showed me the engagement ring. I don't like it." My father laughed. "It was his grandmother's and has been passed on down. I had to pretend it was lovely. He said he'd have it resized. 'Your finger is bigger than grandma's,' he said. I didn't say anything. Just accepted that was to be my engagement ring. My fate was sealed. I couldn't even stand up to him and tell him I wanted to choose my own engagement ring."

"Bellie, part of having your own opinion means you will face opposition."

"Yes, I know."

The house was quiet.

"Where's mummy?"

"She's upstairs. She took a Bex, said she had to lie down. She'll be all right. It was a shock. Shock to me too, but if you promise not to tell your mother, I'm glad you've decided to do something for yourself. I'm glad to see you have it in you to buck the trend. Good for you, Bellie. It's better this way, than bolting at the church."

My turn to laugh. "Yes, I suppose so, I hadn't thought of that. Clive might like to know that."

My father put his finger to his lips. "Better left unsaid."

Four

At a get-together at home with my girlfriends, one Saturday after-noon, shortly after the non-engagement party, I announced I was going overseas. Beyond Clive and my parents, no one knew.

"You're going away with Clive before you're married?" Very modern, everyone agreed.

"No, I'm going on my own, for a year."

"What?"

"What about Clive?"

"Just a year," I said. I didn't give the speech about wanting to know who I was. "I'm staying with Peter in London when I arrive. I've booked a passage on the *Canberra*. It leaves in just under a month." Their collective looks of disapproval prompted me to say, "It's just one year. Besides, Clive wants to put all his efforts into creating a career, which we think will take about a year."

I'd done it again. Found an excuse for my actions, lost the courage to give the real reason.

"I can't believe Clive is letting you go."

"If he's okay with that ... then ... well, he's one hell of a guy."

"Don't go getting any ideas, Jenny – Ken's not going to let *you* go."

"So, tell us ... where are you going, apart from London?" Norma said.

"I've always had a dream to go to the Greek Islands, sail around, go to where daddy's family came from."

"The posters in your room are a bit of a giveaway," said Janice.

I laughed. "Yes, my long-held dream. I'd like to take a bus tour or join a group driving through Europe to Greece. Peter tells me that's what's happening now."

"That's so exciting, Annabelle, I wish I had the nerve to do that."

"Me too."

"Well, why don't we all get together?"

"Perhaps we could join you, Annabelle?"

"Yes, let's do that."

I could feel my freedom being wrapped and squeezed.

"Three weeks. Can you be ready in three weeks?"

"Oh, you could delay it, Annabelle. The shipping company would let you change. I know they will. Tilly and Mark changed their trip," said Nicola.

"I'm set ... sorry."

Although my friends started in on me again, I refused to be budged. This was exactly why I'd announced my plans at such short notice.

My father entered our get-together at about this point. My girl-friends loved him and when it was my turn to host, he usually came in and joined us towards the end of the afternoon. He liked women and they liked him. He always enjoyed himself, as my friends mildly flirted with him. After they left, he agreed with my decision to go alone and admired my forbearance not to bend. Again, with my father's backing, I felt strong.

Most of my friends' reactions mirrored my mother's. And in

turn their mothers'. In those last three weeks, my mother's astonishment at my actions continued, taking Bex after Bex to ease her nerves. Tears erupted. The cause – the wrench of her daughter leaving her and what her friends were thinking. How safe was it for me to travel over there? I would be looked on as a loose woman. Did I expect my father to support me? Would my brother be able to put me up for a year? Most of all, and here her face dropped, how disappointed she was. She'd put so much heart and soul into planning my life, her dreams were shattered.

"People have been travelling overseas for a while, mummy. They want to see the world before they settle down. Lots of people are doing it. Annette's going next year."

"She's not engaged to be married. She's probably going to look for a husband, as she can't find one here."

Not a good example, I realised. There was no one else I could actually name, but people were going, I assured her. They wanted to live a little, see some of the world before settling down. Some of my friends were booking a trip to London with plans to travel around Europe, but they were a group and only going for one month. Not an example I could use. There was no instance of someone travelling on their own that came to mind, but then I did have a brother living in London, settled, with a good job.

My mother joined us after my friends left. She'd been lying down in her bedroom again. I had the feeling my father had spoken to her about interfering in my plans. She sat on the sofa with lips sealed, her inner struggle showing in her twisting hands. She couldn't contain herself for long.

"I heard you talking about sailing around the Greek Islands. That's more a honeymoon. Perhaps Clive could join you?"

"Lucy," my father's voice held a warning.

"All right. But I will say, Bellie's always loved sailing." Off-topic, my mother eased her struggle. "Ever since you were tiny ... a fascination with toy boats, it was then. You remember? You played for hours in the paddling pool in the garden, your little fingers barely able to clutch that motorboat your uncle gave you. Off in another world ... pudgy hands and arms splashing about in the water, making waves so the boat tossed about. Your little mouth making all the sound effects for storms and sea chases.

"And what about our Sundays at the beach? Remember, George? Annabelle, you were always so happy to see the ocean. 'Are we there yet? Are we there yet?' Jumping up and down in the back seat ... then as we crested the hill, your little face lit up at the sight of the ocean. Terry said after he'd given you the boat, that you'd probably make a great sailor one day. How he judged that from a toy boat, I've no idea. But he was right."

"Not at all interested in dolls," said my father. "Remember how upset Vera was when you pushed her present aside, after you opened Terry's? Then Terry gave you a bigger boat ... I think it was your eighth or ninth birthday. I thought you'd perish with excitement ... you took it to bed with you."

"Yes, I remember," I said.

I also remembered, that in my mind, it was real. I imagined it life-sized, and I was in it. It wasn't something that was at the end of my fingertips, which were larger by then. One day I'd sail in a boat just like that.

"You were so obsessed with that thing. Sometimes it was like you were in a trance." said my mother. "Do you remember that day? You were happily playing in the pool and then ... what was that, Annabelle? You went a bit strange. Disappeared in your head with a strange look on your face. Like you'd seen something. It was a little scary."

"Yes, I remember. I don't know what it was. It was a strong feeling. I can't put my finger on it even now."

"Annabelle, you're frightening me. George, this is exactly what I mean." My mother was back on track. "You know how Annabelle knows things." She turned to me. "Perhaps you saw something in the future that's going to happen? You shouldn't go. I think we should get your cards read."

"Oh lord, not this again. No, Lucy, she's not going to any mumbo jumbo person. She is her own woman. She's sensible and intelligent. Simply, no, on that subject."

"No, mummy … daddy's right. It was nothing. I was little. It could have been anything. Kids have imaginations. They're meant to." My mother didn't look convinced.

But I did remember that feeling. One of foreboding. I'd almost forgotten about it. I tried to leave it buried, but once the memory was uncovered, it wouldn't go away. I could not put my finger on the reasons for its visitations. It hovered.

Five

As my departure day rolled closer, my mother toyed with anger, pleaded and sulked, but I refused to budge. This was not something I, or my mother, had experienced before. I'd never given her cause.

"Mummy, stop. I'll be fine. You know I will."

"But I'll miss you."

This put the conversation to bed until woken later. I tried comforting her, but my own excitement was too large to fix her worries.

The night before my departure, I heard my mother's tears. My father's deep comforting voice lulling her to sleep. As I lay in bed, I imagined the trip home from the ship's departure. Stepping from the car, my father would hold my mother to stop her collapsing.

My brother's departure had been one of joy and fun. He was a young man and men must broaden their horizons. The only person crying then was me.

My father's own past, I was sure, was sprinkled with misbehaviour, but men were men. It was expected and acceptable. In fact, his knowledge of the world was what guided my mother through hers and smoothed my own turbulence. My mother came to their marriage unblemished. She had not only been a good student of her mother but read the appropriate books and magazines. She knew the unwritten code. It made life so much easier, she told me, knowing how to be a good wife.

My own turmoil started with that toy motorboat incident and plagued me. My joy in bringing the boat to life in our above-ground pool, had me living a life on the ocean. I imagined that life so realistically, that our garden simply disappeared. I sailed on high seas, passing magical islands.

On a very hot day, the water in the pool was higher than usual and, in my enthusiasm, I wound the motor too tight. The boat took off, hit the end of the pool, spun out and crashed into the rock wall. For a split second, the world stood still. Nothing, and I mean nothing, moved. Birds seemingly stopped mid-flight. All noise muted. I felt frozen as if something else controlled me. The intensity didn't last long, maybe seconds, but I couldn't be sure.

I saw my mother take a look at me, but she stayed inside humming a tune to herself.

My uncle fixed the boat and I continued to play, but every once in a while, from then on, I experienced the same sensation. Once I grew out of the toy boat, it ceased.

At the time, my mother eventually saw me and came down the garden to ask if I was all right. I didn't answer. Apparently, I had a strange look on my face. I hadn't heard her approach. Suddenly she was there, questioning me.

"Hello mummy,' I said. "Is everything all right?"

"Where were you, Annabelle? Didn't you hear me calling?"

I hadn't. My mother insisted on taking me to the doctor, although I didn't want to go. I was fine.

"You said it only lasted a minute or so," I said. "I must have been daydreaming."

There was nothing wrong except a child's imagination, the doctor told my mother.

"Could it be a migraine?" she insisted.

"No, but should she suffer other symptoms, bring her back."

So, it was forgotten. Or so I thought, until my mother mentioned it.

Back then, my (or rather my mother's) life's path continued. She was especially pleased when Clive spoke of his career. The legal firm recognised Clive's ambition and assured him his trajectory to seniority was recognised and would be fulfilled in due course. Something I reminded him about when he complained of my travel plans.

"You will be a partner when I get back. With me out of the way, you'll get there faster, Clive. You'll be able to work longer hours without having to worry about me."

"Yes, and who am I supposed to take to social gatherings?" he said.

Clive had another quality. He respected me. Should I have ever mentioned it, my mother would have been delighted. Even after he proposed, he was polite, talked of our future, where we would live. A little foreplay and then he stopped. 'I respect you too much to take advantage of you now, Annabelle.' What a gentleman. Many times, Clive commented about young women who were forward. Even being engaged was no passport. Part of the blessed act of marriage was the first night. A night of discovery for both the bride and groom. That night should be cherished.

Then there was the ring. Clive must have deduced my feelings towards it. I admired its history, its detail, but never its beauty.

Diplomatically, I suggested he hold onto the ring for safekeeping while I was away. It would be too awful to imagine if I lost it. He reluctantly agreed but felt I should wear a replacement ring in the meantime. He presented me with a simple zircon, in a style much more to my taste.

My mother assured me they would keep Clive close, so he felt part of our family.

"Thank you mummy."

No wonder I was suffocating.

Departure day arrived. The ship docked, hugged the wharf in readiness to scoop up eager travellers. After the ship sailed through the Heads, Clive and my friends were to have a party at my parents' house. Partly to console Clive, but particularly for my mother. It would give her something to do. She loved nothing better than organising and entertaining.

Soon I stood at the ship's railings looking down through the streamers, through my tears. My parents and friends stood at the wharf below, crying, waving and cheering. There I had warmth and support. As the ship pulled away, paper streamers snapped. For one split second, I wanted to leap from the ship and join them.

As the sounds grew fainter and family and friends grew smaller, I turned and walked to the highest point of the ship, to watch the spectacle of sailing out of Sydney Harbour.

It was one of those perfect, cloudless, sunny days when everything sparkled.

It was absolutely thrilling.

PART TWO

Six

Once we passed the Heads, I clutched the plan of the ship and traced my way to my cabin where, I was assured, my luggage had been sent. I had paid the second-to-cheapest fare and was to share with three others. Never having even shared a bedroom, what to expect was beyond me.

Small didn't describe the cabin. Compact was too grand a word. A tiny porthole to view the world was far from my long-ago imagination of life onboard my toy motorboat. Having booked the top bunk, this was to be my private space for the next four weeks. The other girls' stuff was spread across every surface. I was yet to meet them, but imagined they were close friends. I found a small shelf, almost bare, in a cupboard and without hesitating, I grabbed it and unpacked.

Laughter opened the door, followed by abrupt silence.

"Oh, hello. Are you in the right cabin?"

"Hi, I'm Annabelle. Yes, I believe so." I showed them my ticket. "My bunk is numbered A."

"Oh, we thought we had the cabin to ourselves. You must have booked late."

"One month ago," I said.

"That would explain it. We booked six months' ago."

I stood looking at them, still waiting for their introductions. Three girls, not sisters but clearly a sisterhood. Similar in height, each with smooth bobbed hair, styled to their jaw line. Mini dresses just above the knee. One neckline bordered with a large round collar, the other two demurely at the neck. Fashionable stripes and small checks. Their hair hurriedly smooth down when they saw me. I didn't know much about body language at that stage, but I felt their bond as they giggled and huddled together.

"Annabelle," I said again.

"Oh sorry, I'm Janet, this is Sissy and Janeen."

A flurry of hellos and stuff being moved, followed.

"Sorry, we didn't realise," was repeated by all three in intercepting moments.

Once space had been cleared, they left. Travelling cabin-light had been suggested, for which I was extremely grateful. Good start, I thought, as I imagined them on deck barrelling into their plans and lamenting my intrusion into cabin life.

My cabin mates were at a different sitting for dinner, so getting to know them was delayed, their accepting of me in limbo.

I didn't dwell on my aloneness and took it as part of the adventure. The journey to London was not my main focus. However, the girls' plans were to enjoy every moment to the hilt. They liked a drink or three and their laughter could be heard along the passageway long before they reached the cabin. One evening, I had just climbed into bed and was about to turn out the light.

"Oooh, hi, Annabelle. We didn't see you after dinner."

"We were looking for you. We haven't had a chat yet."

"We checked out every bar on the ship and ..."

"Yeah, we like them ALL."

Raucous laughter.

Through serious hangovers the following morning, they remembered I'd been laughing with them the night before. I wasn't so stuffy after all. We were about the same age and I realised when girls get together, they decrease in maturity. Suddenly I felt like a matron. If this was to be my trip, so be it. I didn't want disappointment or annoyance to spoil my dream. And I didn't want to spoil theirs. Whatever came my way was part of my year.

The ship sailed through the Suez Canal and I joined the organised trips. We docked in Aden. Small craft gathered around the hull of the ship, bearing their wares. Trinkets, souvenirs and leather goods were on offer. Warned not to buy anything, my cabin mates couldn't help themselves, as the prices were irresistible. A rope and pulley made transactions possible. Money down, goods up. Nothing was hurt except pride when one of the girls opened the box containing a beautiful leather handbag. Unwrapping the tissue-wrapped treasure revealed the bag to be only one side. To add insult to injury, it wasn't even leather but made of an unknown material. Too late, the money and the seller were gone. Back in the cabin, the girls took it in their stride. They fell about laughing. It was to be kept and showcased.

In Egypt, a full day trip to the Pyramids astride camels was a sell-out. We all laughed and wobbled, clinging to the uncomfortable saddles. 'Don't pay until you get to the pyramids,' was the warning.

Inevitably, someone believed the cameleer, when he said, "Pay now, that's rules." The forlorn passenger was dumped, mouth agape, surely wondering what had just happened to him. The cameleer, not stupid, got two rides for one. Ship's personnel were on standby to help the victim, knowing full well someone would get duped.

Naples, Gibraltar – we were getting closer. By this time, the girls had met their shipboard romances and emotions rose when two liked the same man. On occasions, I had the cabin to myself. Another time I shared with one grumpy cabin mate who'd not got lucky.

I planned to stay unencumbered, so wore my replacement engagement ring. I told various stories, including 'My brother needs me in London'.

Finally, finally we arrived in Southampton. With little communication during the trip, I could only trust Peter would be there. He was.

The girls and I disembarked together. Cabin by cabin, deck by deck, the ship disgorged its load. Now I was the one with purpose. The girls rushed me when they saw I'd met my brother.

They swarmed me in a hug. "You've been such a great cabin mate."

"We've loved sharing with you!"

"Have a wonderful holiday."

My brother stood back, smiling, as the girls flounced away.

"I couldn't introduce you, or they'd have asked if they could move in with us," I said when they had gone.

"You certainly made a hit!"

"I'm more shocked than you. That's the first time they've taken much notice of me. I was just part of the furniture. Like a sink or a wardrobe."

I took Peter's arm, my smile as wide as the ocean. "Let's go."

Seven

We took the train to London. Every so often I grabbed Peter's hand in excitement as my eyes scanned the passing scenes. We sped past lush green fields, grazing cows, visible back yards with hanging washing and scattered toys, then sometimes quaint and sometimes grimy towns.

"I can't believe I'm actually here."

"Better than the ship?"

"Oh God, yes. It wasn't bad, just long. The girls in my cabin ... oh my God. I was never invited to join them, thank goodness, as there would have been no refusing. When they came in at night, I was the mama. They left nothing out. More's the pity."

"Well you won't get that from me. I'll censor everything. Can't have my little sister knowing my secrets."

"I promise not to tell mummy anything if you do?"

"Still mummy, eh? Here ... that's very posh. A bit on the nose. Perhaps just plain 'mum'?"

"Okay."

"Same for dad."

"Okay, big brother ... lessons one and two. Will do."

"There's a mountain of letters from home waiting for you."

We left the train and took the underground.

"Are you showing me all of the English transport system?"

"Easiest way to get to my place."

"You don't have a car?" I said.

"Not many people do, living in London. You don't need one, unless you're picking your sister up from Australia."

My brother lived on his own in a tiny bedsit. I was shocked, to say the least. It wasn't much bigger than the cabin I'd just left. I'd pictured him with his good job being able to afford a more salubrious place. "Oh," was all I said.

"Yeah, small, isn't it? I don't usually have my sister to stay. Anyone else shares my bed."

"You've never mentioned a girlfriend. Do you have one?"

Peter grinned impishly. "Yeah, one or two. I'm not ready to settle down yet, Bellie. You'll have my bed and I'll pull out the sofa."

"By the sounds of it, you're not disappointed I won't be staying long, then?"

"Sis, stay as long as you want. I work different shifts, so it'll work out. They gave me tonight off so we can go out to dinner somewhere. I'm on nights this week."

"Nights? What do you mean? Do the offices here work around the clock?"

"Offices? No. I'm a barman and a pretty good one, too."

Well, this was a surprise. "A barman? Do mummy and daddy know this?"

"There you go again, Bellie ... I never said I worked in an office."

"But mummy ... um ... mum and dad think you have some sort of high-powered job in banking."

"I never told them that. I said I dealt a lot with bankers. Which I do. The pub's in the middle of the city. Bankersville."

"You sneaky sod, Pete."

"Well you don't have to tell them."

"No, I won't. Mum would take to her bed with a Bex." And she'd had more than enough of that from me lately.

Pete and I went out to dinner that night, to a local pub. Music was playing, and the place was packed with people speaking in many different accents and languages. The atmosphere was thick with my dreams, all come true. Many of Peter's friends knew I was on my way. I was greeted like *their* long-lost sister.

"Wow, Pete," I said on our walk home. "That was some night. Do you do that every night?"

"Well, I work some nights, so it varies. I don't always get to meet up with that crowd."

"They seemed to be from everywhere. All nationalities."

"That's London. It's a hub."

"You didn't mention travelling, in your letters … have you done much?"

"Not yet. To be honest I've been having too good a time here in London. I've travelled around England, stayed in some nice homes, in picturesque places. The pub, because it's in the city, has a lot of wealthy clientele and I've been invited to their estates for weekends."

"Estates … well aren't we coming up in the world? No wonder MUM got the impression you're doing so well."

"Well, I am. It's just not my money."

There was barely enough room for Pete in his bedsit, so my stuff filled the remaining space. I slept in his lumpy bed and he slept on his 'pull-out sofa'; a grand name for the plank of wood he pulled from under his bed. He piled it with blankets and pillows.

I stared at him. "Really, Pete? Seems I'd better leave quicker than I thought."

"Nah, I'll be fine."

❧

The smell of toast woke me. Hard to miss as it wafted through Pete's entire home. I took the mug of tea he handed me and sat like a queen in his ramshackle bed.

"Wow, I can't believe I slept so well. How could you manage to be so quiet in this tiny space? For heaven's sake, breakfast as well? I may never leave."

The shock at the size of the place hit me again. It was clean enough, compact and managed like a small yacht.

"All that sailing with dad has put you in good stead."

"... and I don't have much stuff," he agreed. "Come on, get up. You've got all this mail to open while I get us some food. You want bacon and eggs?"

"Yeah, great. Where do you cook it?"

Pete whisked away a tea towel and pulled out a small benchtop to reveal two gas rings.

"Voila! I have to put some money in the meter and then we're away."

He showed me the meter he'd named Cyril, the Coin Gobbler. Since he had never described his living arrangements in his letters, a whole new world was cast before me.

Eight

Cramped as it was, I enjoyed spending time with my brother, getting to know him in his London environment. His air of confidence was new – street smart, so it seemed to me. Two weeks after arriving, I was asked if I wanted work at the Ferret and Fox. So, I joined Peter, but my job was collecting glasses. Shortly after I learnt how to pour an English beer. I also collaborated in his half-truths, telling our parents *I'm working close to Peter in the banking district of London.* All true, technically.

My letters home focused on the people I met, life in London, galleries and other places of interest. My father would think what I was doing just fine, but my mother would have had a meltdown if she knew I was collecting glasses in a pub. A pub. What was her daughter thinking? With her qualifications? What would my mother tell her friends? I was being thoughtful in saving her worrisome reports.

In their replies, my mother did the writing, with a postscript from my father saying he loved me and to remember he was there if I needed anything. In the private talk with my father before I left, he had given me strict instructions to ring him reverse charges at his office should I need to. If I rang home, my mother would immediately assume disaster.

On the periphery of Pete's circle of friends, was a Danish guy who drifted in and out of London. I liked him but there was mystery surrounding him. Pete said he was a human rights lawyer and worked all over the place. His home was Copenhagen. My brother couldn't remember how he'd first met him. He was just there. We both liked him, and both felt that mystery although Pete was less concerned than I was.

"He's interested in you, I think, sis."

"Is he married?"

"I don't know, and I don't know if he's engaged either."

"Mmm ... off limits maybe."

"Ha ha, as are you ... I'll find out."

"I'm not interested."

I reminded myself I was engaged.

"Sure, you're not. I notice you've taken your false engagement ring off, all the same."

I stammered to explain myself.

"For heaven's sake, Bellie, I don't care. You've decided to take a year off. Go for it. Don't tell me deep down that part of your adventure wasn't in that area."

"Well ... Clive made a snide comment about that."

"And what did you say?"

"I don't think I answered him."

"There ... go for it. We could have a drink together, the three of us. Once I've checked on his marital status."

For the first time since arriving, I thought about Clive longer than just to read his letters and reply, mainly on postcards. His comment, 'You want to try out other men and then you expect me to take you back?' reverberated. Putting that aside, I told myself I'd just started my year away, what harm would a mild flirtation do?

"Neills. Does he have a surname?"

"I've never asked, sis. Does it matter?"

"No, I guess not. Not here in cosmopolitan London, in any case. Have you known him long? He seems to like you."

"You make it sound so formal. I don't know. He hangs around with the crowd. Yes, I like him. He's easy, interesting, quite funny. He's also quite reserved. Maybe it's a Danish thing. He probably asks me more about my home and family than most around here."

With my mother no longer watching me, I learned to let go and have fun. I needed to lighten up. Life had no formality here except for the unwritten rule, not to be formal.

We didn't see Neills for a while and I wondered when and if he'd be back in London. Parties came and went and during one I met five of Pete's crowd, who were taking off in a Kombi across Europe. They planned to go for a month, maybe two, whatever. I heard them talk about the route they'd take. They'd planned as far as Turkey via Greece. Greece? My ears walked me over to join them.

"That's quite a trip," I said, butting in.

"Yeah, it's going to be tight, but makes it cheaper with petrol and whatever we put into the kitty for food and booze."

"My dream ... sail around the Greek Islands. See a bit of Europe on the way," I said.

"Yeah, it's everyone's ... my name's Wes," He held out his hand. "You're Pete's sister, aren't you? Fresh off the boat?"

"Yes and yes ... I guess so."

"This is Doreen from the Alice. That's how you say it, isn't it, Dor?"

"Yep. Hi. Pete's sister, eh? What's yer name?" said Doreen.

"Annabelle. Hi."

Canadian Wes continued. "This scruffy mug is Scrub and there's Paul and Joanne."

"Hi." They talked on about their trip. "I'm so jealous."

"Keep your ears open. People are doing this all the time. Good luck with it," said Wes.

Pete and I walked back from the party.

"That's exactly what I want to do, Pete."

"Well, like the guy said, people are grouping up all time. I'll keep my ears open. Do you reckon you could do it? It'd be pretty rough going. You'd have to muck in."

"I'm not a china doll, brother dear."

"I'm not so sure, but you've certainly loosened up since you've been here. Something will come up. Or you could join one of the countless companies who do these trips."

"I've thought about that, but I don't want to do the round trip. I'm after one way to Greece."

"I'm sure you could do that too, but in the meantime, I'll keep my ear to the ground."

I didn't have long to wait.

Nine

I continued to collect glasses and pour beers when the Ferret and Fox was short-staffed. My knowledge and liking of the locals grew. I loved it. It still crossed my mind – how my mother would be so crestfallen.

Pete and I continued to keep our ears open for a travelling group.

As chance would have it, a couple of weeks later an offer came from the Kombi group who had been on my mind, as no other trips had surfaced. Joanne had dropped out. Was I interested?

Interested? Are you kidding?

"Do you think they're okay?" I asked my brother, suddenly filled with the reality of it all. "Do you think they'd be okay to travel with? It's an opportunity too good to miss. Shall I go?"

"Sis, for God's sake ... go. You're driving me crazy. They're fine. You'll be fine. And besides, I want my flat back."

At the morning send-off, once we were neatly packed into the van, Pete called out, "Hey sis, don't forget to send postcards. Looking forward to the big slide night when you get back," and smothered an exaggerated yawn.

I waved to Pete until he disappeared, as we rounded a bend in the road. While we drove through London, I looked around the van. I'd seen the inside before but not packed like this. How the hell was this going to work?

"Are you from a big family?" said Doreen, who was squashed in the seat next to me and must have noticed my look. Short and chunky, not fat, more solid. She had rats-tails blond hair, striking blue eyes and a big smile. A diamond I shouldn't wonder, but rough around the edges. Beating around the bush wasn't her style; she asked like she was interested in the answer. She was typical of someone I imagined from Alice Springs in the centre of Australia.

"No, just my brother."

"Big house at home?" she said.

"Um, yes." What was she getting at?

"Going to be an adjustment then."

I looked at her. She was smiling. Checking me out in a friendly way, I hoped.

"You'll soon get used to Scrub's farts in the night," said Wes. "You won't be able to sleep if he lets one go, but at that point I usually chuck him out of the van."

Wes was Canadian, hailing from Calgary, though he hadn't been home for a while. Tall, dark hair, dark eyes that looked directly at you and held the gaze. He apparently was an old hand at the travelling rough game. Seen it all.

"Yeah, well you won't be able to sleep, period, if you happen to get one of Wes's feet in your face," said Scrub.

Scrub, another Australian and about as far removed from my experience of home as a person could get. A lover of anything he did on a surface, be it surfing or snow skiing. He followed the work. No fixed home, apparently, for a very long time.

Wes and Scrub had travelled before. Doreen had been camping with them, on long weekends. Paul and I were the new ones. I was the freshly scrubbed one and no doubt china doll in their eyes. Peter told me they'd asked him as many questions about me as I'd asked about them.

"So, you've not travelled with this lot before?" I said to Paul.

"No. I'm as pure as you. Scary isn't it?"

Paul was a New Zealander. Short, squat, serious. Away for a year, like me and returning to his farm in the South Island, taking a new MG car, duty free, home with him. I didn't know much about farmers, but I felt his honesty and integrity.

"Don't worry, we've kid gloves in the glove box if things get a bit rough," said Wes.

We were a disparate lot. Again, I thought, how the hell was this going to work? United Nations in one Kombi.

By this stage we were out of London and heading to the Dover coast to catch the ferry to Ostend. Once the initial taunting was done, very little talk took place. Idle comments about the country-side, towns, and the weather of course, which was cloudy and cold. We talked of summer and what it meant. Wes was used to the cold. Too much heat made him anxious. Doreen was good with the heat and the cold.

"It can get pretty damn cold on winter nights."

Paul also knew cold, but he liked the heat of the sun. Dry heat – the humidity wilted him. Scrub wasn't concerned with the weather, just if the conditions were right for him to earn a living. He was an instructor in both his two passions: skiing and surfing. I guessed in time I'd learn why he was called Scrub.

"And before you ask," Scrub said, "no I'm not on the wrong trip. I'm just doing something different."

He knew the others socially and had camped a day here and there with Wes. Although curious, if he wanted to keep his desires private, that was his business.

We'd all been asked to pitch in with running money and I presumed we were all square. Driving, like all other tasks, was to be shared.

Ten

During a quiet spell while we drove on, I found myself thinking of Neills, the Danish guy, who popped in and out of London. He'd come into the pub one day and was surprised to see me collecting glasses.

"Bit of pocket money before my trip," I'd said to his questioning look.

"Oh ... I see. Where are you going?"

"To Greece, via Europe."

"Via Europe? That's a big call. There's a lot to see in Europe."

"I know and impossible to see it all. I'm being very shallow, skimming the surface. I'll see more later. I'm joining a group of others in a Kombi."

"Ah ha, the traditional run for Australians."

"I guess so."

Peter wasn't working that day or night, so the three of us planned to catch up later for dinner. During my break, while the pub was shut for its midday customary closure, Neills and I went for lunch. I was abuzz with anticipation. I'd really become interested in him, but he had boundaries, extensive ones. This kept me thinking he

was married, or at least engaged. I didn't like the idea of an affair –
but if he was single, that was different. I was definitely attracted.

"So why Greece?" he asked after we had ordered our meals.

"I've always wanted to go, sail around the Greek Islands."
I paused as he sat looking at me. "I know. A favourite haunt of
Australians," thinking that was on his mind, "but it's been some-
thing I've dreamed of doing for a very long time."

"And thousands of other nationalities too. I just wondered why
for you. You sound very definite."

"I have big posters on my wall at home ... photos of the Greek
Islands and a map. I've also read heaps of history books about them
and any fictional book that's set there. Maybe I'll get it out of my
system once I go. My father's Greek as well, so that may be a pull.
He's lived in Australia a long time, though."

"Tracing family history?"

"Maybe."

"Peter tells me you're more or less engaged."

"Um yes, although not officially."

"No ring I see. Unless you've taken it off?"

Before I could answer, he went on.

"You say 'not officially'. Do you plan to get engaged, officially,
when you get Greece out of your system?"

His questions were direct, too direct, and they jolted me. Once
I was over the shock, I felt comfortable with his directness. He
seemed genuinely interested, with no agenda. It felt refreshing.

After thinking hard about what I really wanted, I simply replied,
"That's the plan."

"You've never been to Greece?"

I shook my head. "No. I don't think my father's been back either.
In fact, I'm sure he hasn't."

"Why's that?"

"I don't know. I've never asked him. He's been building a life in Australia, I expect."

Neills could jump on me, but I wasn't having him jump on my family.

"What about you? Have you been to Greece?" I said.

"Of course. Every European in their right mind has been to Greece."

Of course, they had, I thought.

There was a brief silence, then he added, "I have a good friend who I sail with in the Greek Islands. His father owns a yacht. Not a particularly big one, but she's beautiful. My friend and his father built it in memory of his grandfather. They are both carpenters by profession. Laars, my friend, designs and makes furniture. They often invite me to sail with them."

His talk faltered. As if he'd not discussed it before.

"That's a lovely thing to do. Build a boat in commemoration of someone."

We sat for a while, eating, not talking.

"I sail," I added. "My father taught both Peter and me. Mostly around Sydney Harbour and further, on holidays."

"Does your father own a boat?"

"Not anymore. We didn't go out so much once Peter left home. Daddy said it was just becoming a money drain, so he sold it."

Ooops, did 'daddy' matter to a Dane?

My obsession with the Greek Islands was finally coming to life. And here was a man who lived my dream. Just an ordinary thing for him. I was a little spellbound, I have to admit.

Neills had a beautiful voice and with his accent, I found him fascinating. And he was good looking. There was something familiar about his look, something that made me feel comfortable that I couldn't put my finger on.

Perfect bloody timing, Annabelle, now you're going away. I guess he knew he was having this effect on me. Perhaps he was used to women falling for him. I shook myself out of it.

"Great story. You're a lucky chap … I have to get back to work now."

The café was only a few minutes' walk from the pub, and I sauntered off. I needed to grab some air. Neills's intensity and directness affected me. Like I said, he was at the same time familiar and foreign. I couldn't explain it. I needed to talk to Pete about it. Pete was good at unravelling emotions – he'd unravelled enough of his own.

At dinner, Pete's presence created an easy-going atmosphere. The intensity was gone. Neills seemed more relaxed, even though he did speak of parents quite a bit. Although not his.

When we got home, I asked Pete to tell me more about Neills.

"Sis, I don't know. He's okay, but we're not close. I get the feeling he doesn't let anyone get too close."

"That's my impression too. Friendly, yet distant. You said he's single, but maybe he has a girlfriend?"

"Don't know sis, never seen one. Anyway, your interest is a bit pointless, isn't it? You're going away, remember?"

"Yeah. Guess I'll never know or get any closer."

Eleven

Wes shook me out of my reverie. "Not far now. We'll have a look around Dover. Stay the night there. All okay with that?"

"Couldn't we stay the night the other side, in Ostend? We'd be on our way then," I said.

"It might be bit late by then," said Wes.

"I'm with Annabelle," said Doreen. The others agreed.

We hadn't even spent a night and we were changing the itinerary. I wondered who had made the initial decisions. I'd put myself in good standing, it turned out, by speaking up.

Prior to leaving, we had decided to draw up a rough itinerary, which could be changed to suit. Flexibility was big on the agenda, provided there was a majority and the minority was listened to. We also prepared for arguments. As soon as one lay in the wings ready to pounce, someone would start singing *Satisfaction* by the Rolling Stones. No one knew all the words, which made it funnier. Everyone knew the chorus. Improvisation helped the humour. It was a whole three days before we needed to activate the song. It worked. Laughter bubbled, then exploded.

After Belgium, the rough plan was to go to the Netherlands, Germany, through Luxembourg and into France. Zigzagging our way, we decided to drive into Spain.

Our first fight started in Holland. The girls against the boys, who weren't pulling their weight with the cooking. Into Germany and the boys again weren't pulling their weight with the cleaning. Good humour was hard to find.

Wes was deciding our route.

"Who made you the boss, Wes?" said Scrub.

"Well, you fuckers aren't making any suggestions."

Wes had to stop the van when internal turbulence became beyond bad. Reenie (Doreen's nickname by then) took over the driving.

"I'm naming the van Poppy. Anyone care to come up with a better name?"

No one was in the mood to carry on the conversation, so Poppy it was. Entering France, the gender wars really took off.

"Who packed? The cutlery's falling everywhere."

"I'm doing all the driving, someone else has to pitch in!"

"I'm sick of finding disgusting socks in with the pots and pans" ... blah blah blah.

But we were soon distracted from petty squabbling.

"Hey ... these German guys have great bums. But so do the Dutch and Belgian guys," said Reenie.

I agreed. The two of us started a bum-rating game. Scrub was driving at the time. We were travelling along a country road as Reenie and I were discussing size and shape, when Scrub pulled over, leapt from the van, pulled down his daks and slapped his bare arse. He then yanked his pants up and clambered back into the van.

"Now shut it, girls. I've got the best arse. I've been told that."

"Wooohooo," we swooned.

The atmosphere in the van changed after that and laughing and singing the latest song kept us from killing one another.

Although classical stuff like galleries, museums and cathedrals were on the sightseeing list, local culture and observations were right up there. But I did manage to see some serious art, albeit on my own.

"Personally, I've died and gone to heaven," said Scrub. "The women here totally knock me out." He went to heaven everywhere we went.

As we entered Spain, our squabble song suddenly stopped working. I've no idea what it was about, but Scrub and Wes got into a furious barney.

"You can fuck off back to England ... or, better still, Canada," said Scrub.

"Hitchhike, then swim to England. You're so bloody skilled at everything, I'm sure you can do it," said Wes.

The fight was so serious that it threatened to end the trip. Wes and Scrub had been squabbling for a few days when it reached its peak. I didn't want us to break up. Life was difficult in such cramped conditions, but we were still miles from Greece. This could be resolved, I felt sure.

As I was driving, I pulled over, leapt from Poppy, and stood by the side of the road with my hands on my hips.

"Stop. You're both being childish ... acting like politicians."

I had no idea about that, but my father said it often enough. Reenie was right beside me. She was Reenie from the Alice.

"Stop it, you mongrels. There are more than just the two of you. There's five. Fit in or fuck off, both of you."

Paul clambered out and joined us, leaving Wes and Scrub in the van. They stopped briefly in shock but continued. Their one-eyed anger got them out of the van and then the fight began in earnest. I watched in disbelief. Paul was about to intervene, when Reenie said, "Leave them to it, Paul." Although Paul was built like a brick shithouse, he was smaller than Scrub and Wes and those two had serious fury on their side.

The occasional passing car's occupants yelled comments in Spanish, but no one stopped. Fortunately. Gradually the fighters slowed down. Bruised, they staggered away, finally collapsing on the grass by the side of the road.

"Do we want to take a vote right now?" said Paul. "We can end the trip here, but I for one, want to keep going. I don't want to go through the breaking-in period with another lot."

We all flopped in the grass, waiting for the two fighters to decide.

"Are you two going to shake hands?" I said.

"Fuck off," said Scrub. Then rolled over to Wes. "Fuck it ... okay."

"Fuck it double." Wes did the same. "You're still an arsehole."

"Not as big as you, you prick," said Scrub.

"For chrissakes ... shut it," said Reenie. They did.

We kept going and made it along the Riviera into Italy, unscathed and intact. The squabble song was dropped and never used again. Although tender and battle-weary, our group relationship had reached a deeper level. We were bonded now from serious highs and similar lows.

Much later, someone brought up the subject of the fight. Reenie put her hand out like a traffic warden. "Stop. We are not going there ... ever."

We stood in obedience like naughty children. She was right and we didn't.

As we travelled this way and that, through Europe towards Greece, my antipodean innocence, as someone called it, fell away incident by incident. When sleeping at camp sites became too much, we splashed out on pensiones and cheap hotels.

One day we'd pulled over for a pee. When we climbed back in, Poppy refused to start.

"She's had enough," was the general consensus.

We were in remote Yugoslavia. It was dark with heavy clouds, inching to evening when it started to pour. Miles from anywhere. There was nothing else to do except sleep inside the van.

To ease the pain, we drank all the alcohol left in our supplies. The more we drank, the more love poured from our hearts.

"I loves you all really ..."

"Me too."

"Hate the lot of yous."

"Nah, come on, you're all a pack of fuckers, but I loves yas."

"It's ya farts I can't stand."

"Me too."

And on and on. Come morning we stumbled, one after the other, into a bright sunny morning, onto damp grass, cradling aches and cramps and hangovers. Scrub volunteered to walk to the nearest village to get help. We watched him stagger up the road and wondered if it was the last time we'd see him. But no, Scrub must have used his charming side; he brought back a mechanic.

The oil-spattered chap had not a word of English and we, non-existent Serbo-Croat. He was cheerful until he looked inside Poppy. Muttering oaths, he got back in his car and drove off.

"What the fuck do we do now?" said Wes.

We decided there was nothing to do but wait. Sometime later, the mechanic returned. Still muttering, clearly swearing with the odd universal 'fuck' thrown in, he fixed our van. We gathered he thought our beloved Poppy was a pile of shit. He had no problem charging us as if we were millionaires. We were at his mercy, as he held the keys, and before Wes got stuck into him, we paid. Poppy ran better than ever.

Despite the inconvenience, arguments and discomforts, I could not have chosen a better way to burst my well-brought-up and protected bubble. On the journey, I met people from all walks of life and nationalities, many of whom spoke no English. I became adept at mime. I was building a confidence I didn't know I lacked.

A shift in world view at this time, the end of 1960s, was bringing in a new movement and hitting the Western world in a hurry. The stuffy old barriers of morality were crumbling and the new were forming. Life became an experiment for those on its threshold.

Despite all the sexual freedom sloshing around, no dalliance ever occurred amongst the van's inhabitants. I think we all appreciated that there were enough tensions already. Scrub disappeared for a couple of days when we'd decided to stay put. We thought we might have to leave without him. On day three of his disappearance, he staggered 'home' with a leery grin. No one asked. He didn't tell.

I met a lone traveller, an American guy, who appealed, but the meeting was fleeting. It was amazing, given how much time we all spent together, how little I knew about my van mates' lives. I knew their habits, their idiosyncrasies, their moods, but not what they did back in the real world. I knew Paul was a sheep farmer, Reenie a nurse. I had a sketchy idea Wes had something to do with the oceans; that is, life beneath the surface. Whereupon Scrub would pipe up saying he lived on the surface, enjoying the waves. He probably spoke more than most, when he did get talking passionately about some of the great breaks he'd experienced. An unwritten code had formed in which we silently and unanimously decided to leave our lives behind, to be picked up later, or not. And what went on in the van, stayed in the van.

Twelve

Reminders of my life back home came in gulps, as we approached any city – time to pick up postcards and letters. We always headed straight for the Poste Restante. Pete was forwarding my mail from London. We tried to keep to our itinerary, time wise, just so our mail was waiting for us. Poste Restante offices held mail for a month.

For Reenie and Paul and myself, the news was quite old by the time we read it. Probably more so for Reenie. Her mail had to travel from Alice Springs to a major city before even leaving Australia.

We all dived into our letters, but Reenie soon noticed that I always hesitated opening one.

"Who's that from?" she said in her direct manner.

"Clive."

"Oh ... okay."

"Why?"

"You're keen to open the rest but hesitate over that one."

"Do I?"

"Yep," said Wes.

"Bloody hell, is there no privacy around here?"

After a minute or two, I realised my annoyance was due to my guilt, not their nosey parkering.

"One day, young lady, you'll get a 'Dear Annabelle, I've met someone else'. That'll make you think."

"Shut up, Scrub," said Reenie. "She's in enough turmoil."

"Shut up, the lot of you," I snapped.

Although I'd never discussed my private life, they'd deduced my situation too bloody accurately. The truth was, I'd thought more of Neills than I had of Clive.

The next day after mail reading, Reenie again noticed how absent I'd become.

"Come on Bell, live today. Let the future take care of itself. You'll be back in the real world soon enough."

"It's how to reply to him ... that's the problem."

"Postcards. Easy."

"I do sometimes, but I owe him a letter once in a while."

"Big writing?"

During our journey I found strengths in myself I never knew were there. Speaking my mind, saying no, saying yes without explanation, saying I was upset or asking people to mind their own frigging business. Appreciating the attention I received from men, without feeling guilty. How anyone interpreted that was their choice. I didn't want to sleep with them particularly, but I was learning how to flirt. Having been told I must always be a good girl and not lead men on, this was ingrained in my upbringing. Unlearning that was a challenge. I heard an American girl say to her friend, "You don't want to be one of those girls who says 'no,' do you?" It was so contrary to my upbringing, a totally new notion. Physically too, I stopped worrying if I looked good. I felt good and that was all that mattered. Long hair, let loose, made me feel carefree. I gave it permission to hang the way it wanted. Besides, there was no other choice.

With the widespread uptake of the birth control pill, life had changed radically for women. I was catching up. Now I'd changed my concerns from not wanting to appear a 'good girl', to not wanting to catch something icky. I didn't worry about the complications of it all, as I hadn't met anyone I wanted to sleep with. A shag, a word I'd first heard shortly after arriving in London, didn't appeal either. Or another expression, a quickie. Whatever word was used, participating didn't appeal.

We travelled on.

One of my brother's postcards mentioned Neills. He'd been in London again. Neills was going to be in Greece, more particularly the islands. How could he get in touch with me?

Catching up with people along the way was very hit and miss. 'I'll see you in a square by a statue and I'll be there every day for five days from midday to two in the afternoon' was about as close as you could get to making an arrangement. Knowing where you would be staying made life easier. Reenie organised a meeting in Madrid and struck gold. Paul, on the other hand, didn't have any luck. His friend was travelling, as we were, and they missed one another by three days.

As we travelled along the coast nearing Greece, I started to feel anxious. For so many years I'd held the dream of sailing around the Greek Islands. What if it didn't live up to my expectations? Now I was so close, would it be as grand in reality?

Travelling now for nearly three months, I was approaching the main event of my one year away. However, I hadn't realised what a highlight travelling with our group would be. Parting company would be like leaving the womb and I was nervous.

"You don't have to go," Paul said. "We're going to be in Athens a few days. We'll be checking it out and if you want to come back with us, you can. You know you can."

"Yeah," I said.

But I knew this was something I really, really had to do and I couldn't let myself down. And now I had Neills to meet. He'd sent me a letter with the phone number of someone in Piraeus, with instructions: 'Ring Takis when you arrive so he can tell me how to contact you'. On our travels, people we had met had given me the names of various places in Greece to stay and the Islands to visit. By the time we reached Athens, I had a fistful.

Our first stop was again the Poste Restante. Flicking through my mail, I saw handwriting that I was only a little familiar with. On the back of the envelope, 'Neills Pedersen'. I wanted to rip the letter open then and there, but the group were watching me.

This was my departure. I was so divided. I wanted to be with the group every single moment before we parted, but I also wanted to open the letter. I decided on reading it later once I was in bed. We were all staying in a cheap hotel in Piraeus and for the first time I wouldn't be sharing with Reenie.

"I'll open it before I go to bed."

"Go on, open it," said Scrub. "Before you make it all wet salivating over it. Read the others later. Besides, we want to know we're leaving you in good hands."

I looked at them all looking at me. "Okay."

I found more instructions on where Neills would be, and what islands they were sailing to, but otherwise more or less a repeat of the previous letter. He was obviously keen, which was the important thing.

Sometime through our farewell dinner, we inadvertently took over the small restaurant with our raucous celebrations. The owners and staff were very accommodating. It was a total piss-up. I can only imagine how our singing, laughter and tears obliterated every other patron's nice evening out. During the night everyone joined us. What else could they do?

After our arguments during the trip, the smelly socks, laughter until we nearly wet ourselves, we'd grown into a very tight group. That night we hugged and bellowed how we loved one another. We said this in as many languages as places we'd visited. It had always been a priority, after learning hello, how much, goodbye, please and thank you, to learn to say, 'I love you'. It's amazing how fluent a drunk becomes in any language. We'd 'mastered' Greek by the end of that night, much to the amusement of the staff.

For the occasion, Reenie and I had put on make-up: a rare occurrence. We saw our reflections later in the bathroom mirror – what ghouls we looked. By the evening's end, rivulets of black mascara streaked our faces and our lipstick was smeared, the rest covering the guys' faces. The photo of us all taken by a waiter is one of my most treasured.

At one point, I remember slurring, "Scrubby babe ... I never did get to find out how you earned that name and why you came on the trip."

"And Bellie dear ... you never will."

Thirteen

The morning after everyone left, I woke bereft. An emptiness filled my heart. I thought of the gang waking somewhere, who knows where, with Scrub's morning fart, Paul's cheerfulness no matter how hungover, Wes's grumpiness and his smelly socks or just plain dirty feet, and Reenie's silence until at least ten thirty.

The day they left, I stood in the street and watched as they piled into Poppy with comments from Scrub and Wes, about how much space they had now and they'd never known a woman to have so much stuff. Which wasn't true. It was better to have a laugh right then, than more tears. Once that van turned the corner, I could no longer hold back.

My hotel room was clean but dingy. It was cheap, which was the norm. Occasionally we splashed out, but not this time, as I was not sharing the cost. It was a whole lot worse with no one to laugh about it with. I showered as best I could, under a shower head left over from the golden age of Greece, with water pressure to match. The floorboards creaked as I made my way along the corridor and down the stairs. Early morning, I left for the day.

The alleyway, also dingy, smelling as it did of Ancient Greek sanitation, did not entice a tourist out for a happy day. I walked towards the strong scent of the port; salt water and ferry fumes. Infinitely more encouraging.

As I turned a corner, bright sunshine gave me a feeling of hope and adventure. Instantly I felt different. Instead of alone, I felt supported by my now-departed friends. What an experience they had given me. I found a café where I could look at the sea. I ordered a Greek coffee and pastry, sat and watched the world go by.

Out of the blue came that feeling, the frozen moment – I hadn't experienced it in years. Everything stood still in a frozen moment. What was it? The same question I'd asked every time it happened. My parents couldn't answer the question, nor could doctors. When it passed, the full force of the sun and squawking seagulls gave me energy. The sea too, ever calling me.

I read Neills's letter again. As I'd been hungover the previous day, I hadn't yet rung the number he'd given me. After our drunken celebrations were finished, I'd fallen into bed fully clothed. Sometime during the night, I'd thrown off my clothes. I woke naked with imprints in my skin from the springs in the thin mattress. My mouth felt like a camel's armpit, to use a Scrub expression. Before going to bed, I'd drunk the provided bottle of water, but it hadn't made much difference to my hangover.

Now, sitting in the sunshine, I clutched Neills's letter. He'd thought of me. This charmed and scared me. I still felt his intensity. My coffee finished, it was time – time to move on to the next chapter.

PART THREE

Fourteen

Dear Annabelle

I saw Pete the other day, we had an evening in the pub. He told me of your plans and approximate arrival in Athens, so I hope you get this in time.

I'll be leaving Piraeus on the 14 April with my friend Laars and his father. You can ring me on Laars's number (below) but if you arrive after that date, you can ring Takis, a friend of ours (below). We'll be sailing out from Piraeus. If you have any idea where you'll be, we can meet up. You mentioned the Cyclades. As it's a favourite for most people, I imagine you'll be sailing those islands.

The 14th of April had passed. "Shit." My outburst caused a ruffle, but nearby patrons quickly lost interest.

How the hell will I find him? I now felt doubly distraught, with no gang to talk it over with. Another coffee and I still didn't know what to do. Neills was right. The Cyclades were a bunch of islands I planned to visit. Should I just take the first ferry out? No.

I wanted to do it properly. No rushing. I'd waited a lifetime to do this, I wanted my trip to last. It would be part of the adventure to meet up with him.

A passing motor scooter smacked the air, puffing smoke, which shook me into action.

Join a yacht as crew. With my fistful of things to do and contacts from travellers, I knew this was possible. Like my trip to Greece, it must be, and I would get off before returning to Piraeus. That way I could catch up with Neills. With that in mind, I walked back to the hotel, taking a circuitous route and seeing what caught my eye on any of the noticeboards. I hadn't walked far when a flutter of paper got my attention. As I came closer, possibilities were pinned one on top of another, flapping like gulls' wings. Something for everyone.

WANTED – RIDE TO GERMANY –
leaving 15th – meet at Bar Zeus

Lost camera – reward – go to Hotel Nikkos

Camera for sale – ask for Janie Watson, Hotel Storm

SHARE – hotel room, male or
female – come to Con's bar at 6pm

Car FOR SALE – URGENT –
cheap – see Joe at Tappas Bar

... on and on.

Some notices were curled brown and weather-beaten, others new and crisp, pins in short supply, space claimed by the latest hopeful, all hung precariously.

Me – Me – I'm what you're looking for – I'm the answer to your dreams.

No telling how old many of the notices were. Fifteenth could relate to any month.

Nearby, equally weather-beaten and offering to make reality out of long-held dreams, boat-hire offices hunkered with doors flung wide, waiting for the full season to start. The entrances yawned, along with the proprietors.

As nothing in the notices jumped out at me, I wandered all the way around the harbour and into the next bay. I stopped for lunch as by then it was early afternoon. My hangover gone, I was famished.

With a full stomach, my spirits lifted and my head sharpened. I continued back to the hotel. As I approached my laneway, I discovered a bar. I hadn't noticed it in my sad, hungover state on leaving. A bunch of travellers sat discussing the places they'd 'done'. Easy going and from all over the world, judging from the accents. I sat and ordered a coffee. But I was soon drawn into a conversation on the next table and moved to join them. Travellers' adventure stories were being shared: travel tips, stories of the sea, the dos and don'ts of crewing. More people wandered in. Among them were the ripped off and the pissed off. Rumours, rumours, rumours. I was no longer alone. I hung out there until authentic Greek dinner and Greek wine arrived, then it was an easy stagger back to my room.

Come morning, I resisted calling Takis and repeated what I'd done the day before. The next day and the next, I embraced my new chapter. I enjoyed just hanging out and getting to know the locals. Three days brought longevity in that part of town.

My father's offer crossed my mind. More than asking for money, which I didn't need or want, chatting with him would have been comforting, but the time difference was usually wrong. In reality, I had nothing more to say that I hadn't already said in my letters. Although I wrote with the censor button on for my mother's sake, there wasn't too much more to say to my father. I didn't want to put him in the position of not telling my mother something.

I would have mentioned Neills, but then a lot of that was only in my head. I wasn't supposed to be interested in anyone else as I was unofficially engaged. The subject had not been discussed with my father before leaving and he never asked me how I really felt about Clive. I believed there was an unwritten understanding that he knew my position. All the same, to hear my daddy's voice would have given me such a lift. I could describe Piraeus and ask if he remembered anything. I continued to send postcards and a letter or two.

A week later, on my walk, I saw it. Simple and to the point.

PERSON TO CREW WITH THREE OTHERS –
TWO TO THREE WEEKS. SHARE COST OF HIRE,
FUEL AND FOOD. LEAVE PIRAEUS AS SOON AS
POSSIBLE. ITINERARY TO BE DISCUSSED.

Fifteen

A shattering explosion punctured the peaceful morning, as I sat with my coffee waiting to meet Danny. Blue smoke belched with an acrid smell from the hurtling motor scooter. The noise alarmed the gulls who half-heartedly took to the air, as if familiar with the din, then lazily resettled once the interruption had passed. Local patrons barely raised an eyebrow, engrossed as they were in their game of Tavli, cigarettes and black coffee. The noise startled me too and I absent-mindedly brushed the smell away. My book lay open, but my concentration had lapsed. A little early, I relaxed as I waited. I'd suggested the café as it had become my favourite. It was close to the action of departing and returning island ferries.

A shadow fell across my book. "Annabelle?"

I looked up to a tall, lean, tanned and dark-haired young man. He was dazzling. His frame momentarily shielded two women around the same age. As they came into view, I saw a stunning dark-haired young woman and another with light-brown hair, highlighted by the sun. The man's smile was huge.

"Yes, I'm Annabelle." I stood. His handshake was warm, as he introduced himself.

"I'm Danny."

The two women offered hands, then all three dragged chairs into position, giving the women a chance to check me out from under their hanging locks.

"This is Kate, my sister and our friend Clio."

I smiled and nodded.

"You're Australian?" said Kate.

"Is it that obvious? I've hardly said anything."

"Either that or English," Clio added.

"But you've got that Aussie look ... long legs and a friendly smile," Danny said.

"That's it?" Mmm, too easy to tell where they were from. "You're from the United States?"

They were.

"We know some Strine," Danny continued, before I could say more.

Oh dear. We'd only just introduced ourselves and my hackles were rising.

"We've been travelling long enough to know an Australian when we see one, and hear one," Danny said proudly.

"We met some Australians the other day," Kate said. "We had dinner with them and they told us all about speaking Strine." Further destroying the encounter. She too, with pride in her voice, said "G'day."

"I've been away for a bit, so I may have forgotten some of the lingo." Clearly, I hadn't. "And what part of the States are you from?"

"California. Clio's originally from Oregon," said Danny.

"You're travelling alone?" asked Kate, with more in her voice than words.

"Yes. Now I am. I travelled with a bunch of friends from London in a Kombi. We took about three months. I got here about a week ago. My brother lives in London."

"We're on summer vacation," said Kate.

They spoke briefly about where they'd been. Their journey matched mine, but a cut-down version.

"So, let's get to our plans," said Danny. "We want to hire a yacht, probably from that company over there." He pointed to one I'd noticed. "We've checked them out and they have a yacht available; two in fact, so we have a choice."

"We'd like to go for at least two weeks, maybe three," said Kate.

"... and we thought it would work out cheaper if there were four, rather than three of us," Danny said. "If we find the right person, we're ready to go straight away."

"Sounds all right. How's your sailing experience?" I asked. I'd been warned to ask that one and watch how it was answered.

"Danny and I are about equal, we've done a fair amount of sailing at home and some in England," said Kate.

"I haven't had as much experience as Danny and Kate," said Clio, "but I'm pretty good crew. I used to go out with my pop when I was little. I can vouch for Danny, being a really good skipper."

"Okay," I said. That sorted the hierarchy out. Fine with me.

"... and you, Annabelle? How's your experience?" said Kate.

"I've crewed around Sydney Harbour and the inlets. Pete, my brother, and I used to sail a lot with my father. I was about ten when I first learned the ropes. Ooops, pardon the pun. I'm seaworthy." I was rattling a bit, being out of interview practice. "I'd be happy to try out if you want me to."

"Not necessary," said Danny.

"Does the yacht hire require certificates or anything?" I said.

"They seem satisfied with what we showed them. I sailed with the North American Yacht Racing Union and they gave me a reference. Kate and I also have a reference from our sailing buddies in England.

This yacht charter company's motto is *Mutual trust is the basis of yacht hiring*," Danny recited. "Guess with the bond, the charges and insurance, they're covered. Kate and I will put our names down, as Clio doesn't have any references. We thought we'd split the bond and hiring charges equally."

"Yep ... that sounds fine." In discussions with those back at the café, this was normal practice. And common sense. "A friend of mine is currently sailing around the Cyclades. I'll be joining him, so I'd only be coming for two weeks and finish up on one of the islands. Is that okay?"

"Ah ... yep, guess so," said Kate.

I felt confident I would meet up with Neills but, if the worst came to the worst, I'd stay on an island at the end of two weeks, wherever that was.

"Are you planning on the Cyclades? Sorry I should have asked that earlier."

"Yes, seems to be the area to head for first. But we don't mind where we go," said Danny. "Cyclades is okay with me." Danny looked to the women. "You happy with that?"

"Yes," they said in unison.

"Do you know which island? The one where you're meeting your friend?" asked Kate.

"No, not yet. He's travelling with his friends who are on their own yacht. They have no strict route. I have to leave a message with a friend of theirs in Piraeus, telling them approximate dates. They'll be ringing in to check."

"That's leaving a lot to chance. Too risky, if you ask me," said Clio.

"It is, but you know how it goes when you're travelling with no set schedule."

Clio looked mortified.

"One question. I nearly forgot," I said. "Have you experienced storms? I believe they can come up pretty quickly in the Aegean."

"Fair question. You want to know if we panic?" said Kate.

"Yeah ... I suppose so."

"Well ... we were out sailing with our father one time," Kate said. "We were only little, maybe nine or ten." A quick glance from Danny and in reply, Kate gave the tiniest shake of her head, more a muscle movement.

"The boom swung round and knocked dad flying. We laughed because he was always yelling at us to mind the boom. But then we noticed he hadn't got up. We both stopped laughing and rushed to him. He was slumped on his side. I told Danny to drop the sail, tie the boom as it was still swinging around, and get the motor going. Danny was on to it before I'd finished. I shook dad and lifted his head and rested it on my ... what was probably back then ... a bony lap. He was breathing okay. By the time we got to shore, he was sitting up and talking. Very scary at the time. There was only the three of us on board." She paused, remembering the moment. "I guess that's not a storm answer, but a crisis answer."

"Scary," I said.

"Dad told mom," Kate continued. "He was mighty proud of the both of us. How we'd handled everything so well."

Danny laughed and said, "We've watched out for the boom more than ever since then."

"What about you, Annabelle?" asked Kate.

"Sydney's known for its southerlies ... southerly squalls ... and I was out with my boyfriend, Clive and another couple. We were sailing home and we thought we had enough time, but the clouds built up and came in really quickly. Well, we weren't quick enough. We got the sails down but not before the boat listed and we lost Jenny. She didn't have much sailing experience but was a good swimmer. It took me three goes before she grabbed the lifebuoy. We were all quite shaken, but Jenny said she couldn't have chosen better friends to fall overboard with. Not sure if that's a good sales pitch … but it's all I've got." As an after-thought I said, "Can you all swim?"

"Yeah," they said together.

"I can't share anything like that," said Clio, "so I don't know how I'd react."

"I can't remember you being panic-stricken for any reason. You always seem calm," said Danny.

"So," said Kate, "are we good?"

"Good with me," I said.

We chatted for a while. Should I get to know them better? In a situation like this at home, I would have spent a few days thinking it over. Even in London, I had Peter to bounce thoughts around with. If they didn't find anyone else immediately, they were going with just the three of them and I didn't want to waste any more time looking.

"Do you want to think about my joining you?" I suddenly realised they may have hesitations about me. "We can leave it until tomorrow if you want to sleep on it. I don't mind."

They looked from one to another.

"Or I can take a walk now and you can let me know when I get back," I said.

I'd only walked a short distance when Danny ran up. "It's fine, join us."

We walked over to the charter company. Kate and Danny signed up. We were to set sail the next day.

The hire company wanted an itinerary. I was sure everyone changed things when they were out on the high seas, but the rough plan was something I could pass on to Takis.

As we walked away, Clio said, "We thought we'd have a kitty for food and wine and beer, or whatever you prefer ... if you'd like?"

Danny said, "Do you know a kitty is not a cat?"

"Yes, I do. We have kitties too."

"Yeah ... see," said Kate and gave her brother a sibling shove, "we'll all be speaking the same language in no time."

The day had broken into glorious sunshine. The few clouds that had hung around earlier had moved on, their job done.

I had time to write letters to mum and dad, Clive, and Peter. I thought about ringing dad, reversing the charge as he suggested, but I figured he might panic if he was out of the office.

That just left my important phone call to Takis.

Sixteen

We ate dinner as an ice breaker that night. The restaurant was cheap, the clientele local, and the food delicious, with plenty of it. Danny and Kate told their life story in bursts of energy, as they enjoyed a new audience. The siblings were close in years and brought closer by their fun-loving mother, who apparently flitted from one good time to another. Their father always knew he had his wife's loyalty; it was friends who weren't so sure.

"Dad loves mom the way she is," said Danny. "Inside the walls of our home, it's clear mom adores dad."

"The nay-sayers don't see that," said Kate. "And besides, she's quietened down now dad isn't so busy with work."

I looked at Clio, as the conversation slowed.

"We all met in college," Clio said, picking up my cue. "I'd just come down from Oregon and felt quite nervous, but I met these two and everything fell into place." It seemed Clio had a brother she didn't like. "He's older than me and he's always been a bully. Still is. Going to school was a break for me. Mom and pop preferred my brother to me. Him being a boy."

A reassuring touch from Kate. "But you had a good teacher, didn't you?"

"Yes, she was wonderful … she said I had talent as a writer. I was always writing stories. My mother said the teacher was talking hogwash. I'd never get a husband if I spent my time hidden in my own little world. Men don't like that. I'm still single so maybe she's right," Clio said.

Danny shifted uneasily.

"My mother has her definite ideas about getting a husband," I said. "She had … still has … my whole life mapped out for me and that was by the time I was about five. A legal degree would find me the right husband at university, rather than the arts degree I wanted to do.

"While I'm away, she invites my boyfriend over once a week. She's terrified I'll lose him. Him being the 'right chap'. This trip wasn't part of her plan. She stopped nagging me in the end though. My father was all for my trip in private. He was the one who got my mother to see travel broadened the mind. I doubt mum went for it, but she stopped nagging me, at least in front of my father." I took a breather. "She was brought up in different times."

"This trip will take us all away from our worries," Kate said and glanced at Danny.

"Yeah, we'll have fun and sail the seas into new adventures," said Danny with hands that traced the horizon.

After dinner I climbed the stairs to my room, feeling much easier about the forthcoming trip. We were to sail the next day.

I'd called Takis and given him our rough itinerary. His English was very broken so I could only hope he got my message correctly.

As I closed my eyes, I thought *Wow this is it. I'm finally doing it.* The smile was still on my face as I fell asleep.

Seventeen

A Crete-sized smile broadened beneath Nikos's prized moustache. The man was loud, big and hearty. His was a name everyone gave for boat hire in the area, as well as for general knowledge and a good laugh. He knew the Aegean intimately and his maps and tips, printed on an old Roneo machine at the back of the shop, were pages in length. Splotched from too much ink, we learnt it was often a guessing game as to what lay beneath.

Danny had his own notes and a book. He came prepared. He took his skippering seriously, which was comforting.

Nikos wished us safe travels, as we took possession of our yacht, *Osprey*. He winked at Danny, wishing him a very bon voyage. "Half your luck," he said with eyes heavenward. Seeing us off, he shrugged and sauntered back into his office. Just another day.

The air was crisp at that early hour. Excited gulls competed in daredevil manoeuvres in the breeze that ruffled across the harbour of Piraeus. Danny took the helm and my first instructions were to make fast the fenders and lines.

"Make sure the dinghy's lines are secure too, Anna, while you're at it. Clio, batten down ... the wind should be okay, but better secure everything."

Clio went below where Kate was unpacking and storing the supplies. I checked the dinghy and ensured the oars and rowlocks were locked down.

Anna was not my favourite abbreviation of my name. In fact, it irked the hell out of me. When all was stowed and in place, I went below to join the giggling.

"Look what I found in the market, Anna ... the perfect tin for our kitty," said Kate.

"Purrrrfect, a Greek cat," said Clio.

"Very kitsch ... perfect," I said. "Please, Annabelle or Bellie, which is what my father and brother call me. I'm really not an Anna."

"Oh sorry. I heard Danny say it, I thought you must have mentioned it to him."

"No. That's fine, perhaps you could mention it, or shall I?"

"You, me, whatever," said Kate.

"Okay, I will."

We sorted out our stuff, cramped as it was. It was a long time since I'd been able to spread out, so the confined space felt natural.

"Hey Anna, up on deck please," Danny called.

"Coming," I said. My preference was to be on deck anyway, but felt I needed to pitch in with packing things away. I was anxious to see the departing sights. The others followed.

"You can't just down tools, Anna. You're needed here."

"Annabelle please. I went below to help the girls."

We approached the white stone breakwater. The wall was reflected in the rippling water and the distortion gave an impression of waving us a fond farewell. Excitement tingled every cell in my body.

"Conditions look good, Danny," I said.

"Weather forecast is good, Annabelle – let's see how it is when we're out at sea."

Strong emphasis on Annabelle.

The harbour was busy with life – colour and movement everywhere. Our yacht was a speck in the scheme of things. *Osprey* held her ground and motored proudly out of the harbour. Kate and Clio readied the halyard to hoist the mainsail. With this done, Danny called out "Okay girls … let her go."

White sails unfurled and billowed with a thwack, as if gasping for air and thrilled to be free. Yachting-wise, it was my favourite sound.

It became obvious that Kate, Clio and Danny worked as an efficient team. Danny was used to his captaincy, and I wasn't sure if he was up for change. I wondered whose idea it was to get a fourth person. Maybe it all came down to finances. This was my dream. I had to make it work. I'll fit in wherever needed, I thought. I just won't be called Anna or Ann.

The breeze blew soft and steady. Scattered, pillowy clouds moved casually across the blue sky. The horizon was softened by a faint haze. Birds swooped and soared, sending us on our way. We sat in silence in our own thoughts. Strands of my hair escaped my white cotton cap and whipped around in the breeze, taking me back to the day I left Sydney. Setting sail on the big ship, out of the harbour had taken my breath away. Already I had experienced more than I ever imagined. That girl seemed so long ago.

Osprey was a lived-in thirty-footer, immediately making me feel comfortable and at home. I could tell she had a cranky nature, even though I hadn't taken the helm. She had a will of her own if she wasn't mastered from the start.

We were headed for Kea, a destination bypassed by most tourists. Only forty-two nautical miles from Piraeus, yet decades away from crowded Athens and the busy harbour. Danny had picked this route as he felt we'd meet traditional and friendly people, similar to those in the small villages on the mainland, where they'd travelled.

Was this my father's island? He never did tell me. I guessed I'd be wondering about every island I visited. He'd said, "Too long ago, Bellie. Please, it's not important to you or me." A strange answer, but I couldn't force him to tell me. He'd taken on his Australianism very seriously. He would not be questioned further, so I dropped it. Pete was none the wiser, but he had never asked the question either.

"There it is," said Danny, pointing to the horizon. "We're here quicker than I thought; we've barely got our sea legs. Lots of history on the island, lots of walking to be done. We should be able to get about by donkey, too."

"Suits me," said Kate.

"Me too," I said.

Danny decided to sail into the small harbour of Vourkari first.

"Another name for this harbour is Vurkarion," Danny read from Nikos's copy. "Seems like there's two names for everything around here, including Kea, which is also spelt T-Z-I-A. On the western side of the island there's a bay called Agios Nikolaos, where we can get to the port of Korissia."

As we closed the distance, Danny said, "I thought we should stop here first. We can sail around to the other side tomorrow, if we want.

"The meltemi, that infamous wind, doesn't usually blow at this time of year, so we should be okay with just the anchor. Vourkari is more a yachties' inlet, Korissia probably busier, more touristy."

"No other yachties here yet," said Clio, sighting only a few local boats of varying sizes.

"We're going in bows-to, if you could get the anchor ready, Annabelle," he said. "We need to be a bit careful as the bottom comes up quickly, so we'll stay out a bit. The notes say the anchor chain and rope have all the length we'll need around the islands."

Danny had mastered my name and now I hoped he'd loosen up.

Observing the fishing boats berthed at the waterfront by the little village, I thought it would be better to anchor at that end.

"Does it say anything about being able to berth there at the waterfront, like those boats?" I said as casually as I could.

Clio's face showed a look of disapproval. Day one and pecking order rules were showing themselves.

"No, it doesn't," Danny said. "They may have special permission ... it may only be for fishermen."

I would have sailed over to ask, but I wasn't the skipper, as Clio had just silently reminded me. I dropped my critical thinking, along with the anchor and let it drag until I felt the pull. A hard tug and it was secure.

"Anchor's secure Danny."

"Double make sure. Clio ... can you check? Give it a minute to check for drift."

In Danny's mind, I still had on my training wheels.

Clio tugged. "Anchor's good."

"Shall we have something to eat on board?" Kate said, "I'm starved."

"Yeah, why not." Danny said.

Kate and Clio prepared houmous, cheese, bread and sun-dried tomatoes. We ate on deck as the gulls swooped, squabbling, 'gimme gimme' ... 'no, me, me.' Our silence as we ate only enhanced the beauty of the bay. The small village lay curled in the hill and I had a strong feeling collective eyes were watching us.

"Ready to go ashore?" asked Danny. "Annabelle, can you bring the dinghy round?"

After I got the oars ready, we eased ourselves into the dinghy and Kate rowed us to the quayside. After finding a metal hook inlaid in a concrete pylon, we stowed the oars and rowlocks under the dinghy's bench and tied it fast. Clambering out, we walked towards the small cluster of buildings along the other end of the foreshore.

The village watched.

Eighteen

An easy walk of maybe five to ten minutes eventually led us to the white-painted buildings. Danny consulted Nikos's notes.

"There's a giant smiling stone lion somewhere, that has guarded the hills since before the days of Socrates. We'll have to find that."

"Let's wander around the village," Kate said.

"Do you get the feeling we're being watched behind these closed doors?" Clio said. "It's very quiet. Is it siesta time?"

Danny leafed through pages of a small book.

"They call it *hor..es..kinis..iisi..hias.*" He liked to be accurate. I noticed his well-leafed miniature English/Greek dictionary. "Translated in English, it means 'time of movement quiet' or 'time of little commotion' or 'quietness'. From our previous experience, this time could be anytime from midday, one o'clock until it ends."

As we approached, we saw an elderly man sitting outside a building. "Kalimera," I said.

He looked like he was welded to his chair, a fixture. He replied to my greeting by lethargically lifting his head, raising a strong, ferocious bushy eyebrow.

"That's good morning," Danny said. "I'll find good afternoon. It's almost that now," and peered into his miniature dictionary again.

"It's a greeting, Danny. He's probably just not overly responsive," said Kate.

"Is he outside his house, do you think?" said Clio. "Maybe it's a café?"

"Not sure we'd find any provisions here, even if we wanted them," said Kate. "Hang on ... looks like it's a taverna. The door's slightly open. Let's go in and see."

"Wait a minute," Clio said. "It could be someone's house."

"Too late," Kate said. "We might get a beer later," and she disappeared inside.

"Maybe we can get donkeys here too," said Clio, following her into the darkness.

The space was like a cave, with a pungent smell of tree roots. A few old tables and chairs were scattered in no particular order, on an almost-level tiled floor. A bar jutted from the end wall, with stools of various heights beside it. On one of the stools sat a very old, very bent man who barely acknowledged our entrance.

A cork wall near the bar was chaotically pinned with curled-edged photographs. One, hung prominently in the middle, was a snapshot of Steve McQueen. On closer inspection, I saw it had been cut from a magazine. A young woman's heartthrob. Three male patrons sat motionless, and another man hovered around the bar. He could have been a barman or another customer. The patrons stayed seated, showing little surprise or curiosity at our arrival, but I had the feeling they were aware of everything.

"Maybe they saw us anchor," said Kate. "They must've known we'd eventually end up here."

With sign language and the odd Greek word, we were able to find out when the tavern closed. It didn't. It didn't open either. If you wanted something, you asked. I guessed you chanced getting what you wanted.

"I'm going to ask if they have donkeys for hire," said Danny, having leafed through his dictionary.

"Do an impression, Danny. That'll get a quicker response than you trying to say, 'donkeys for hire,' in Greek," said Kate.

Danny faced the seated men, "EEEE AAAAWW."

Bewilderment.

"Maybe they think you're calling them donkeys," I said.

"Hell, I hadn't thought of that," said Kate. "Besides, it sounds like a stifled chicken."

"Maybe they think you're asking for a chicken," Clio said.

Danny had another go. "... eeeeaaaawww ... gai'daros ... eeaawww. That's what it says here," said Danny, enthusiastically.

"What ... really?" said Kate.

Crouched over and using his free hand, the other holding the dictionary, he imitated ears and plodded around the floor, doing his best donkey impression.

We started to giggle. The patrons started to giggle. Giggles turned to laughter. With the laughter audible, the taverna became a magnet.

"Where have these people come from?" said Clio.

Black-clad women snickered behind their shawls. Children appeared from nowhere, along with pregnant women and old wobbly men. Toothless smiles erupted into gales of laughter. The more Danny tried to ask for donkeys, the louder the laughter became. Some of the children joined in and mimicked Danny around the room. Laughter was raucous. Danny began laughing too and couldn't go on.

"Doubt the locals have had so much fun in ages," said Kate as she caught her breath and laughter eased … "and neither have I. They are making me laugh as much as Danny."

We were beckoned outside. A crumpled old man with a big, single-toothed smile and sparkling eyes, stood proudly next to two donkeys.

"Donkeys! That's fantastic. It's a miracle," said Clio. Everyone was excited, including the ever-gathering crowd. We all clapped, much to the donkeys' annoyance.

"I think the word is out that there are fresh crazy tourists in town," I said, as an assortment of villagers continued to laugh and jabbered to one another in gunfire Greek.

"Do you think the donkeys will live very long if we get on them?" said Kate.

"Why don't you and Clio go first," said Danny.

"Okay, we'll be the guinea pigs. You up for it, Clio?"

The whole scene was a photo opportunity with the assortment of locals in the background. "Smile," I said.

"Us or the donkeys?" said Kate.

Kate and Clio clung tightly to the tufts of manes at the base of the donkeys' necks and intertwined the string reins around their hands. It was hard to tell whether Kate was riding the donkey, or just sitting astride and walking. With a whack on their rumps from the old man, the disgruntled donkeys took off along the path, as Kate and Clio bobbed around on their bare, knobbly backs. Suddenly the donkeys stopped. As I watched, I could only assume the shrewd animals had nearly succeeded in dislodging their loads, intending to return home. Gales of fresh laughter erupted from the watching crowd and the donkeys' ears flipped around as if sharing the humour. After much coaxing and heel-kicking, the donkeys trundled unwillingly along the path, ears laid back in annoyance, their peaceful afternoon interrupted by this unscheduled form of hard labour. Kate and Clio's squeals could be heard as they disappeared around the bend.

"Let's have a beer while we wait for them to get back," said Danny.

"Bit early?" I said. Then I thought better of it, "Na, let's have a beer."

The word beer sprang life into the quiet bar. Two chairs and a table appeared out front, along with two bottles and two glasses.

"My God, that's quick," I said and thanked the bartender.

Once we were settled, Danny said, "So, have you got a boyfriend back home?"

"Erm ... yes. I'm supposed to be getting engaged when I get back."

"Supposed to?"

"Well ... um ... yes."

That all seemed so far away, but I figured it would come up sooner or later. But I wasn't here in my dream place to think of my responsibilities.

"My boyfriend wanted me back in six months."

"Or what?"

"Marriage. Or ... I'm not really sure. Anyway, we negotiated a year."

"Oh ... how much longer do you have?"

"A little over six months."

"You weren't ready to settle down? Or are you looking for a better offer?"

"I'm just travelling before I get married. Then I'll settle down."

"With the current boyfriend?"

"Spect so."

"Mmmm."

I thought for one second about asking Danny what his situation was. But after that second, I realised I didn't care and really didn't want to know. Clio had thoughts there, I was sure, but I didn't care about that either. One thing I did care about was not talking about my future life as a tamed wife. Danny pressed on.

"This guy you're meeting up with here in the islands ... possible better offer?"

"Danny ... he's a friend of my brother's and he happens to be in the area with a boat. What would you do?"

"We'll deliver you to him ... don't worry."

I hoped Danny's curiosity was satisfied.

"What else is there to see on Kea?"

Danny read more from the notes and chatted on about the group's experiences in Greece.

"Shall we have another?" I said, now getting a taste for the beer.

"Yeah, why not, we're on holiday and not sailing this afternoon."

Before we could ask, two more beers appeared. "These people amaze me," I said. "How do they appear so sleepy, yet know what we want without asking?"

We sat in silence gazing at the sea. Tranquil and heavenly, as far as I was concerned.

"Hope Kate and Clio are okay," said Danny. "They've been gone a while."

"Well, they're both competent women and their sense of adventure may have overtaken them."

"Or the donkeys have refused to move."

With beers infusing happiness, I could have stayed all afternoon. It was a warm spot and so peaceful. I loved the untaverna-looking taverna, the gnarled old men, the sea and swooping gulls. The assortment of locals had dispersed, seemingly into the craggy earth itself.

Two old men sat nearby. They smiled at us and nodded. I lifted my glass to them and wondered if they spoke English and hadn't let on. With my 'back home' life closed down, all was well in my world. Peace eternal.

A slight shift of breeze tickled my skin.

Nineteen

At first, I thought it was the 'frozen moment' revisiting, but then I realised a physical breeze had stirred.

The old man welded to his chair muttered something unintelligible. Neither Danny or I reacted, unsure if he was talking to us or himself. He could just be a mutterer. He spoke louder. We both looked at him, as it was now obvious he was talking to us. He inclined his head towards the sea and repeated his utterings.

"What's he saying?" said Danny.

"No idea, but maybe it's something important."

Danny spoke loudly and slowly in English, "What-is-it?"

"I don't think he's deaf and he probably doesn't speak English," I said.

The man continued to mutter and tilt his head towards the bay. One of the patrons from inside came out and spoke to the man, then turned to us.

"He say storm coming."

"The man's wacko," said Danny to me. He turned to the two men, raising his voice. "I don't think so. I looked at the forecast, no storm."

"Danny, he's a local, he'd know." Twisting around, I looked towards our boat and the hill beyond. "When did that happen?"

White gulls shone bright in contrast to the dark clouds.

Danny turned to look. "That was not in the forecast. The anchor's secure, isn't it?" said Danny.

"Yes, it is, but I think we should go out to her all the same."

A small crowd had gathered outside the taverna. One of the old timers said, "Better there," pointing to where the fishing boats were moored.

"As I thought," I said more to myself. Danny gave me a look.

"What about the girls? They'll worry we've gone," Danny said.

"They'll be fine, Danny. They'll speak to the men here."

Danny sat hesitating for a moment. "Okay … let's go." He pointed in the direction of Kate and Clio, "Girls … you tell them?"

The men padded down with their hands and nodded they understood.

By the time we got to the dinghy, the clouds had grown. The sea was whipped and dark. With the wind and sea against us, the short distance to the yacht was a struggle.

"Annabelle, I thought you'd secured the yacht. She's drifting. She wasn't that far over."

"Shit."

By the time we got to the *Osprey*, she'd dragged and swung around on the anchor rope like she was trying to free herself. Danny leapt on board and rushed to start the motor. It was a fight to get the dinghy secured.

I climbed aboard and clung tight to the rails, fighting against the wind. My hair whipping my face, I made my way to the bow.

Danny shouted, "I'll get the load off the anchor, so wave when you're done."

I lunged for the anchor. Against the wind I yelled, "Go forward …
a bit more … more … I can't get the anchor up." I heaved, as Danny
moved the boat forwards. Slowly the anchor released and banged
against the hull on the way up. I dragged it aboard and gave Danny
a thumbs up.

Then Danny was suddenly behind me, clutching the rails and
shouting into the wind. "What the hell are you doing? This is a hire
yacht you know."

"Why aren't you at the wheel?"

"Because I have to be here, supervising you. Seems I have to do
everything."

He stomped back, clutching at anything as *Osprey* rolled, waves
tossing the yacht like a ball.

"We'll take her to the other end of the bay like the old man
suggested," said Danny. "Stay there … I need you as lookout."

I clutched tightly to the rails as the lashing wind and rain bit
into my skin. My hair now wet, the salt stung my face and eyes.
I could see Danny struggling to get the boat into the angry waves.
He needed help.

Tight grip over tight grip, I made my way to him.

"Don't come here … don't come back here," he shouted in a
staccato beat. "I said to stay there, go back to the bow … guide me
over … we'll end up on the rocks." Then Danny started gibbering,
with many words inaudible. "I'm not going below, stay here, stay
here," and his eyes flicked from left to right. "Haven't had a chance
to check the depth here." His lucid words interspersed with crazy,
that crackled with terror.

Osprey rocked and rolled.

"We need to go windward," I yelled and went back along the rail
again to the bow. I gripped tightly and held fast against the lashing

waves. I couldn't think what was troubling Danny. Something was, something that was affecting our safety. Right then we were in trouble.

"Starboard ... windward ... more ... Danny starboard," I yelled as water and wind took advantage of my open mouth. The waves struck: 'take that and that' they seemed to say.

"Oh, for God's sake," screamed Danny, "you take the helm ... I'll go up there."

I couldn't believe what he was about to do, then he did it. He left the helm. "I'm coming ... I'm coming." Christ, he's losing it. "What are you doing? Didn't you hear me?"

"Shut the fuck up ... just take the helm," Danny said as he shoved past me. A crazed look in his eyes told me he was totally panicked.

Now at the helm, I had to right our predicament. I turned *Osprey* windward into the waves. The boat settled. The squall subsided. Having done its damage and become bored, the storm began to move on. Danny was still shouting something, but not only could I not hear him properly, I decided it was best to ignore him.

Gradually we had the yacht at the other side of the bay. Considerably calmer, I motored in towards the fishing boats.

"You little darling," I said to *Osprey*, "at least you've got your wits about you."

I knew she was feisty right from the start. We motored calmly up next to the end fishing boat.

"Anchor up, Danny."

"What?"

"Drop the anchor".

"No, go further over," he said. "Over ... further over." Hysterics still crackled in his voice.

"Here is fine. It's okay. Drop the anchor," I said, lowering my voice to calm.

Danny opened his mouth then shut it and dropped the anchor. He tugged the line over and over, then slumped down. His foot and leg beat out a quick jerky rhythm. I thought it best to leave him. I went below and the mess hit me. I stowed everything back in its place, partly to give Danny time to collect himself, hoping against hope Kate was back and could come aboard. At least nothing was broken below.

Kate hadn't arrived when I went back up on deck and Danny still looked shaken. "Shall we go ashore?" He showed no response. "Danny ... Danny ... are you okay?"

"Danny, are you okay?" It was Kate shouting as she ran along the shoreline with Clio trailing her.

"Danny's not okay," I said quietly as she came aboard.

Kate rushed past me. She huddled down with her brother. Clio stood on shore. I joined her. Neither of us said a word, but waited for Kate to get Danny off the boat.

"Everything's fine," Kate said, her arm around Danny as they joined us.

Everything did not look fine, but at least Danny had regained his composure.

"Let's go get a drink," I said. "I want to hear about your donkey ride."

Twenty

A crowd had gathered. The locals certainly met us at our most vulnerable moments. As Clio and I walked through them, I smiled and mumbled, "Everything's okay." I noticed the old man who'd originally warned us, still sitting outside the taverna. He was dry, so he must have gone inside while the squall was on. I smiled at him. "Efkharistó." I hoped he understood my pronunciation as I raised my hand in the universal drinking action. His eyes twinkled and in response he tilted his head. At the bar I ordered four ouzos and whatever the old man wanted outside.

"Is good now?" the barman said.

"Yes, all good now."

Miraculously quick again, a table and four chairs appeared outside, the storm now a memory. Thick silence swelled amongst us four. The drinks came. We raised them and sculled silently. Without a request, four more arrived.

Unbidden, Kate and Clio tumbled out their experiences, blurring their sentences one into another, breaking the weighty silence. The storm, their storm, differed from ours. On the journey, the had donkeys stopped at every bend, looking back longingly. Often

98

dismounting and pulling on the rope-reins, Clio and Kate tugged and tugged. One step, maybe two. They clambered back on the donkeys but had to wait until the beasts saw there was no other option.

"It was fine, as we had time to take in the magnificent views," said Clio. "We saw the storm coming and thought we were about to drown."

"Thank heavens it didn't reach us. I think the donkeys would have raced home no matter what we did," Kate said.

As the storm had passed, they'd decided to return.

"No need to coax them then. The donkeys trotted for their lives," said Kate. "A firestick up their backsides wouldn't have made them move any quicker. They'd done their hard graft for the day. You could see it in their ears and faces. I thought their spindly legs would break."

"Mine stumbled and I nearly went over his head, but he was in too much of a hurry to get home to waste time falling," said Clio.

"The path is a mass of rocks and gravel, but they must be used to it. They bounced us around like we were bags of sugar. I'm sure I'll be bruised. It's a wonder my spine wasn't dislodged," said Kate. "Bony buggers ... them not us."

Danny sat, remote, listening. Kate glanced at him from time to time.

"My face is aching, we laughed so much," said Clio. "Poor donkeys."

"Poor donkeys? They tried every trick in the donkey book to get us off their backs."

"That storm was amazing. We saw it come in and head out to the next island," said Clio. "Good thing you moved the boat."

Clearly Clio was unaware of the severity of our chaos. It was Kate's knowledge of her brother that had brought her onto the boat. At that point it must have looked like we'd simply up-anchored.

I said nothing.

It was dark when we finally left the taverna. Food was simple but plentiful and delicious. Fresh produce, no doubt. We were all quite inebriated by then too. Danny had hardly said a word and I imagined there would be a private conversation between him and his sister. I felt my side of the story should be heard, but with the three so close, I guessed it would go unsaid.

The moon was at its brand-new sliver when we boarded the yacht; the sky so clear, the abundance of stars were brilliant against the dark space they inhabited. I looked heavenward and felt so small, the events of the day so insignificant. With few village lights, the glow from above reflected and shimmered in the dark water. The calm was deafening after the ferocious seas of the day. 'Who, me?' the night seemed to say.

Once we were settled on board, Kate said in a whisper, "You okay, Danny?" Whispers shout in stillness and I felt sorry she couldn't console her brother with more privacy.

"Fine, Kate, I'll tell you later."

Twenty-one

Deep sleep engulfed me as soon as my head hit the pillow. The following morning, sunshine pierced its way into the cabin and startled me awake. A little hungover, I opened a bleary eye to an empty cabin. Then I heard voices above. Splashing my face, I tottered up top, banged my head and remembered yachts. So bloody amateur, I chastised myself. On deck the others looked crisp and clean. Did I drink more than them, or were Americans made of sterner stuff?

"Ouch … morning Annabelle," said Clio, as she heard the thump.

"We've had breakfast. Yours is here. Did you sleep well?" said Kate.

"Like a baby. What a beautiful day." The bay and the day were stunning. All that I could have asked for. "This makes it all worthwhile."

"You have regrets already?" said Kate.

"No of course not." I avoided looking at Danny. "It's just more beautiful than I'd hoped."

They'd done an excellent job. The table was laden with fruit, cereal and coffee. "This is excellent."

"Yeah, Danny makes the best coffee," said Clio.

"How are the legs ... the muscles, the bruises?" I said.

"Not so good. The insides of my legs are red raw," said Clio.

"I have both sore muscles and bruises ... in abundance," said Kate. Danny remained quiet.

"We were talking about going round to Korissia for the day," said Kate. She looked at Danny and picked up that he didn't intend to add anything.

"So soon?" I said.

"We can come back here later. Might be nice to see what's around there. We'll have a choice then, see which is the most protected, which looks the most interesting."

"Fine. Can I make a suggestion, first?" I said. Danny stiffened. "We make it a rule to stow everything every time we leave the boat. The mess below yesterday was unbelievable."

Clio was about to speak but Kate spotted it and jumped in. "Good idea."

We readied the boat and Danny silently took the helm and charted the course. I tidied away the breakfast things while Kate and Clio untied the halyards.

Out of the blue, a shift in temperature. Not another storm. I grasped the rope to steady myself and the rope's tiny fibres came alive, electric. I let go immediately and pulled back. How peculiar. Then the world stopped, and I felt frozen, out of control. No noise, not even the sound of gulls. Not again, I thought. Please, not again. I looked up and all seemed normal, no storm was brewing, no threatening clouds, the gulls still flew but the hairs on my arms stood on end.

"You okay, Annabelle?" said Kate.

I was about to explain but thought better of it. It passed like the storm yesterday. No point giving it airtime.

"Yeah ... fine. Think I'm still a bit hungover."

I did wonder if the storm was linked to my toy boat crashing all those years ago. That first time I'd had the weird, frozen experience. If so, all was squared away now.

We were about to motor out when one of the men from the night before shouted out. "You go now?"

"Yes, we're going to Korissia," said Danny.

"Okay ... but safer here. Korissia ..." the man flicked his hand as if to say, 'dodgy'.

"Is another storm coming?" said Kate.

The man shrugged and waved goodbye. I looked at Danny. He looked away.

～

As we sailed out, another yacht sailed in and came alongside.

"Were you here last night?" said the man on deck.

"Yes," said Danny.

"Did you get the storm?"

"Yes, in the afternoon but it was calm last night," Danny said.

"Apparently, it's safer here than Korissia. Are you coming back?" said the man.

Another man came on deck. He looked like the father of the first man who was in his early thirties. Both sailing fit. The younger man spoke English with an accent from somewhere, perhaps Scandinavia. The yacht looked new. Immaculate timberwork. A thirty to forty-footer with *Olin II* on her side.

"Well, if you think it's more protected, then probably ... are there more yachts round there?" said Danny.

"There are, but they may come here ... the storm yesterday spooked a few people."

"Do you know the area?" asked Danny.

"Yes, some," answered the older man.

"Well, we'll go round and have a look and possibly come back," said Danny.

"We'll save a spot for you," the one at the helm smiled and waved.

Out of earshot, as they set sail, with a twinkle in her eye, Kate said, "He's all right. The older one's not bad either."

"How do you know they're all right?" said Danny, peevishness in his voice.

"They may be drug runners, axe murderers, anything," said Clio.

"Oh come on, Clio ... they were polite," Kate lowered her voice to a deep husk, "... and very gorgeous. What do you think, Annabelle?"

"I'm with you on that one, Kate."

"Gorgeous maybe, but that's about all we know," said Danny, "... and all we may ever know."

Danny took *Osprey* around the point. Kate gave me a wink. Hmm, a party girl and an insecure brother.

Twenty-two

The day continued perfect, as we sailed into Agios Nikolaos Bay, which was the mouthpiece to the village of Korissia. Yachts were anchored sporadically in the bay and at the waterfront. There was definitely more going on here than in Voukari.

Peace had settled on our yacht.

"Well, here we go again," said Danny, "Korissia is also known as Livadia. Just in case anyone gets lost and thinks they're somewhere else."

"No problem figuring out which are the tavernas here," said Kate. "That's if the chairs and tables are anything to go by."

"Feels good, doesn't it?" I said.

"Yeah, not as busy as I thought, still early in the season I guess," said Danny.

With the boat moored and secured at the small concrete quay, we clambered ashore and ambled along the front. Electricity pylons guarded the foreshore. We followed them around the bay to the right-angled pier. A few yachts were moored, along with faded fishing boats, which created a patchwork of colour with odd angles and gently bobbing shapes. At the water's edge, rippled reflections of white houses and coloured boats gave the little harbour a painterly effect.

"I guess, as night gets closer, the rest of the fishing fleet will be back," said Danny.

It was one of those wonderful spring days with promise in the air. The sun gradually warmed the hills, sending in the smell of summer to come.

"Let's stop for a coffee and watch the world go by for a bit," I said. Always a favourite pastime of mine.

"Good idea," said Kate.

"Wonderful, just for us," said Clio as we came across a taverna with an empty table out front.

Like Vourkari, although with a few more buildings scattered about, Korissia, I was learning, was a typical island village, standing its ground close to the front with the brown hills arched up behind. Olive trees struggled, as if seeking forgiveness for their occasional need for water, which the dry, history-burdened land seemed reluctant to give. Even the storm had not revived the parched land. The old people, like the land, carried history in their bones. Dry and brittle, but resilient. The young, biding their time. Life here, despite seasonal tourists, I guessed had changed little.

"I feel I could sit here forever, and it wouldn't matter," I said.

"What wouldn't matter?" asked Clio.

Is Clio on my case, or just a very literal person?

"Don't know. No clocks. No time."

I didn't know what I meant. I just didn't want to think beyond this moment. Anything could be going on anywhere and here you'd never know, and it didn't matter.

Four sweet Greek coffees were ordered. Clio ordered a pastry.

It looked so good, we all ordered one. The talk was easy but mostly we sat and people-watched.

As if propelled by a remote source, Kate's antennae sensed something even before her eyes did. She sat up, neck craned.

"Is that the yacht that came into Vourkari as we were leaving?" she said.

"Where? ... mmm, think it might be," I said.

I caught Kate's eye, and we shared a smirk. We watched as the yacht slid into a mooring.

"Wow, that is one sleek yacht," Kate purred and cast me another look.

"Sure is," I said.

I'm not sure either of us were looking at the boat. There were now three men aboard. The older gent and maybe his two sons.

Twenty-three

Lines secured, the three men from *Olin II* stepped ashore. Picture postcard stuff. They looked a better fit for Monaco, freshly washed and sun-dried, tanned, wearing the latest fashion sunglasses and boating caps. Comfortable in their bodies, they took the promenade with unpretentious confidence, wholly aware of being observed. They stopped at a doorway, a little distance from us.

Whether it was just Kate and I who were glued, I'm not sure, but they must have made an impression on others too, although Danny refused to notice.

"Do you think they've seen us?" said Kate.

The men talked to someone inside the doorway and a table and three chairs appeared.

"Oh, that's a taverna too," said Clio.

Danny laid out his notes on the table, "Well, what shall we see today?"

"Isn't there a stone lion somewhere?" said Clio.

When one of the younger men glanced in our direction, Kate's hand shot up and waved. She tossed her long dark hair, strikingly contrasted by her white cap.

"Hi there," she called.

Americans have it all over us for confidence, I'd noticed more than once since leaving home.

A wave back, surprise written on his face, which not for one moment did I believe. Kate beckoned them over. The one who'd waved said something to his friend before leaving. As he approached, Kate's tanned arm stretched forward, and long elegant fingers offered a seductive handshake, as she smiled from under her cap.

"Hi, I'm Kate," she said in a lower-than-normal timbre. "You decided to come back here, hope it was for us."

Oh God, she entirely bypasses go.

He smiled at Kate's proffered hand and shook it in greeting.

"Hello ... my name is Laars."

He turned to me, but in contrast to Kate and as naturally as I could, I went with the girl-next-door approach.

"Hi, I'm Annabelle."

"Oh, you are Annabelle. My friend thought you might be."

Kate's look stirred an already boiling pot.

"You know Annabelle?"

"Really? Um ... who's your friend?" I said.

"Come and join us," said Kate. "Bring your friends over."

As they carried over their coffees and chairs, I saw the third man.

"Oh my God, Neills. What a surprise ... I didn't recognise you with the cap and sunglasses." Surprise was understating it. He was obviously below deck before in Vourkari.

I turned to the others. "This is Neills, the friend I'm meeting in two weeks ... but looks like a lot sooner now." I turned back. "Is this a coincidence?"

"I guess it is." He shook my hand. "Please meet my friend Laars and his father Ute."

We all shook hands as Kate did the introductions. I was dumb-founded. It was day two of my two-week trip. Was I jumping ship now? Or was I getting ahead of myself?

"It seems all share-and-share-alike around here," said Danny. "They don't seem to mind if you move to another café."

"Nooo, it's very casual here," said Laars.

Danny's notes were shuffled out of sight, as our coffees and pastries squeezed for space.

"Too quiet in Vourkari?" asked Clio, almost accusatorily, having noticed Danny's slight displeasure at the invasion.

"Yes, we thought so," said Neills, his tone smoothing sharp edges.

Determined to get matters back on the right track and with one man not spoken for in her age bracket, Kate said, "Do you know these islands well?"

"Yes, quite well, we've been coming here for a few years," said Laars.

"You must tell us about the Cyclades: best places to go, sailing pitfalls," said Kate, as she leaned a little closer to Laars and oozed sultriness.

Still gobsmacked at meeting up with Neills, I had trouble concentrating on the idle chitchat.

"And the rest of you? I know Annabelle is from Australia, but you ...?" said Laars.

"We are from the States ... California. We all know one another from way back," said Clio.

"Ahh, so not from Australia. Have you visited?" Laars said.

"No. The country sounds so beautiful and wild. We must all go there one day," said Kate in a dismissive tone, to bring the conversation back to its proper place. "And where are you from? I just love your accent ... let me guess, Denmark, Sweden?"

Danny glowered.

"We are from Denmark," said Laars. "Copenhagen ... well, close by."

"We were in Copenhagen about a year ago, wasn't it Danny? Lovely city," Kate said.

"It sure was. We rode bicycles but the distance around the city area was much more spread out than we'd expected. We went way over our hire time," Danny said.

"That's the five-finger plan," said Laars.

"Five fingers? What do you mean?" said Danny.

"It's a plan to spread the city out so parks and recreational areas are interspersed with buildings, so everyone can enjoy an open space. It's a long-term plan. It's not finished yet, but it looks like it's working," said Laars.

"No, it's not, son. It'll be a disaster. Wait and see," said Ute.

"Are you in urban planning?" said Danny.

"No. I'm a carpenter." Laars turned to his father. "Okay. We will drop that subject."

"We visited the Royal Hotel in Copenhagen. I wish we could have stayed there," Kate said and shrugged at Danny. "Way beyond our reach. We heard The Rolling Stones stayed there."

"Yes, I believe so. It's popular with a lot of stars. It is very expensive," said Neills.

Kate's flirting was irritating her brother. So far, Danny wasn't faring well on this trip. The storm and now male competition.

Twenty-four

Reenie and I had had fun on the trip across Europe, flirting and mock fighting over guys, but this was out of my league. This was how it was done to win. I wondered if Neills was getting caught up in it.

My thoughts drifted to Neills's arrival at Kea. I'd given our itinerary to Takis but I hadn't expected we'd meet up so soon. Was this really accidental? My feelings were a mix of being enamoured, overwhelmed and curious. That kind of perseverance was foreign to me. Was it a Danish thing? Besides, my mother, along with girlfriends' mothers, all had the same advice: 'A man must do all the chasing but be gentlemanly about it. Be wary of a man who is too pushy.'

"How was Peter when you saw him last, Neills?" I said.

"Yes. He was good. The usual. He's very easy-going, your brother, very likable."

"Yes, he is, always has been."

Ute was saying, "My family have been sailing here for a long time. My father and uncle taught me to sail and some of it was done in these islands. Now my son must sail with his friend."

"I usually join them in the summer months for a couple of weeks," said Neills. "We've been to most of the islands over the years."

Something I had noticed about Neills, in London and now, he didn't appear to concentrate on what was said, but at the same time, he heard every word. With you but not with you. Just out of reach. Maybe that was an attraction for me. He was good-looking, with his thick, tousled sandy-coloured hair, bridged nose and strong body. There was something about him that reminded me of my adorable father, my role model. That was the type of man I wanted to marry. Now I was at a distance, I didn't see that in Clive, and until now, I had never realised that I used my father as a comparison. I dismissed my thoughts of Clive, just as a pat on my hand brought me back.

"Where are you, Annabelle?" It was Neills.

"Oh sorry, miles away."

"We were asking if you've done a lot of sailing in Sydney," said Neills.

"Yes, yes I have. With my father, uncle and my brother, but not so much since Pete left."

"Is your boat new?" asked Clio. "It looks new."

"Quite new. We built the boat," said Laars.

We all looked to the boat, although it was too far away to see detail.

"Amazing," I said. I'd always been impressed with people who could make things. My father could turn his hand to anything.

"Which island is your favourite ... in the Cyclades?" said Kate.

"Mmm, that's a hard one. They all have their own personality," said Laars.

Kate and Neills talked as I drifted again. I caught the tail end "... great idea, Neills. We took donkeys out in Vourkari ..."

"What's a good idea, Kate?" asked Danny, who'd been talking to Ute.

"Neills was saying we can ride to some of the sites by donkey, if we want. He was suggesting we visit Ioulidha, where some fifth-century poet was born ..."

"Sounds good to me," I said. I smiled at Neills. Was he taking up Kate's flirting now?

"Hey, why don't we all meet up for dinner tonight?" suggested Neills.

"Here, or in Vourkari?" said Danny.

"Oh, there's more to do here, I say," said Kate. "What do you think, Laars? Here or Vourkari?"

"What do you want to do, Danny?" said Clio.

Danny shrugged, "We've got a good mooring here. Suits me."

"Then that's settled," said Kate, "we stay here. Is that okay with you three?"

"We can drink some retsina," Neills said, "a little ouzo, eat excellent lamb, listen to some music. They don't eat until late so we could meet for a drink beforehand, at say, seven-thirty, if you like."

"OK ... shall we meet back here?" said Kate.

"Fine," said Neills.

We stayed at the crowded little table for a while longer. Laars went on to explain the art of good cooking.

"They do enjoy their evening meal and when there are some tourists around, they like to make a fuss of them, especially at this time of year, when there aren't so many yet," said Laars.

"And they like to dance too, especially with strangers. They like visitors to join in. Do you like to dance, Annabelle?" said Neills.

"Yes ... yes I do."

"These people are warm and friendly and very lively," said Laars.

"Oh that sounds like so much fun … don't you think, Danny?" said Clio.

Danny grunted a smile, "Would be good to experience some local tradition."

"Will they throw plates?" asked Clio.

Neills laughed, "Oh you've heard about that. Yes, they sometimes throw plates, if they enjoy themselves."

The day had stretched past midday.

"If you will excuse us," said Neills, "we are meeting some local friends. Let's meet up back here this evening." As an afterthought, he said, "Oh, save something of your sightseeing, we can all go together tomorrow."

They wandered off along the waterfront and disappeared into another building.

"This trip is really looking up," said Kate. "Neills must be keen, Annabelle. This meeting is no accident."

"You think so?" She was the professional in the romance stakes. "It seems all so remarkable with all the islands in the Aegean."

"Yes girl, I'm sure." Kate studied me for a minute. "You're on holiday Annabelle, on your dream holiday, if I need to remind you. Don't get bogged down in your thoughts. Have a good time."

"You're right."

"She might be thinking about her fiancé," said Danny.

"What?" Kate and Clio turned to me.

Shit. "Not officially Danny. It's my year off from that life before I take it up again."

"Well then double go for it, Annabelle," said Kate. She pushed back her chair, already bored with the subject. "I'm famished. Shall we go back to the boat and finish what we have?"

Twenty-five

Danny was struck with moodiness as we walked back to the boat. I was fast realising he was a man who liked to be the centre of attention and in control. Male competition did not sit comfortably. Kate spoke quietly with him, but not quietly enough, as I overheard the discussion.

"What's up?"

"It feels we've been lassoed."

"What? By those guys?"

Danny must have shrugged.

"Isn't this why we're doing this trip? To experience the local life?"

"Not exactly local, if they're from Denmark?"

"What is it, Danny? I know the storm hit you. It all came back. Forget it. I think Annabelle has."

"It's awkward. With Clio and Annabelle."

What? Clio and I don't have a problem. Do we? What's he on about?

"Annabelle?" said Kate.

"Yeah ..." And then I couldn't hear what he said.

"That's awkward Danny. In fact, it's stupid. She has a guy back home, a guy here, forget it."

Oh Christ. I hadn't thought that for one minute. And Clio? I thought there was something going on there. One-sided. Her to him. Bloody hell. A boat is not a place to get embroiled in other people's infatuations, or to become one. I stopped listening.

After lunch, I announced I was going to take a nap. "Might be a late night."

"Me, too," said Clio.

"Danny, you wanna take a walk?" said Kate.

Danny seldom refused Kate anything, I'd noticed fairly early. I was going to take Kate's advice – take a nap and be ready for a good time.

An hour or so later, I climbed up on deck. No one was about. The sun was lower on the horizon. The day had slumber to it. It must be the ongoing siesta time. Clio emerged. We sat, said nothing. Later Kate and, finally, Danny appeared. It was beautiful to sit in the stillness. No one spoke. Gradually we came to life. Kate went below to change first, then Clio and me a few minutes later. Danny waited for us all to finish.

Kate's long, dark hair hung casually over her high-collared, red sleeveless shirt, buttoned to reveal cleavage. Her tan looked great under the red cotton, the corners tied high at the waist, setting off her taut, slim frame and deeply tanned body. There was an Ava Gardner look about her. Levi jeans and leather sandals set the picture perfect. She shouldered a denim jacket.

Clio, also squeezed into Levis, wore a small, flower-printed, pale blue, short-sleeved shirt, tucked into her jeans. A small white cotton scarf was knotted at her neck. Her fine fair hair was tied high at the back, with a narrow blue ribbon. She was delicate and quite beautiful, like a bird. Clio climbed aloft, then it was my turn.

As I was sorting my stuff, I discovered postcards and a letter I'd written, but not posted from Piraeus. Nothing was important except the ones to my parents and Peter. I'd written regularly to both and, knowing how long it took mail to reach home, I knew my parents would be worried.

"Oh shit," I said, more to myself.

Clio and Kate peered down into the cabin, "What's the matter?"

Danny called from the deck, "Is everything all right down there?"

"Oh yes, sorry, it's okay, well it's not okay. I wrote these post-cards and letter in Piraeus and forgot about them. I didn't send them. A letter was to my parents. They'll want to know how I am and where I am. Also, a postcard to my brother, but he'll know where I am, through Neills."

"There may be a chance we can send them from here; we can ask the guys tonight," said Kate.

"It's okay, I'll send them when we get back."

"Better get a move on, Annabelle," Kate called down. "Danny still has to change."

"Sorry, coming."

I wore my favourite tight Levi jeans, the ones you had to lie on the floor to do up. Not the most sensible attire on board with stairs to climb; nevertheless, they were sexy. Well, they made me feel sexy. I teamed this with new white sandals I'd bought at The Plaka in Athens, and a new white cotton-knitted cardigan draped around my shoulders over my electric blue t-shirt. My hair had grown and lightened in the sun and waved down over my shoulders. I got an 'ooh la la' when I finally made it up on deck.

Danny took his turn, wearing a white polo t-shirt, jeans and leather sandals. He wore a peaked white cap. He scrubbed up very handsome.

Daylight saving had just begun, giving extra light to the end of the day. The sky was painted a light turquoise, with flashes of sunset piercing through the soft evening clouds.

We strolled along the foreshore, as if we were a group thrown together in conviviality. I'd always envisaged myself with a group of fun-loving people, in the Greek Islands. This was certainly better than nothing.

Neills, Laars and Ute were already at a table, larger than the one we'd sat at in the morning. The feeling at night was totally different to daytime. Still early in the season, the heat of the day had not extended into the evening. It was warm, but I was glad I'd brought the cardigan.

On the table lay fresh local olives, bread and retsina. The men stood when we joined them. I've no idea what we chattered about, but it was as delicious as the olives. The night was young, as were we. From my wonderment at everything, I tuned into Kate, who was doing all the talking.

"I love your accent," she said, "your English is flawless" – addressing Laars once again.

"We learnt English when we were very young. Not everyone does, but we were fortunate."

"Thanks to their mor and far," said Ute.

I hadn't been sure how much English Ute spoke or understood. He didn't speak so much. I realised he probably understood everything. He had a twinkle in his eye. He obviously enjoyed the company.

"The three of you have known each other a long time?" I said.

"Neills has been part of our family for a long time, yes," said Laars.

"Like another son," said Ute.

I didn't know anything about Neills's family. Did he have siblings? I would get to know all in good time.

Kate was in good form but, rather than find it irksome, I remained fascinated as she used her mascara-layered dark eyelashes to full advantage. Ute watched on, as his son was earmarked for some serious work during the evening. He caught me watching and whispered to me, "Women love my son".

Neills was smart – so as not to alienate Danny, he said, "Sounds like you've done a lot of travelling, Danny, but your first time to the Greek Islands?"

"Yes, it is. Our parents love to travel. Dad took us to Europe every two years for a bit, so we have seen a lot. Mom prefers the cities and the nightlife. The Greek Islands would be too quiet for her."

"Some of the islands are lively, but yes, not like cities," said Laars.

"You have yet to see how these quiet islands come to life," said Ute.

"Yes, we have a surprise for you," said Neills. "We only found out about it this afternoon. There is a special party on tonight. One of the local young men has just returned from studying at university in Europe. His family and friends grouped together enough money for the fees. He's done them proud by gaining his degree. Tonight, will be his homecoming party. We were invited and we mentioned we had friends here, so they invited all of you as well."

"Oh," said Clio. "How wonderful!"

"That is very big-hearted of your friends," I said.

Danny finally beamed. "This is a very generous invitation. This sort of thing happened to us on the mainland. The Greeks are very hospitable people. And a big thanks to you."

"We should take something too," I said. "What should we take?"

"It is fine. We have provided lamb and retsina, it is from all of us," said Laars.

"We should get going," Neills said, as he took the bill and paid for everyone.

Danny leapt up behind him, hand on shoulder, "Thanks, mine next time."

"So where is this place?" asked Kate.

"Hidden away along the end of the quay," Neills said, and pointed in that direction. "It's a private taverna, for locals. We have been there before. You'd never find it on your own. The food will be excellent, I guarantee. I hope you like lamb, it's their speciality. I promise you, it will be delicious." Neills closed his fingers around his lips and exclaimed, "Nostimo."

"They love to eat and there will be lots to choose from, or you can try everything, if you can fit it in," said Laars.

"So ... let's go eat," said Neills. "Let's go eat and dance."

He clicked his fingers, spun around and offered an arm each to two girls who just happened to be me and Kate. Clio, in the spirit of the moment, grabbed both Laars's and Danny's arms.

Twenty-six

We followed Neills, as he took us on a journey first to the far end of the quay, past a hotchpotch collection of houses, through a narrow, cobbled passageway, to arrive in a big courtyard, in which sat a nondescript taverna. Stunted buildings stood guard around an off-centre square. Tables and chairs were set out in no definite plan. Coloured lights were strung higgledy-piggledy from one roof to another. The 'welcome home' sign, hand-written on a big white cloth banner, hung from two roof corners at the far end of the square. A quick guess would estimate seating for one hundred and fifty people.

Neills, Laars and especially Ute, were welcomed with hugs and handshakes and children clambered for surprise presents. Out of the Danes' pockets came little treats, sweets and small toys, making the children squeal in delight.

"Yiasas ... elate mesa ... elate mesa ... yiasas ... kalos orisate," said a short robust man with a moustache as wide as his face and an apron circumnavigating his paunch.

"Come in, my friends, you are welcome, we have a table over here for you," said a younger man, coming up behind.

"Galeespera," said Danny.

"Ah, you are learning to speak Greek and good evening to you," said the waiter.

Before they sat down, Neills called out, "Everyone, this is Danny, Kate, Clio and Annabelle, and of course you know Laars and Ute." Neills gestured to the gathering guests, "... and this is everyone."

Hands squeezed with nods of approval. We were welcomed in a collective hug.

Our table was off to one side. Retsina, already poured into rough glass tumblers, was placed amongst earthenware plates and bowls filled with olives, bread, dolmades and locally made fetta cheeses. A feast before we'd even begun the feast.

Chatter, laughter and greetings reached dangerous decibel levels, and one-on-one conversation soon became cheerily impossible. More people straggled into the square, accepting hugs and kisses. Children ran and jumped into strong loving arms, were scooped up and spun around.

The food arrived. A procession of plates piled with souvlaki, salads, moussaka and an array of succulent lamb and vegetable dishes, were held high by waiters as they twisted and turned around chairs and scampering children. And the meals kept coming. Tables overflowed. Glasses were refilled, time and again with beer, retsina and ouzo.

Amid the noise and chatter, musicians appeared unannounced, took their chairs in an area set off to the side and tuned their instruments. A chord strummed and the square hushed. The outi player paused, struck another chord and the crowd went mad with cheers of encouragement.

I doubted the stars would get any rest.

Next, the sazi, tambouras, guitar and finally the bouzouki rolled in. The square exploded. The musicians abruptly paused and waited mid-strum. Hush fell. From an alleyway, a youth, high on the shoulders of two men, was carried around the courtyard, to claps and cries of, "Nikos ... Nikos ... Nikos ... bravo ... sigharitiria ... sigharitiriapaidimou ... kai s'anotera ..."

The music struck up again. This was the returning hero of the moment, fulfilling the dreams of many, waving his degree atop strong shoulders. When the thunderous applause quietened, the music continued and guests resumed eating and drinking.

A man seated near the band stood and flung a plate close to the musicians' feet. The crowd cheered. The tempo climbed in appreciation. Another plate joined the first and smashed with gusto. The crowd deafening again.

Clio seized her moment, leapt to her feet, reached for an offered plate and scrambled to the front, close to the musicians and in a magnificent gesture, twirled and flung the plate to the floor crying, "Opa!"

Laars leaned across to Kate and Danny, "Clio's taken to this very quickly."

"This is a rare sight, like she's been waiting to do this her whole life," said Kate.

When not a morsel more could be eaten and tiny ones' smeared faces were wiped clean while their eyelids drooped, tables were cleared away to reveal a trampled earth floor, compressed over decades by pounding feet.

"Ah, now I know why they put us here. I think we're going to have front row seats," said Danny.

"More than that," said Neills. "You are the front row and the performance. You must dance too."

"Oh no no no, I couldn't dance. I don't know how at home, let alone here," said Danny.

"I've seen you do the donkey dance, Danny ... no excuse," I said.

The crowd began to clap to a single beat. The music paused. The crowd waited. Hushed.

An old man entered. Short and solid in stature, he stood off from the centre. The crowd held its breath. Waiting. From the gnarled leather boots to the top of his etched, weather-beaten face, the old man's countenance told the history and wisdom of his ancestors and the island. Slow and strong, he began the story. Eyes closed, arms raised, he clicked his fingers and paused. The music paused. With one foot raised, his body shed its age. The first step settled gently on the ground. His upper body steady, he glided into the second step. The old man was eternal, young yet old. Step by step, click by finger-click, he moved with grace, passion emanating from every cell in his old frame.

The crowd roared their appreciation and encouraged the old man on. His pace became faster and faster, then slowed as he gestured for the crowd to join him. The musicians, conducted by the old man, enticed more and more dancers to the floor. The tempo increased. A circle of arms on shoulders formed until it became too wide. A second circle joined and finally children created a third. The lame or too old clapped and cheered the dancers on. One by one, a dancer stepped forward to take a solo turn in the circle centre.

Despite Danny's objections, we were all up and in the circle. A solid, no-nonsense woman, many years his senior, grabbed Danny's hand like a prize and led him into the centre. Like the old man, as soon as she started to dance, still clutching Danny's hand, she became young again. With caring dexterity, she led Danny step by step. The old woman was obviously another favourite. We followed the crowd as it moved to the side. Danny, first-time Greek dancer, was centre stage. The crowd clapped to the beat of the music.

Clio giggled as a young man took her hand. Everyone came back to the dance floor.

"The whole island seems to be here," I shouted to Neills, as we shouldered around the floor.

"They've been coming in all night. Look, more."

Night moved into morning's early hours. We offered to help clear the tables but were shushed out with weary smiles, "No, you go, eees ok, we do."

"Efghareestoh … efghareestoh," said Danny to everyone.

"Good night, ora kali, bye bye," they replied and waved us out.

When we were back at the quay, Clio said, "That was so exciting … smash … smash …" She twirled and demonstrated her newfound skills. "I'm taking that ritual back to the States."

"They're going to love you," said Kate.

Clio continued to twirl. I'd not seen her so loose and free before. I formed a different impression of Clio from then on.

"Looks like all the stars in the heavens have joined us tonight," I said. "Millions and millions … isn't the sky exquisite?"

"So now you see how these people enjoy life, eh?" said Neills, squeezing my shoulders.

"My hands are raw from clapping," I said.

Clio kept dancing, twirling and opa-ing her way along the foreshore.

"You're a good dancer, Ute," I said. "You've obviously done this before."

"Ah yes, for many years. These people are warm with a magnificent heart, and dancing is a way of expressing it."

The night was so still after the noise. Other guests peeled away, some with sleeping children draped over burly shoulders. Traces of tired chatter could be heard, drifting into the hills.

"I didn't think I could dance like that," said Danny. "Hey guys, thanks so much for inviting us. An unforgettable night."

"It is our pleasure. I think that's one of the best nights we've had here too, wouldn't you say, Laars?" said Ute. "That young student brought them all together."

"I think so. I haven't seen so many people before," said Laars.

"I don't think I'll be able to talk tomorrow," said Kate, "my throat's already sore from cheering."

"Well, here we are at your *Osprey*," said Neills. "I think you will all sleep well. I know I will. I'm happy you joined us. Shall we see you in the morning?"

"Let's meet back at our table, but not too early," said Kate.

With that Neills, Laars and Ute were gone. No special good-night. My wistful imaginings dashed, but imaginings cannot ruin a wonderful evening.

Twenty-seven

We emerged one by one. Four foggy heads into the blinding
light of late morning. I was the first and watched as each
scowl appeared squinting into the sunlight. With casual time
constraints, we washed and wandered to the café to meet the Danes.

Neills's nonchalant attitude the night before created an eagerness
within me. We'd all been intoxicated. I thought so anyway. How
could a person not be? After a few drinks everyone goes a bit nuts
on the romance level. Neills had drunk enough to make a play for
me. Kate and Laars, I suspected, had had a moment. Peter, my dear
brother, in correspondence, said I should go for it after seeing Neills
the last time in London. I was only used to romancing Australian-
style and, in my mother's words, a girl should always play hard to
get. That was then and back there; now I needed to watch and learn
from Kate – there was no better teacher. Then again, maybe Danes
had a different approach. I didn't know. Suddenly I felt like there
was a floundering fish flapping about in my head. I decided on the
'sit back and see what happens' approach. My mother's, I suspect.

We arrived before the Danes. Kate and I were quietly discussing
the men and possible expectations. Then we saw them, bright-eyed

and bushy tailed. Don't Danish people suffer hangovers? They joined us. No emphasis on where to sit, just grab an extra chair and sit, so neither Kate nor I was sitting next to the man we were flirting with.

Pleasantries first and why weren't they hungover? To which they shrugged a reply. Clearly, we were rank amateurs. We settled down to map reading.

"We think motor scooters," said Laars.

"Donkeys would be too slow if we want to see what the island has to offer," said Neills.

"More fun," said Ute with his twinkling eyes. "More danger." He laughed.

"Far ... stop," said Laars. "It is not more dangerous." Laars turned to us. "One of the men who helped organise last night is a mechanic. He has a scooter and I'm sure there are more we can hire. We need four. I know for sure there are more in Ioulida. We'll need to get there, though."

"Does anyone have an international driver's licence?" asked Neills.

"I do," I said.

"Me too," said Danny.

Kate and Clio looked at one another. "We both drive," said Kate "and I have my U.S. licence with me."

"You may need an international one, but we have enough just in case they ask," said Neills. "Depending on how many scooters we can get here, Annabelle and I and Laars and Danny can ride to Ioulida and pick up more."

Laars continued, "Far can ride his own if he's going to be dangerous." Ute nodded in appreciation.

"Then Laars and Danny can ride back here and pick up you two."

He looked to Kate and Clio. "We'll meet you in Ioulida." Neills faced blank stares. "Does that make sense?"

"Yes, sure," said Kate. She paused. "No ... not really. And what about Ute?"

"Thank you," said Ute.

"Let's see how many scooters we can get here first," said Neills.

"I think we should pick them up today and have an early start tomorrow morning," said Neills. "There's plenty to see so it would be best to have a full day. That way we can stop where and when we want."

It was then early afternoon. Laars, Neills, Ute and Danny left in search of scooters.

"We'll be back on the boat," said Clio.

"Unless we're not. We might still be here," I said.

Kate, Clio and I spent an easy afternoon taking in the little township. I was quite happy not to do anything but watch the world go by. The smells, voices and general activity were enough. Kate wanted to explore continually, which she did with Clio. We were to have a big exploration day tomorrow and, with my hangover lingering, I was happy to mooch around locally by the foreshore.

The girls and I decided to meet back at the café and, much later in the afternoon, the Danes and Danny joined us on battered and spluttering scooters.

"There was no need for my licence, they were hired on a handshake, all down to these guys," said Danny.

"Will they make it? They look a bit dodgy," I said.

"Dodgy?" said Ute.

"Yes ... old, decrepit, falling to bits," I said.

"I said dangerous earlier but maybe dodgy is better," said Ute, chuckling. "Mmm ... dodgy. I like that."

"They'll be fine," said Laars, "they're ridden all over the island."

Ute snorted with disbelief and a smile.

"Far," said Laars, warning in his voice.

Ute looked at me and leaned in. "In my son's eyes, I'm being naughty. I say I'm being dodgy."

Three scooters were secured at the back of the café overnight. In the early morning, with a coffee and pastry on board, we retrieved them. I pillioned with Neills, Laars with Danny on the other. Ute on his own, triumphant. The scooters moaned and spluttered into life.

"Be interesting to know what make these are … they look pre-war," said Danny.

"Probably bits stolen from the Germans during the war, then used as spare parts," said Laars.

"Dodgy," said Ute.

We waved Kate and Clio goodbye, noticing Clio had her fingers crossed. I felt the same but away we went, puffing and spluttering. The bumpy, bendy road wound up to Ioulida. The mechanic had already made contact by the time we arrived. Two scooters were proudly displayed outside a café. Rust and bumps gleamed in the sun. They were a similar vintage to the others. Just as hardy, no doubt, and just as flamboyant. Cheap paint had been used to cover some of the rust, which was flaking. Like our three, they puffed and shook into life. More handshakes and instructions about the scooters' idiosyncrasies, and Danny and Laars headed back to Korissia.

Ute, Neills and I enjoyed another coffee. Ute knew the mechanic and walked away to talk to him.

I took the opportunity to ask Neills something I'd noticed. "You call Ute 'Far'. Is he like an adopted father or a good friend?"

"He's been like a father to me."

"What about your own father?"

"Not around."

Those words had an air of finality, so I asked no more. Neills wasn't particularly communicative after that. I'd hit a nerve. Ute returned to our table and later we heard the noise of popping scooters approaching up the hill. They passed through Ioulida's town gate and joined us.

"Touch and go there for a bit," said Danny as he waited for Clio to dismount.

"We made it," said Clio, as she thrust her arms in the air.

"Such a quaint little town," said Kate. "There's barely enough room here for chairs and tables."

"Wait until you see the main square," said Neills, "it has room for at least one more table."

"I think you're teasing us," said Kate.

"No, it's true, we can go there later. When you're ready, let's climb that path, it will take us to the ancient fortress and the magnificent view I told you about."

Twenty-eight

Colours so vivid and the sea so clear, I swear we were looking into the depths of eternity. This had to be the earth's inspiration for her precious jewels. We were hushed by the sheer magnificence.

Breaking the spell, Neills said, "The hill we're standing on looks barren but it's catacombed with many tunnels. There are thousands of years of human history right under our feet."

"Can we visit the tunnels?" Clio said.

"We would have to get permission and that requires time," said Laars. "Red tape rolls slowly on the islands."

The vastness of the shimmering island-dotted Aegean, the history, the gentle breeze and warmth of the sun; we fell once again under her spell.

"Let's go," said Neills abruptly. He saw my disappointment. "We have a lot to see."

Back at the village, we found another path that led to the Stone Lion.

"At last," said Clio, "we've been talking about this Stone Lion since we arrived on Kea."

"Lion of Kea, a statue from around 600 BC, that is to Kea what the Parthenon is to Athens," Danny read from his notes.

Returning to the little square and our scooters, we puffed our way from the square, leaving its inhabitants to their peace and tranquillity. We wove our way down hills and along winding roads and across the countryside. When an exotic view was too good to pass, we stopped and sat on tufty grass or a warm rock. Occasionally we passed a villager walking along a track or another riding a donkey. "Yassas," Danny called out. In reply, the donkey flicked an irritated ear.

We were forced to stop at one tiny village as a procession passed through. White-robed men, belted with colourful sashes and carrying banners of gold-painted religious icons, slowly made their way, swaying from side to side. The gold shimmered in the sun, as bells clanged.

Danny read: "When someone dies on Kea, the family hosts a Dinner for the Dead. It's a celebration rather than a funeral. The dead person passes on to the next phase of the cycle. It's called mini-moso or something like that, it's spelt m-n-i-m-o-s-i-m-o. I wonder if that's what this is all about?"

"They look kinda happy for a funeral procession," said Clio.

We eventually passed through the few clusters of buildings. Dotted on the hillside, goats, sheep and the odd shepherd could be seen, the animals' bells clanging a hollow ring. A gentle breeze cooled the land, which would later burn in the shimmering hot sun of deep summer. The grass and trees seemed tethered to the soil in survival bondage, but looked content, not yet parched, as would soon be the case.

"It's so tranquil. I imagine life doesn't change here," I said at one stop we made. "There's something comforting in that."

The warmth of the late afternoon sun on my back and wind in my hair, the Greek Islands and a gorgeous man, who could ask for more?

We arrived back at Ioulida where we had to do the motor drop off. From there we were on the last leg of our day. Neills and I pulled our scooter over for a final view. "We're not too far from Korissia now." He took out a jacket from his rucksack and laid it on the parched grass for me to sit on. "Are you enjoying your trip so far?"

"This trip we're doing now, or do you mean the islands trip?"

"I mean meeting up with the Americans and sailing."

"Well, it's only been a few days … it feels like weeks, though. Yes, I am. So much has happened, I can barely catch my breath."

"Are you getting on well with the others?"

"Yes, I guess so."

"You don't sound so sure."

"There was an episode with Danny on the boat in the squall, but that's passed now. I'm not sure if we'd be friends long term, but things are fine. Yes, it's good. I was really shocked to see you that first day. Was it a coincidence?"

"Why do you ask?"

"Um … well … we were only a day out and I was meant to be meeting up with you in two weeks' time. That's all."

"It could only be a coincidence, although you did give your itinerary to Takis. We were very close to this island. Laars and Ute were happy to make a small detour. Why not?"

I chuckled. "Easy."

"I can see Danny is interested in you."

"Really? I don't think so. I'm pretty sure Clio has her eye on him, though I'm not sure it's returned."

"Mmm … I do think so. And you with him?"

"Not at all."

"So ... you still want to come sailing with me?"

"Yes, that would be lovely, if the offer is still open."

"It is. Laars and I will take Ute back to Piraeus first. We can meet on Paros. It can get very busy there in peak season, but now should be okay. I'll give you the card of a small hotel. When we get back to Piraeus, I'll ring them and tell them you will be coming. We can use that hotel as our point of contact. We know them. It might be easier than finding our boat, in case we have to anchor further away. But look out for our yacht. You might see her when the Americans drop you off. I expect we'll be there before you. We leave Korissia tomorrow morning."

"Okay. Thank you."

"I will probably have a special trip for you too. I'm checking on that when we're back in Piraeus."

"Really? What sort of special trip?"

"A friend of mine has invited me to join him on his yacht. Well, it is more than a yacht. It's a luxury motor yacht. No sails. He designed it himself. It's big. It's beautiful. He asked if I would like to invite someone, someone special, to join me. There'll be other people on board also. Would you like to join me?"

"Wow," I said quietly. "Umm ... I'd love to." Then I had a thought. "Will I need to dress up? I don't have fancy clothes, just one black dress and sandals."

"That will be fine. See what the shopping is like in Paros or anywhere else you may stop. Don't worry too much though. It's a fun boat with a party atmosphere. Casual, not formal. We will also get to see more of the Aegean islands."

"And it's okay for me to come along?"

"Of course," said Neills. "You will be my guest."

I was speechless. It was all beyond my dreams. More than I could have hoped for. I had been thinking, perhaps I could get some work for the season somewhere, but this seemed too good an opportunity to pass up.

"That sounds fantastic. I'd love to join you."

"Good," said Neills, beaming his winning smile. He stood and kissed me on the top of my head. "We'd better get back to Korissia."

Twenty-nine

We gathered early by Greek standards, or perhaps our standards. Neills and I discussed the arrangements with the others, and everyone was happy. The Danes planned to leave early the following morning. We agreed any number of things could go wrong, but we had a plan to follow.

Walking back to our boat, I spoke with Ute, saying how good it was to meet him. "I believe you have been like a father to Neills."

"Yes, we have. My wife and I helped out Kirsten, his mother, when Neills was small. She worked and found it difficult caring for her young son."

"No father, I hear."

Ute laughed. "There was one obviously, but not in Denmark. She was alone with no parents. We don't know what happened and we've never asked. She never spoke about it and we didn't like to pry. She is a very sweet woman. Very pretty. I think men have taken advantage of her. Now she is much stronger, but still alone. Her son is her life. The same for Neills. He cares very much for his mother. They have a tight bond."

"Being a human rights lawyer takes him away from her quite a lot, I imagine."

"Oh ... he told you that?"

"Um, yes. I think I have that right. I know he spends a lot of time in London. He's a friend of my brother's. He's often there. He must go to other countries too, unless it's just London he visits."

"That's something I don't know too much about. Titles mystify me. I'm a humble carpenter." Ute chuckled in that mischievous way he had.

"Yes ... sure you are," I said. "You just threw that little boat together."

He laughed again. "More or less."

We eased our way into the day; lunched, took walks, rested and finally had an early farewell dinner.

I slept well that night, even though I expected excitement to keep me awake.

Early morning and I was the first up on deck making coffee for everyone. The smell stirred them. I enjoyed that moment of stillness and solitude. I looked across to where *Olin II* had been moored, now an empty space.

As I sat, a breeze suddenly took hold. Touching hurt my fingers again. It was the 'frozen moment,' revisited. The water stopped lapping. Then it was gone, leaving me feeling weak and shaken. It was happening too often. It hadn't touched me in years and now it was three, four times in as many weeks.

"Talking to yourself, Annabelle, or can anyone join in?" said Danny.

"Oh, was I?" I laughed. "That's a bad sign." For once I was glad of Danny's company. "I've made coffee. Shall I go to the café and get some pastries?"

"Wait till the girls get up. Maybe we'll all go."

We decided on one more breakfast at the café we'd become so familiar with. It was time to consider the rest of the trip. With the map spread across the table, we planned our route. We decided to sail to Kythnos next, Serifos, maybe try for Syros and then over to Paros.

"We have a week and a half with Annabelle," said Kate. "We may be pushing it to fit all those islands in and enjoy each one, but let's see how we go. We need to keep our eye on getting Annabelle to Paros by the due date. We can do the others in our final week. What do you think, Annabelle?"

"Look ... I'm happy with any of it. It would be nice to spend time getting to know an island, as you say, Kate. See what we think of Kythnos and go from there. But having those islands as our itinerary makes it easy. There are so many, we could get carried away and go off course."

"It's also what we told the charter company, but I'm not sure how much they worry about it," said Danny. "I suppose they need to have an itinerary for insurance and if their yacht goes missing. All good with you, Clio?"

"Like Annabelle, it's all good with me. They all look wonderful. I wonder if any more have plate-smashing restaurants?"

The proprietor, Aléxandros, came over just as we were packing up. "You leave too?"

"Yes, tomorrow," said Kate.

"Then we must have farewell dinner, here, tonight."

"Oh great," said Clio and leapt from her seat. "Do you smash plates?"

"No ... sorry. But you have very good time," he said. "So ... it is settled. We have the best menu for tonight."

For the rest of the day, we hired four clapped-out bicycles and rode around the flatter areas, as the brakes were practically non-existent. Some yachts were coming into the bay, some leaving. Peak season activity could be felt, even though it was still a few weeks away. We decided to get ready for an early-morning sail, as we didn't know what condition we'd be in after the evening dinner.

Aléxandros greeted us like long-lost friends. The dinner was indeed grand, with similar food to the night before. Beer, ouzo and retsina flowed. After other patrons left, Aléxandros, waiters and the dishwasher joined us. It must have been the Danes' introduction that gave us status. The combined English of Aléxandros and the rest of the staff was good enough for them to share stories of tourists' histrionics, and I was sure we would be included in the next episode. We learnt more about local folklore, sailing tips and unpredictable weather. As other tavernas closed, the remaining patrons and staff gathered around. Tables and chairs shuffled to create an ever-growing party. No one wore a watch, but as the night didn't really start until at least ten o'clock, it was early hours before we returned to the yacht.

By mid-morning, when we woke, we were well happy we'd done the packing the day before. With all the activity we'd shared, I felt that my relationship with the others had become inclusive and fun. A happy bunch of people left Korissia late that morning.

Thirty

In no hurry, we talked as we readied to sail. I decided to broach the subject of the latest offer from Neills. I hadn't dug deep enough to know why I felt hesitant, but I needed to share.

"Neills has a friend who has a big yacht, like a 'yacht' yacht, motor yacht, you know, the big kind," I said. "The royal kind, the magnate kind." As soon as the burbled comment sprang from my mouth, I felt its snobbishness.

"That's nice," said Danny.

"Neills has been asked to invite a friend. He's invited me. He's just yet to confirm it."

"Nice," said Kate.

"I might have to get some better clothes, the next town we're in." I definitely had the snob trowel out, but I couldn't stop. I guess their reaction was predictable.

Danny said, "What's this yacht's name?"

"I don't know," I said. "There are going to be others on board. Party atmosphere, Neills said."

"Okay," said Danny.

"You guys don't seem too interested."

"What do you want us to say?" said Kate. "You don't seem to know too much about it. I've heard about some of those party yachts. They can get pretty wild. So long as you're up for it, Annabelle."

"I'll be with Neills," I said.

"It might be one of those keys-in-the-middle-of-the-table kinda parties," said Clio. "But maybe not keys."

"I was trying not to get into that, Clio," said Kate. "Annabelle's a big girl. She can look after herself. I'm sure she's sussed it out. I hope you have a good time, Annabelle. It sounds plenty luxurious."

I hadn't, of course, sussed it out. I only knew what Neills had told me, which didn't amount to much. Why would I need to investigate the boat myself and how in hell could I do that? But the thought hadn't even occurred to me. I was to be with Neills. He was a friend of my brother's. My brother thought I should go for it, if I was interested. Peter trusted him, otherwise he wouldn't have suggested I meet up with him.

"What do you know of Neills?" said Danny, interrupting my flimsy thoughts.

His question was quite valid, which annoyed me. I thought my travels had smartened me up – I now considered myself quite savvy. Of course, I was. Neills was who he said he was. Friend of Laars and Ute. Why should he not be okay? I was not being naïve. The idea that I needed to explain to Danny and the others annoyed me. I couldn't answer, which also annoyed me. I was back with my mother. My mother who had all the answers. All these thoughts buzzed around my brain a fraction of a second before I opened my mouth and the words spilled out.

"He's a friend of my brother's ... Peter knows him ... he's in their group ... Peter knew I liked him, knew Neills liked me ... Pete said I should go for it ... Neills had been asking about me ... keen enough to keep in touch with me ... invite me to sail with him on his friend's boat. He told me about his friend's yacht in London." After I said it, I couldn't remember whether he had or not. "I've received mail from him ... he's a human rights lawyer ... Danish ... lives with his mother and very close to her ... Neills said Ute had been like a father to him ... his mother raised Neills by herself ... Ute and his wife helped as best they could ... Neills and Laars met at primary school ... Ute said Neills's mother is a lovely woman."

My gabbling stalled as I looked to the shoreline, searching for more to tell. I'd run out of what I knew about Neills. I turned to face startled expressions. I searched for something to appease myself, that I had this. Everything was fine. Of course, it was. No one said a word. After an uncomfortable moment, they got back to the business of setting sail. I sat gazing out to sea. I was not going to let anyone spoil this for me. Even myself.

Back when I was in Sydney and gazing at my Greek Island-covered wall, I knew amazing things would happen when I got here. And they were happening. I shook myself out of doubt. Everything would be fine. Everything would be just fine.

Action calmed my bothering thoughts. No more was said on the subject. The sail to Kythnos was about four hours. The sea was calm and friendly, with only a slight breeze, making our sail easy and slow. Time was of no essence. My unsettled thoughts blew away with the breeze.

We sailed into Loutra, at the north-eastern end of the island, more yacht-friendly than the main ferry area of the harbour. We prepared anchors, lines and fenders, ready for the L-shaped break-water. Fortune favoured us as we slid into a vacant mooring.

Another pretty anchorage. We ate a late lunch sparingly, as we planned to have dinner at a taverna, or whatever we could find.

Ashore, we hunted for two motor scooters. Kate and I were eager to try out a spa in one of the springs we'd read about. By evening we'd found our taverna and two scooters for the following day. We all enjoyed the spa. Relaxed, we joined another table of yachties swapping sea shanties.

We woke late the following morning and breakfasted at the taverna we'd been at the night before, then took our scooters for a spin for a couple of hours. We decided to stay for three days, and these days effortlessly repeated themselves. In no hurry, we scootered and swam at a small beach we'd discovered. When we returned to the yacht later, we all decided to rest before the usual late dinner.

One morning, motoring to Chora, a village of wedged-together little white houses, we parked and walked the cobbled paths that wove shyly through the town, as if not wanting to cause a fuss. The hooves of horses and donkeys over many years had flattened and polished the inlaid stones, making them dangerously slippery to the untrained walker. I wished I had my daggy rubber thongs from home; they would have given me a better grip than the new leather sandals I'd bought in Athens. Although we were over religious buildings, we couldn't resist one particular Orthodox church. Its white exterior was in sharp contrast to the gold splendour inside. Intricate carvings adorned every space. It was so small, the four of us filled it to capacity.

Even though my time with Danny, Kate and Clio was winding down, days were splendid and stretched endlessly. The weather was glorious. A breeze caressed our skin and cooled us from the hot sun. Hues from sunsets reflected and dappled the water. The lowering sun freshened the sea air, providing a peaceful end to the days.

No further mention was made of the yacht I was soon to join.

The following day we rose late after a farewell dinner and set sail for the island of Serifos. We arrived at Livadhi, where we once again found ourselves in luck. Another perfect mooring. We soon discovered one drawback: mosquitoes. They loved Clio. A storm was also imminent.

"The winds can get up here," Danny said quietly to Kate, although I still heard. I felt for Danny, carrying a fear that could surface any time a blow was likely.

"Don't worry about it, I'll make sure we're fast," said Kate. Whispers carried again.

Clio had a ritual we'd all taken to. First, it was imperative we were on board as the sun set. Looking to the horizon, just as the sun hung at its lowest point, we'd be ready. Watching, waiting ...

"There ... nearly ... just about ..."

Breaths were held.

"Now ... yes ... woohoo."

Cheers, hoots all along the mooring just as the sun kissed the Earth. Yachties on both sides caught the fever.

Thirty-one

It was on to Serifos and another township named Chora, which was off the beaten track for most tourists, especially early in the season. Its rocky bareness did not provide a parade of beaches. So, we trailed seasoned yachties for the best mooring and enjoyed ready-made friendships. This Chora was bigger than the one on Kythnos, but just as pretty.

We went all out: a bus ride, hiking and scooter hire. As on the other islands, we feasted on fresh local produce with plenty of retsina, ouzo and beer, along with hot sweet coffee. Lamb and seafood were plentiful. I couldn't take to calamari, seeing the squid hanging like old socks on lines.

The sun-kissing ritual had evidently been passed on. Word came back that it was an ancient custom in the Greek Islands. We felt no need to explain and toasted the very ancient Clio.

We'd been told to visit Kamares at Sifnos, so we shortened our Serifos stay and set sail. Its speciality was potters, whose strong hands turned great lumps of clay into beautiful organic vessels. Way too big and heavy to purchase.

Photos mounted up and I stored the films in their tinfoil bags.

Getting them developed on the islands was out of the question and would also weigh more. In the meantime, I mailed postcards, knowing it could be weeks before they arrived at their destinations.

The letters I'd written and forgotten to post I still held and decided to keep until I was back in Piraeus. They would get there quicker and have more likelihood of actually arriving.

Another farewell dinner, my final one with Kate, Clio and Danny. Other yachties joined us. We dragged in anyone around, to join us. Greek dancing, arms locking shoulders, forming circles into smaller circles, we became more Greek than the Greeks. Even Danny danced, no longer worried about his technique. We stumbled into bed as dawn approached.

By early afternoon, bleary-eyed, we finally set off for Paros. Kate, Clio and Danny had wormed their way deep into my heart.

They came with me to find the small hotel Neills had recommended. It was delightful and the proprietors had received word to expect me. They had known Ute and Laars for many years, Laars since he was a little boy. Neills was a new addition.

My room was clean and basic. If I stood on tippy-toes, I could see the sea. At street level, the houses were higgledy-piggledy, with lanes winding their way, randomly it seemed, to mysterious destinations. It wasn't far to the sea front and I walked back to *Osprey* with the others. They planned to sail to another part of the island to moor.

Having hugged a teary farewell, I watched *Osprey* and her crew disappearing from my sight. A cold shiver ran through me. End of a chapter. Now alone, I was excited but anxious, which must have been why the 'frozen moment' came upon me again. I was getting used to it, knowing it would pass. When it passed, I went shopping.

Thirty-two

Dressing to wow was far in the past. I thought back to my farewell in Sydney. Heated rollers to set my hair, sprayed within an inch of its life. Step-ins and waist-length bodice bra. All holding me together under a strapless dress. I looked pretty on the outside, a prisoner inside. My mother had suggested I take the dress with me. I didn't.

Now alone with time to think, I ran through my travels right up to the group who'd just departed. My experiences, learnings, my reactions to people and theirs to me. Dan, Kate and Clio's lack of interest in my next venture, although put aside for a time, now returned and plagued me. Were they just not interested or did they genuinely not like the sound of the invitation? In which case, they had been too diplomatic to express their true feelings. Instead of ranting to them, perhaps I should have put the idea forward for their thoughts? Shared rather than informed. Too late now. It was my own hunger for adventure and infatuation with Neills, that caused me to rush in and accept the invitation. Everything will be fine, I assured myself.

Hunger on another level caught up with me. I hadn't eaten since breakfast and it was now late afternoon. I would have to dine alone, something I'd never done. Suppose Neills didn't come? Suppose? What if? I realised I'd spoken aloud – if he didn't turn up, I'd become the local mutterer.

Back at the hotel, I asked the owners, Elena and Dom, if they could suggest a friendly taverna. Yes, their cousin's place. More than that, they had their eldest daughter accompany me. Thea wanted to improve her English.

Neither Dom nor Elena had heard from Laars as yet. Sailing in the Aegean, unexpected weather conditions often occurred. I should not worry. In the meantime, I should enjoy their hotel and they would look after me. For the following days they commandeered a nephew, Con, to take me around the island, since he also wanted to improve his English. Improve was generous, we had to start from scratch, but we had fun miming and swapping words in English and Greek.

Twice daily I checked the waterfront, with no sight of *Olin II*. I began to make plans of my own. The ferry service was now in full swing and there were many islands to explore. Planning an itinerary kept my mind occupied.

Day five: I came back from being out all day, to find Neills and Laars happily chatting with Elena and Dom, while they waited for me. I hugged them both excitedly, which made me realise just how anxious I'd become.

We decided to leave in the morning, after one more night in the hotel, where Neills and Laars would take a room. That night, the private dining quarters of the hotel seated everyone who'd helped me during my stay. Even though they were purchased locally, everyone was overjoyed with the presents I'd bought them.

Mid-morning Elena and Thea walked us down to the waterfront. I hugged a final goodbye. "Keep safe," Elena said close to my ear, as Neills offered his hand for me to step aboard.

Thirty-three

Finally aboard *Olin II*, I could experience and see the exquisite workmanship of the yacht, expertly crafted and lovingly maintained. My father would have been crazy for her. And Peter, I suspect.

A smorgasbord lunch had been set out in the galley, along with a little pot of wildflowers. My curtained-off bed was already made, with more wildflowers carefully placed on the pillow. We sailed to another area of the island. I thought of *Osprey* but imagined she had long gone.

"We'll eat now on board. For dinner we'll eat at a little taverna we know along the waterfront. Tomorrow morning, we'll leave early," said Neills. "Elena told us you've seen a lot of the island already, so we'll go straight back to Piraeus. Laars has work and we have a boat to catch." Neills beamed.

Rye bread with cheeses and finely cut meats were laid out, along with a fresh pot of coffee. Later we took a walk. In the evening, we changed and dined at the taverna. There was still no discussion about the forthcoming trip. Who, what and where? I tried to bring it up, but Neills gently changed the subject. I did manage to dig a little further into Laars and Neills's friendship.

"You two are like brothers. Close brothers." Why beat around the bush.

They looked at one another and smiled.

"We are. I have a sister but no brothers," said Laars.

"And I'm an only child. Laars and his family are like a second family. Well, a first, as I always think of my mother as my ma and me. We barely make a family. Laars's family adopted both of us a long time ago."

I wanted to approach the subject of Neills's father but thought better of it. His reaction before had shut me down. Now he changed the subject again and talked about Laars and Ute's boat-building skills. We got onto the subject of my brother, and Neills's trips to London. He always looked forward to catching up with Peter, he said.

Although Neills and Laars were about the same age, Laars appeared to be more like an older brother, taking care of his younger sibling. Laars was totally comfortable in his skin, Neills a little wary. His good looks and studied charm had carried him through life, I imagined. Underneath, Neills wore a vulnerability. I found the quality charming. I held a natural desire, I believe most women share, a desire to care for someone. Perhaps that's how Laars felt. The whole package had certainly struck a chord with me.

Back on board after dinner, Neills was warm and friendly but beyond that, nothing. Fine, we had time. Maybe he was a shy person in front of Laars. I wondered if I passed muster. I wanted to speak with Laars on his own, suss out the big yacht to come and Neills's friend, but the opportunity never arose. There was a niggling feeling that Neills had orchestrated that. He was obviously a private person, keeping certain doors firmly closed, even with his close friend.

"Big day tomorrow, Annabelle, we had better get some shut eye," said Neills. "I'll say goodnight. Would you like to use the head first, or after us? We'll be quick if you'd like to take your time?"

"OK, you go first, that's fine."

"We'll have breakfast on board. Sleep well," said Laars.

"Okay ... goodnight."

"Goodnight Annabelle," said Neills.

No kiss goodnight, or even a peck on the forehead from Neills, as he'd done before. No rush, plenty of time.

Thirty-four

The sound of the sea's regular rhythm scudding the hull, gently woke me into wakefulness. A particularly loud thwack had me sitting bolt upright. Oh my God, I'd slept in. I had no clear idea of my duties but felt I should help. When I finally scrambled up on deck, we were in full sail.

"Morning, Annabelle," said Laars.

Neills was forward and didn't see me straight away.

"Good morning, Annabelle, did you sleep well?" he shouted from the bow.

"Good morning. I slept like a log, but I feel bad I didn't help you guys."

"No need," said Neills, as he came towards me.

"Well, let's get some breakfast, I need a coffee," said Laars. "We thought we'd wait for you."

"Well let me at least do that."

With coffees in hand, I said, "How far are we?"

"It won't be long before we reach Piraeus."

"I didn't mean to sleep so long ... you must be ravenous. Thanks for waiting."

With my previous experience of Danish food and what we had eaten yesterday, I searched and found rye bread and cheeses. There was more coffee in the pot. The sea was calm, sailing steady and talk sporadic, as we sat with our mugs of coffee.

"What's the meaning of *Olin II*?" I said.

"My grandfather's name was Olin," said Laars. "We originally had a boat called *Olin* and, like my grandfather, it became old. We built *Olin II* in remembrance of him. He was a wonderful man, tough and disciplined with his children and grandchildren, but we loved him."

By late morning, Piraeus came into view. We moored away from the mayhem of the main harbour. I sat and watched as Neills and Laars took the boat expertly into a mooring. Once we'd docked, I went below and finalised packing. There was little to do. Their efficiency ran to below deck as well. The only things out of place were mine. The mooring was booked for a couple of hours, and after that Laars would sail the yacht to its permanent mooring, which his father kept around the other side of Piraeus.

"Laars will join us for dinner," Neills said, as we took our luggage ashore and waved goodbye to Laars. "I've booked an hotel not far from here. I've already booked two rooms for myself and Laars, let's make sure they have another."

"Okay." Separate rooms, nice, no pressure. My trip with Neills was really happening.

The hotel was certainly an upgrade from the place I'd stayed when I first arrived in Piraeus. We checked in and as Neills was about to pay, I said I could pay for my room, I didn't expect him to. He wouldn't hear of it.

"Let's make sure your room is okay, then I have to make some phone calls and arrange a few things. Reception had a message from my mother. I am trying to buy a house for her, so I need to speak with her immediately. I'll see you in reception in two hours. We'll meet Laars there too."

Thirty-five

I still knew nothing of the forthcoming trip. I wanted to write home and to Peter. It would be good not only to tell them what I had been doing, but what was planned. I went for a walk and bought postcards and stamps and two airletters, one for mum and dad and one for Clive.

I found a café, ordered a coffee and wrote. As I'd written postcards earlier, I numbered them, so they knew which to read first. It took me longer than I thought, and I realised two hours had elapsed. I didn't have time to get back to the post office. Besides, I still hadn't finished my current letter to my parents or another to Clive.

"How's your mother?" I said, when I saw Neills waiting for me.

"Oh, she's fine. She panics when she's given legal forms to fill in. They can wait until I get home. Did you have a nice couple of hours?"

I told him about the café and writing home. "I must finish my letters and get them posted before we leave. So, are you going to tell me what we're doing?"

"Oh, haven't I? Sorry."

"Only that your friend has a luxury yacht, there'll be other people on board and it would be okay to dress casually. By the way, I couldn't find much on the islands in the way of any formal wear, do you think I should look around Piraeus?"

"No. I'm sure whatever you have will be fine. Anyway, we don't have time. You will look good in anything." He smiled.

That was the first compliment he'd paid me and I blushed.

"Laars will be with us in ... oh there he is."

Talk of the forthcoming trip was dropped.

"Where shall we eat?" said Laars.

"There's that rooftop restaurant we've been to," Neills said, as we stepped into the soft, beckoning twilight. "Shall we go there?"

"Oh yes, good choice," said Laars.

A narrow network of laneways led us to a flight of stairs. In single file, we trod carefully across a rooftop, onto unsteady and uneven timber walkways. I stopped for a brief moment, to lift my gaze from careful footsteps. Vast hazy views of Piraeus, with gentle light reflected in the water, took my breath away. An emotional view for me, but at dusk, the less than attractive side of the harbour looked misty, giving it the look of a Monet painting. We continued on, jutting in and out over two more rooftops, until we finally arrived at a large terrace built out from a room under a roof.

"This is amazing," I said breathlessly, my concentration divided between the view and the precarious walkway. "How on earth did you learn of such a place? A casual tourist would never find this."

"And I hope they never do," said Laars.

"It's amazing, isn't it?" said Neills. "Just getting here is an adventure in itself."

Delicious smells wafted from under a tarpaulin, attached to the edge of the roof and stretched over a timber frame. The kitchen was set deep into the roof at the back. The end of the terrace was free of overhead cover, giving the feeling of sitting at the end of the world, with another world laid out below. Our table was at the edge of the terrace, barricaded by a fragile-looking railing.

"I don't think I should put any weight on this," I said.

"Mmmm ... probably best not to," said Laars.

"We got here just in time," said Neills, as we saw more people arriving.

"You have to be quick. They don't take bookings and it's first in, first served," said Neills.

Still more people arrived but were turned away. "A night like this, everyone has the same idea," said Laars. "Not a cloud in sight."

The evening was warm and sultry. The sun still not set. I told them of the sun-kissing-the-earth ritual and how important it was to be observed.

"What a great thing to do," said Laars. "I'm not sure we'll actually see the sun kiss the earth from here, but we'll get a rough idea. There's still a horizon it will touch and sink behind."

We raised our glasses and praised the moment even though we'd missed the touch-down from our viewpoint. The sun was touching down somewhere.

The menu was whatever they were serving on the night. The main dish of course, was the ambience with lashings of romance. I sat with two wonderful men. How could it be any better?

"This is fabulous." I raised my glass. "Thank you, both of you, for bringing me here ... and for the chance to sail on your beautiful boat, Laars."

Neills pointed out various landmarks scattered around the 180° view. The hues of light changed as night closed in and the water picked up pastel colours and swallowed them whole into its inky depths. Lights flickered into life and their reflections fractured in the wake of motoring boats. Smells of cooking, salt air and diesel wafted around on the light breeze.

"What will you do now, Laars?" I asked.

"I'm going back to Copenhagen. I have a business to run, not like some," he laughed and indicated Neills.

"Hey, hey, not so fast. I am on holiday now. I've been working very hard."

"What sort of business, Laars?"

"I am but a simple carpenter." He laid out his broad hands, a smile creasing his face.

"Oh yes," I laughed, "just like your father."

"He's much more than that," Neills said. "His chairs are much in demand. From time to time he designs interiors of houses and then renovates them. But his chairs have won awards in Denmark."

"I won't win any more if I don't get back to work. This year is very busy for me."

"Are you married?" I said. It suddenly dawned on me I'd never asked Neills if he had ever been married. I knew he wasn't then.

"No, not yet, but maybe soon," he said and smiled at Neills.

"She's a lovely woman ... of course you know that, Laars."

"Yes, she is."

This time I changed the subject. I didn't want to talk about my situation. Neills already knew and I certainly didn't want to harp on about it.

Back at the hotel I said a final farewell to Laars. "It's been very good to meet you and a pleasure to meet your father. Please pass on my regards."

Such a full day. I said an exhausted goodnight to them both.

Too tired to finish my letters, I hoped I'd have time the following day. Not knowing how long I'd be on the forthcoming trip, I wanted to get them posted or my parents, in particular, would worry.

Thirty-six

I woke refreshed and early after a deep sleep. Stretching luxuriously in the double bed; with all that space, no wonder I slept so well, I placed my feet on the floor and sprang to a tall stretch. I was so looking forward to this trip. Not knowing exactly what was in store seemed to make it all the more exciting. I looked out at the sky and saw the makings of a beautiful sunny day.

Neills was waiting for me in the foyer.

"Let's have some breakfast on the way. It's a nice walk and your bag isn't too heavy. Are you okay with that?"

"Yes, sure."

There was a disparity between our bags. Me with my grubby rucksack, which had been thrown into the back of a dishevelled Poppy and then chucked into available space on the yacht; it groaned from overwork. Neills's bag, on the other hand, shouted elegance: a carpetbag of the designer type with worn leather handles and a bronze metal clip. Worry about my clothes surfaced again.

"Let's have a coffee here," he said.

We settled and ordered a pastry each. Determined not to badger him, I let Neills talk in his own time.

"*Sea Falcon* is a beautiful boat," he said finally, as if he hadn't held me in suspense.

"Mm ... interesting name ... what's your friend's name?"

"Fahim. I won't bother you with the rest." Neills chuckled. "It goes on and on in true Saudi style and I don't always get it in the correct order."

"He's from Saudi Arabia?"

"Yes."

"Okay. I don't think I've met any Saudis. Either in London or on my travels." How many Saudis did a Western person meet in their life?

"I doubt you'd meet any hitchhiking around Europe. Or travelling in a van. If they travel, it's usually in style. You wouldn't meet any unless it was by appointment."

My thoughts jumped to my clothes again. I'll have to wear the little black dress every day. Certainly, every night. I waited for Neills to continue.

"Where to start."

Neills, I was learning, was linear. The sequence of events was important to him. He had no time for randomness or spontaneity.

"Fahim is from a wealthy family. His father owns several companies and consequently sent Fahim to be educated in England and the United States. Now Fahim is wealthy in his own right. Not only does he chair some of his father's companies, but he also has companies of his own. He has made his father very proud. He's the eldest son, and that's important in their tradition. Now that oil is making Saudi Arabia a wealthy country, there are expectations for the top families to be well educated and expand that wealth. He is doing well in that respect, in fact ... very well indeed."

Neills was obviously very proud to know this man.

"Is he married ... does he have children?" I asked.

"Yes ... two sons ... and at the moment he has only one wife and I think he's happy with that. His wife is well educated too, which is unusual. He regards education very highly. He wants his wife to be able to communicate intelligently with their sons. Also unusual in their society. I imagine they will have more children."

Knowing very little about Saudi Arabians or Arabs in general, or their world, I thought back to what I'd heard. Stories of women markets in the desert, keeping them in cages to fatten them up for sale. Ghastly beyond imagining. There was talk of blond Western girls being offered highly paid work in harems. No one ever heard how they fared.

Now, hearing Neills talk about his friend, I thought a lot of it was probably hearsay. This man, Fahim, didn't sound like that. That he was a Saudi was maybe why Neills hadn't told me about him. He didn't want to scare me off. I'm sure he'd heard those stories too.

"I heard the women were not allowed to be educated ... or work," I said.

"You're right about work, in the context we know it. But I suppose you could say running a household in a large mansion and managing servants, is work. Some of the Saudi women are educated. Home educated."

"Mansion, servants .... sure takes the wind out of my nine-to-five job. Have you seen this mansion? What's it like?"

"I haven't been there but apparently there are greeting and enter-tainment areas, many bedrooms, servants' rooms, all housed in a large walled compound. Fahim can show his racehorses to prospec-tive buyers in the compound. They have many guest quarters, being very hospitable people."

Neills's tone told me he wasn't amused by my flippancy. As he had a beautiful voice and I loved his accent, I was happy for him to wax lyrical about his friend as long as he wanted. But I did bolt up at the last item, in the list of his friend's assets.

"He has racehorses too?"

"He owns a few, but he's planning to build on that ... so he's told me. And what might appeal to you, I imagine, Annabelle, is his interest in art. You've spoken of yours."

"Really? Yes, that is intriguing. Do you know if he has a specific interest?"

"No, although he likes both classical and modern art, I believe."

"And what about you, Neills? Do you share his interest?"

"Not so much. Well, I have never studied art. When Fahim was in America and London, he spent a lot of time in museums and art galleries. I believe he collects too."

Of course he does, I thought. With wealth, a person can. That much wealth had never been visible in my life. My father was considered wealthy, but nothing like this chap. Owning your own home, a beach shack, a couple of cars and a boat was doing more than all right.

"Will his wife and children be on board?"

"No. His yacht is his getaway. It's where he can have a break from his day-to-day responsibilities. He takes his wife and children to Europe quite often. His sons will be educated in England and the United States as he was, so he wants them to experience Europe before they start their serious studies."

Neils went on to say Fahim's wife would not be on board. She was educated, but not equal. Women weren't exactly equal anywhere. Life for women was the same no matter where you were, to a greater or lesser extent, I'd learned.

It was then I remember the Americans' words. A party boat.

Thirty-seven

My thoughts about a 'party boat' must have shown on my face. "Annabelle, you look worried. He's a good man. You've heard terrible rumours and stories about the Arabs, haven't you ... I can tell that's what you're thinking. That's what they are: just rumours and stories."

Neills was more astute than I realised, but he was right, it was the party boat that concerned me. From what I'd picked up about Neills, he didn't seem the partner-swapping kind and, as I would be with him, I relaxed. But there was no point lying.

"Yes, I have heard those stories." I paused with a new thought. "Have you been on his yacht before?"

"Yes ... as I say, it's large and beautiful. But Annabelle, don't worry about anything. Also, you will have your own cabin." Neills paused. "Fahim was educated in the West. He likes having Western people around him. Also, his wife doesn't like the sea, that's why she's not coming. He sometimes takes the boys out as they love the sea and the boat. But not his wife. And besides, you are *my* guest on his boat, Annabelle, not his guest."

I smiled, reassured. But Neills had not finished with Fahim's life story.

"He has built an art gallery in his compound at home. An air-conditioning unit is kept at the perfect temperature and moisture level to preserve his collection of paintings and sculptures. You will see on board copies of some of his paintings. I believe you will have this in common. He loves to discuss art, but only if people are interested."

"Does he paint?"

"Yes, a little. He gets frustrated that he doesn't have a great talent, though. He's such a perfectionist. He told me when he was going to university in the United States, he would visit as many galleries and museums as he could. He'd stand for hours looking at works of art and try his hand at what he'd seen. Sometimes he'd take a sketch pad to the gallery and draw. His talent, he says, lies in collecting and appreciating art, rather than trying his hand at it, but he does dabble from time to time."

There was no doubting Neills enthusiasm for his friend.

"He's certainly a well-rounded person." I felt faintly concerned that none of this was mentioned to me in front of Laars. "Has Laars met him?"

"No. Why do you ask?"

"No reason. You're very close to Laars, I thought he would know this part of your life. It seems quite a big part."

"Laars doesn't govern my life. They're like family to me but they don't own me."

Mmmm. There are strong boundaries with this man. "It was just a question, Neills. I meant nothing by it."

He was silent, then got up to pay. "We should go. I'll tell you the rest on the way." We walked. "Fahim is very down to earth. You'll find him easy to talk to. But I should be letting you make up your own mind. I've said enough."

"One more question though, while we're on the subject ... how did you two meet?"

"Ah, that was interesting. We both love falconry ..."

"Falconry as well ... okaaay."

"Yes, you've heard of it?"

"Of course, it's just ... well ... I haven't met anyone who's been involved in it before. I don't know much ... well, anything about it."

"That much wealth gives a person the opportunity to indulge all their fantasies and others like me enjoy it too. Though I don't own a bird."

I waited for more as we walked.

"It's been around for hundreds of years ..."

"I meant the story of how you met."

"Oh yes ... but falconry comes into it and a bit of background won't hurt. You said you don't know anything about it. We have time."

He smiled his disarming smile. He liked to share his knowledge, but not his personal self, something I was learning about him.

"Falconry has been practised in Europe for a long time. In fact, there's a place in the Netherlands called Valkenswaard, where falcons used to fly over on their migration south. Valk, it's Dutch for falcon. The birds were caught on their migration, then trained and used in the Dutch royal courts, as early as the seventeenth century. So ... I was a little interested in the sport of falconry and I'd met a few people in Holland and Germany who were falconers. Then when I was in England one time, I heard of a well-respected falconry club in the north. They sometimes have guest speakers, so I went along and the speaker ..."

"Don't tell me ... it was Fahim."

"Well, no … it was his father. Fahim was with him. His father's English is not so good and Fahim was there to interpret."

"… and you struck up a friendship."

"We did indeed. He was soon going to be in Denmark, so I gave him my phone number and we've been friends ever since."

"Lovely story."

"But you find it amusing."

"No, not at all. I was imagining friends in Australia swapping tennis racquets for leather-hooded falcons. I don't even know if it's legal in Australia."

"Tennis is an honourable sport too," said Neills.

"Of course, it is … I guess we're just not that broad in our interests in Australia."

We were close to the water and the area where a large boat could dock. Neills suggested we sit on one of the benches dotted around.

"*Sea Falcon* will moor here. Not long to go."

We sat still and quiet. Neills's story of his friend and their meeting eased me into this new world I was to meet. The Americans and the little yacht we'd hired seemed a lifetime ago. My mail completely forgotten.

"I think that's *Sea Falcon*." Neills shielded his eyes. "See … look … she's a hundred-footer, three decks … hard to miss."

"Where … oh my goodness … I see what you mean."

Shivers ran down my spine. The boat sailed closer and reminded me of something. Then the 'frozen moment' came again. Stillness. A strange cool shift in the air brushed across my face and over my body. I was frozen to the spot. The hairs on the back of my neck and body stood on end. In my mind, I was back when I was little, playing with the motorboat my uncle gave me, sending it up and down the paddling pool, as I made wave noises. I realised then, I had imagined such a boat.

As abruptly as the sensation came, it went.

I was looking at a sleek, enormous white yacht with a great deal of attitude, gliding silently towards us.

PART FOUR

Thirty-eight

Neills continued to talk, "... he had his own architect design it and contracted it to a company in the Netherlands. No expense spared, the engines ..."

His voice trailed away. I didn't hear or listen anymore. I didn't care about engines. I was spellbound. I knew this boat. Why did I know this boat? I didn't know this boat and had never seen it before, but I had a sense of knowing it. My little-girl self knew it.

Standing a few metres away were another young couple. Had they been there a moment ago? I wasn't sure how long I'd been wrapped up in my mind. The woman was young, younger than me. She bubbled with nervous excitement, bobbed from foot to foot, shimmered and grinned. Her companion, a few years older, approaching thirty, recognised Neills and touched his forehead in a mock salute.

"Are they passengers too?" I said.

"Yes."

With exterior cool, the man smoked a cigarette and draped a languid arm around the girl.

"Do you know them?"

"A little."

The *Sea Falcon* eased into her mooring, barely ruffled the water. As she came to rest, the gangplank slipped across to the wharf and two male crew came ashore to greet people and collect the luggage. Sleek and unobtrusive, the crew were dressed in navy pants and white-collared, short-sleeved t-shirts, with a gold crest embroidered on the breast pocket. Navy and white plimsolls fitted expensively around tanned, sockless feet.

The gangplank's timber was smooth. Polished handrails welcomed your hands and eased you forward. At the end of this short journey, a welcoming committee greeted us. Crew and general staff stood behind a man who could be none other than Fahim. He smiled warmly.

We were first on, and Fahim and Neills hugged. Then I was introduced.

Clothed in blinding white cotton everything, the man looked spectacular. Good looking, about Neills's age, with confidence to spare. Why would he not be? Fahim stood exotic, masculine and friendly. Around five foot ten, comfortably proud in his soft flowing, white attire. His national dress. A broad, trimly bearded smile showed perfect white teeth. Expensive leather sandals held him elegant and firm to the deck. The sea breeze caressed and fluttered his clothing. Picture-perfect for any high-end glossy fashion or travel magazine. I took it all in, suitably impressed, as I moved along that gangplank.

He shook my hand, which surprised me. Neills had mentioned that Saudi men don't shake women's hands, but, as he said, Fahim enjoyed the company of Westerners. More than just shake my hand, Fahim held it with his other hand, like you would an injured bird. He seemed to study me, rather than greet. His brown eyes were warm and his smile came from the depths of his being. His intensity unnerved me.

I had never been close to a traditionally dressed Arab man before. There was no comparison with the men in the streets of Aden and Port Said we'd seen on the way over by ship to England. This man owned his space, personal and physical.

Another couple arrived and we were ushered aft. Two couples were already aboard and, with six new arrivals, we were ten guests in all. Drinks in beautiful flutes were proffered and introductions made by an older woman, immaculately dressed in similar style to the greeting crew, though more befitting her age. She introduced herself as Lucile. Introductions were made to crew and staff, which included the Dutch Captain, Eduart. One staff member was assigned four guests and was to look after their cabins and personal needs. Our luggage had already been taken to our cabins. I knew Fahim's wife would not be aboard. This woman must be his assistant. I didn't know how it worked on a yacht like this.

Again, in my head, I heard the Americans' voices, or rather their silences on board *Osprey* that day. What did I know about this trip? I was Neills's guest and he had assured me of that. I wouldn't be expected to play around, if that was the game. With that in mind, I was not going to miss out on this trip, no matter what.

When crew and staff took their leave, we were invited to sit or wander the aft deck. The area was huge. Another drink was offered if we wished. Small chit-chat, mingling, things you say when you don't know anyone, but will get to know them. None of the women knew each other. The men did. Not best-buddy knowing but acquainted. I had the impression the other women knew their men only casually. Neills was talking with Fahim on another part of the deck, so I wandered away and took in the décor and view.

Beautiful didn't really describe this boat. I had nothing to compare it with, so I didn't know what other yachts of this grandeur were like. It was minimalist in style; exquisite soft white leather seating curved around the aft deck. Passing the drinks table, I noticed the champagne was Krug. Sparkling mineral water was available, which would be my next drink, if I could drag myself away from the expensive stuff.

Still concerned with my evening wear, I looked around at what was being worn. Was that a Mary Quant outfit? To hell with it. That Dutch woman wasn't so up to the minute, so I relaxed. I heard English and European accents speaking English.

Neills and Fahim separated. Bringing the crowd together, Fahim tapped a glass.

"We are just about to set sail and I want you all to enjoy yourselves. The first island we'll be stopping at is Delos, then Amorgós on the western side of the Cyclades, and wherever else takes our fancy. I'll speak to you later in more detail, but in the meantime, enjoy a drink as we leave Piraeus."

Neills was at my side, as we watched the harbour and the approaching whitewashed breakwater.

"Everything okay?"

"More than," I said. "It's all so very beautiful. Thank you for inviting me." I looked at the passing harbour. "I love this bit." I laughed. "I talk like I'm an old hand, but I loved watching the harbour recede when we set sail in that little yacht. Now here I am again, from one extreme to another. I've only been here about a month, and this is my second time sailing from Piraeus."

Thirty-nine

As we stood looking at the passing buildings and boats, Neills put his arm around me. Apart from a peck on the forehead, that was the first physical contact he'd made towards me. I moved closer.

"He doesn't drink ... Fahim ... is he a strict Muslim?"

"He doesn't drink alcohol and in that he's strict. But he doesn't object to others enjoying it, as you can see."

"What does he get from being so hospitable to strangers?"

"They're not all strangers. They're bringing their latest loves, mostly. And the rich are happy to share their wealth, Annabelle."

His tone again. I needed to be on my toes. Latest loves? I wondered. I wanted to pursue the reason more deeply, but at the same time I didn't want to antagonise Neills, or look a gift horse in the mouth. Maybe I just needed to lighten up.

"We'll be having lunch soon," Neills said. "All your things are in your cabin if you want to unpack, otherwise you can stay up here. By the way, in your wardrobe you'll see a surprise. They're all yours to use for the evenings."

He smiled and squeezed my arm. "See you at lunch."

Having passed the breakwater, a wall I was beginning to love, I re-joined the chit chat.

One of the English accents belonged to a young woman, whose parents were from Trinidad. Her deep throaty voice matched her dark cascade of curls. Her boyfriend, the total opposite, was from Sweden, with blond hair and pale blue eyes. The Dutch girl was languid, with perfect English; her boyfriend from the Dutch Caribbean, with closely cropped tight curls. Another English girl was from London. Both she and her boyfriend had Cockney accents. Both were very savvy and quick-witted and were wearing the latest gear. There was also an English guy from Brighton and his girlfriend from New Zealand. They were the couple I'd seen waiting at the wharf. Most guests were holidaying in Greece or travelling through. None of the girls had been on board before and were invited by their boyfriends. Boyfriends; a loose term I suspected.

We excused ourselves to check out our cabins. Mine was a large bedroom. There was space to move easily around the double bed. Clean lines, a minimum of fuss, exquisite luxury.

After gasping at the grandeur, I took a tour of the bathroom and lapsed into childish glee. I smothered my face in the thick, fluffy, white towels, breathing in their freshness. I ran my fingers across the expensive brands of shampoo, conditioner, moisturiser, hand cream and talcum powder, and the five miniature bottles of expensive French perfume. I sniffed them all. A fresh white orchid was reflected in the mirror. The detail; a woman's razor and soothing gel, separate soap for the shower and a smaller one for the basin, both embossed with the same emblem I'd seen on the shirts of the crew. Up close, I could see it was a bird. A sea falcon, if there is such a thing. I doubt Fahim would leave that to chance, unless this was the one and only sea falcon. Proud in gold outline, its head was in profile, under-laid with blue wavy lines.

On the bed I noticed more big, fluffy, white towels, skilfully folded into a flower, with a large bar of sweet-smelling soap, in the centre.

A large porthole gave me an expansive view.

I sat on the bed with my hand sunken into the towels, staring at the room. Then I noticed a Picasso on the wall. It looked so real, I inspected it closely. It was paint and this must be one of the copies Neills had spoken about. Did Fahim own the original somewhere in his compound? I was gobsmacked. This was one of Picasso's disjointed portraits of women. It was disturbing and mesmerising at the same time. Colours from the painting, I noticed, were picked out in the décor. Cushions, a throw and pillowcases on the bed. Everything else was white. The rest of the cabin was pale timber, so flush it was difficult to find the wardrobes or cupboards.

Then I remembered Neills had mentioned a surprise in the wardrobe. Having figured out that the doors opened with a gentle push, I swung open both doors. My jaw dropped.

Six full-length dresses in basic block colours, with matching sandals beneath each dress. I plonked myself on the floor and stared. There was no way those sandals would fit. I hauled myself up and tried on a pair. Perfect. I guess you can't go too wrong with a sandal. The shoes fitting my foot fascinated me more than the dresses at that moment. I tried all the sandals.

The dresses. No way would they fit.

Removing one of the dresses, designed so a bra would not be seen, I slipped it over my head. Crosscut, it hugged my body and flowed to ankle length. A mix of silk and cotton, smooth and sensuous. I gasped again, a perfect fit.

Presumably, we were to be on board for six nights. I had never asked how long. I'd forgotten that detail. I remembered that the surprise was for my use in the evenings. Nevertheless, there was room to hang my little black dress.

The cabin's carpet was like running your hand through a sheep's fleece. I had become accustomed to timber floors on a small yacht, and crappy hotels where rugs and carpets were sticky and thread-bare – and who knew what the Kombi's floor was like? Seldom seen. This carpet was like walking on fluffy clouds. I dropped to the floor once again, gawped into the wardrobe and turned to take in the cabin, from a different viewpoint.

No wonder Neills had said not to bother too much about evening wear. He knew? Of course, he knew. I stared and rambled though the idea of whether the clothes were chosen to match the woman or the woman to match the clothes. Was this a job lot? I had to admit all the women on board were slender, about the same body size as me, some taller, but not by much.

The dresses were in a rainbow of colours. Blue of the Aegean sky, sunshine yellow, fire engine red, soft green, burnt orange and finally navy. All those colours suited me.

Were other wardrobes the same? I'd find out soon enough.

Forty

At an endless buffet lunch, accompanied by Krug and other wines from Europe, I forced myself not to be a pig. I didn't want to get too used to so much wine, so I interspersed with mineral water, but that only lasted so long. Catering must have thought we were over local alcohol, as it was beer from the Netherlands and Belgium and other parts of Europe. The chilled bubbles in sparkling bowl-shaped glasses, made it difficult to pass up just one more glass of Krug. That I managed to find a modicum of control, I put down to Neills. The thought of him seeing me two-parts drunk as soon as I was on board was underwhelming.

Neills sat next to me at lunch. Attentive and sociable, the perfect gentleman. He knew how to charm. Perhaps he acted as Fahim's assistant. Sharing the load. A fleeting thought crossed my mind: did Neills work for Fahim? His comment: 'I have been invited to bring a special guest.' Well, what a job if that was the case.

Fahim, exuding warmth, welcomed everyone on board. It was to be a wonderful few days, he hoped, for everyone. He then left. I didn't see him eat.

Once we'd had our fill, I suggested to Neills we stand at the rails, watch the waves and catch the sea breeze. He was to be my companion on this trip and I wanted to talk with him. Get to know him. There was a gap that needed filling.

"I need a moment with Fahim. I'm speaking for him this evening. Just give me a minute."

I stayed seated and joined the other guests. Eva, the Dutch woman, was nearby. We were about to speak, when Neills tapped a glass.

"For the women, you have by now seen the dresses in your wardrobes. Fahim enjoys a theme. This theme expresses his passion for art. He takes the colours from a favourite painting and brings the mood of that painting into the room. The painting comes to life through you. Wear whatever colour you like but wear a different colour each evening. Tonight he's taking colours from Gauguin's Tahitian paintings. The men know what to wear. We'll see you for aperitifs at seven-thirty."

While I waited for Neills to return, I made my way to the side. So, there we have it. Fahim's passion for art coming to life. Theme parties I'd attended were usually on the crazy side. This was elegant. I was deep in thought when Neills joined me.

"A penny for your thoughts, Annabelle?"

"Oh ... I was thinking about my father. Nothing in particular."

"And what were you thinking about your father? What led you to those thoughts?"

"Um ... well I don't like to be disrespectful, but there was always an issue with my parents on theme parties. My mother loved to hold them, while my father was not so keen. He refused to dress up."

"Is he an angry man, do you think?"

"No, not at all. He loves my mother dearly and will let her do anything, up to a point. That point is telling him what to do."

"Did they marry young?"

"My mother was young, but my father is older, by about ten years."

"Was he married before?"

"No. He never wanted to settle down, until he met my mother. Between you and me, I think he enjoyed being a bit of a lad, before he met my mother."

"Bit of a lad?"

"Well, to be blunt, played the field. Ladies loved him. Still do." I giggled at the thought. Women were always flirting with daddy.

"Have they been married a long time?"

"Um ... going on twenty-three years, I expect. My brother is twenty-two. Then I came along."

"Bit of a player then?"

"Yes. You know that expression?"

"Oh yes."

"But in the nicest way and before he met my mother," I said with loyalty. I couldn't be sure, but was that recrimination in Neills's tone?

"By the way, the dresses and sandals are beautiful. How on earth did you get the right foot size?"

"Just a guess."

"Men don't normally guess such things. My father, my brother, Clive, would not have a clue about women's sizes. Slim, big, tall, short is about it. Is that a trait of Danish men? They take notice of such things?"

"I know from my mother. I shopped with her when she wanted to buy a new dress. Sometimes I still do, if it's a special occasion."

Neills took me on a tour of the boat. Part of it was cordoned off for Fahim's private quarters. Everything was stylish, carefully chosen, Scandinavian in style, elegant and simple. This gave the copied Impressionist and Classical paintings more emphasis.

"Six dresses," I said as we walked. "Does that mean six nights?"

"If you want."

"What do you mean? This trip has no end date?"

"Of course there is an end date. The others will be disembarking in about four days. We will be going to Idhra after we drop them off in Piraeus. There are many artists on the island and Fahim likes to see their latest works. You can stay on if you like."

The others only have four dresses in their wardrobes, was my first thought. Did Neills know I'd accept the invitation? He was right, and yes, he probably knew.

Staying on board after the others left would give us extra time together. I was thrilled.

"I've heard about that island and the artists and writers who live there."

"And musicians, all kinds of people."

We arrived back where we'd started on the aft deck and sat on the soft leather seating that hugged the interior. We were both quiet, listening to laughter, calls from gulls and the lap of waves. I could feel myself slipping into sleep. It had been a big day and I didn't want to fall asleep in his company, but I couldn't hold out.

"I'm going to take Fahim's advice and take a nap, Neills. What time shall I see you?"

"Canapés are being served at seven-thirty, so from seven? Get there earlier if you wish. I'll be here."

"Do you want to pick me up on the way?" Someone had to make the first move.

"If you like. I'll knock at seven."

Not the outcome I was after. A man can take gentlemanly

behaviour too far. The night had not begun, so maybe I was rushing things. This swapping of the chase was unfamiliar to me and I had no guidelines to follow. I needed Kate. Certainly the Krug helped, gave me courage.

Peggy, my allotted cabin crew, had left her greeting card on the pillow. I was to call her any time. A phone sat on the bedside table. In the meantime, the towels on the bed had been moved to the towel shelf and the bed turned down, presumably because Peggy knew I'd take a nap. Is that what everyone was doing? The wine had gone to my head and my anxieties and excitement had taken their toll.

I showered, barely dried myself, put on the bathrobe, lay on the bed and instantly fell asleep. The bed felt more comfortable than any I'd ever slept in. The movement of the boat lulled me like I was two years old. It was six o'clock when I woke. One hour to make myself beautiful.

Forty-one

Neills was prompt, as I expected. I'd just finished combing my hair and dabbing on one of the perfumes, when I heard three taps on the cabin door.

He stood back, "Wow, you look amazing, Annabelle."

I felt amazing. The red dress was soft and feminine, especially after my shorts and t-shirts. The fabric alone made a girl feel sensuous.

"Everything fits so perfectly." I spun.

Neills took my arm and we walked the short passageway to the aft deck, where we'd lunched. I accepted a Krug. As everyone arrived, the effect was astonishing. The colours blended beautifully and matched the coloured lights strung around the deck. The men, in contrast, wore chinos and white shirts, the *Sea Falcon* crest on one turned-down collar. Soft leather sandals shod their feet. The whole scene was elegant, where it could have been gaudy.

The centre table was decorated with a melting ice falcon. Frangipani flowers were sprinkled around the large dish it rested on, waiting to float as the bird became water. Aperitifs and hors d'oeuvres adorned the table. Cabin crew, now waiters, weaved in and out, offering morsels from the table.

During mingling, I asked Neills how he managed to get the right size for my dresses.

"I gave Fahim, or rather his assistant, your sizes."

"But how did you know?"

"It's not hard, Annabelle. I can judge sizes."

"Do you have a background in fashion?"

"No. I know my mother's size. As I mentioned, I go shopping with her. I judge from her size."

"What about shoes? That can't be so easy."

"Sandals are easier, but I noticed what you were wearing and it's the same story as with my mother's foot. Fahim has many sizes and styles available."

Aah, so that was it, truck in a load of designer styles ready for the next occasion. "Sounds impersonal."

"Annabelle, I observed your size."

"Sorry, I sound ungrateful … it's more wonderful than I hoped."

Neills gave me a loving squeeze, "I hope so."

My thoughts didn't rest. How many of these gatherings occurred? Carefully constructed with pre-sized women ordered ahead of time. It sounded like a factory and sent a shudder down my spine. There's a wardrobe mistress on the payroll.

"What other themes does he hold?"

"I believe they're all to do with art. Not everyone will get it, but it's for Fahim's pleasure, so that doesn't really matter."

"Have you been invited to many of these parties?" I couldn't let it go. The words fell before I had time to stop them.

"First time."

I looked at him as I wasn't sure if this was a truthful answer. His face was a mask.

"Oh, then I'm doubly honoured," I said.

Why was I nit picking? Let go, Annabelle, and enjoy.

We were called to dinner around eight-thirty. Glass-panelled doors slid across part of the aft deck to give protection from the evening chill. Soft, hidden lights glowed inside and out. The guests gathered around the table and the shine on their faces reflected the splendour. Thick, white gold-crested napkins, folded in the shape of falcons, lay neatly next to etched crystal glasses. Candles threw shadows and shards of light. Settings of fine white porcelain dining ware, embossed with the golden falcon emblem, were placed around the large table. Smooth Danish-style silver cutlery glistened as each knife, fork and spoon waited for the many courses to follow.

The waiters, both women and men, were dressed in starched white, high-collared shirts hanging low over black pants and topped with black bow ties. Name cards placed the guests and would be changed for each course. During the meal, Fahim spoke quietly with his immediate guests. He ate little and drank nothing. Smiling, calm and attentive, only his eyes were animated; they sparkled and observed. I couldn't believe he enjoyed all this so passively. This luxury was ordinary for him – surely he wasn't just acting as a benefactor to give the less privileged a peek into his world? I've no idea what I ate. I was so overwhelmed, I couldn't take it all in.

Neills chatted easily with everyone. Some of the girls were off their heads by the time dinner had finished. When dancing started aft, we were all sozzled, though I was still steady on my feet. Sober enough to wonder what Neills planned when dancing finished. Intimacy had begun amongst the couples. Neills, it seemed, liked to talk. I was watching the scene and, encouraged by the Krug, turned to Neills to suggest we dance, but he'd gone. He hadn't even excused himself. What was this?

When couples started to drift away, I ensconced myself on the leather seating, draping myself over the railing to watch the night waves churn, lit by the boat's lighting.

Fahim left after watching the dancing. He looked so splendid in his full Arab dress. White on white, complementing his brown skin and white smile. No one was missing after he left. The couples were all still intact. I wasn't sure if there were exchanges to be made later, from cabin to cabin. Nothing of that sort came to my attention, so I remained sure I was with Neills and only him. Swapping wasn't on my agenda.

I stayed watching the dark sea beyond the boat's lights, wondering where Neills was. The sky was pitch black, speckled with blinking stars. The velvet air and light breeze were warm and romantic.

"Penny for them?" Neills's sudden arrival made me jump.

"Oh, stop doing that. No thoughts ... other than perhaps you'd gone to bed."

"I was on the bridge talking to the Captain."

"Anything interesting?"

"I like maps and how the course is charted."

Of course he does. What else would you do if you have a friend on board at a dance party? Never mind. I stayed schtum.

"I wasn't really thinking anything, just enjoying the warm night air and being out here on the Aegean Sea." I guess we all lie in our own way. "It's not very far to Delos, is it?"

"You'll wake to Delos. We'll be going ashore after breakfast. It's a very interesting island, if you like history."

"Sounds great." I moved closer to Neills. He put his arm around me.

"How about we call it a night?" he said. "Let me walk you to your cabin."

That was the size of the conversation. I walked with him and behaved like the girl my mother would be proud to call her daughter, as we said goodnight.

Peggy, once again, had my cabin sorted. The lights dimmed just enough to make the room look inviting and, dare I say, romantic. *Wasted, Peggy dear.*

I undressed and fell into bed naked, thinking that tomorrow was another day. I didn't stir until morning.

Forty-two

I woke with a headache. I thought quality champagne wasn't supposed to give you a hangover, or so I'd been told on our trek across Europe. Who, I wondered, had drunk enough of the best to give such learned advice? I'd forgotten to drink any water before I fell into bed too. Maybe that was the reason. My addled brain was on other matters at the time.

The ship was still, engines quiet. The previous night, Peggy had closed the drapes across the porthole. Wobbling out of bed, I pulled them aside, immediately struck by brilliant light. The porthole was not a hole but a massive expanse. The sea sparkled beneath blue sky. The view gave me a feeling of looking back through the ages, as if into another world. I imagined Poseidon himself rising, as the waters cascaded from his body amid froth and rage. His wife, Amphitrite, by his side, peering in at the curious onlooker, a mere mortal.

I must still be drunk.

With my imagination put back into one of the indiscernible cupboards, I quickly showered.

On the aft deck, others straggled to the breakfast buffet. The thought of food didn't stir me; however, some stodge would help.

All I could see that satisfied was toast. Lunch would be provided picnic-style. I could hold out for more until then. Once we were all present, Fahim appeared, this time wearing long cotton pants, t-shirt and a cap. He looked ordinary. Quality ordinary.

We were shepherded into small zodiacs, fortunately, across tranquil water. Resting my hangover on wobbly water would not have been a good look. The vessels were to remain in the bay, should anyone wish to return to the yacht before the day trip was over. Prewarned, we were dressed for the occasion with hats and good walking shoes. Anyone lacking this attire could borrow from the yacht.

We gathered around Neills, who provided commentary on the history of the island.

"One of Delos's main claims to fame in ancient times, was the birth of the divine twins, Artemis and Apollo. Delos became a place of cult practices. Ionians moved in around 1000 BC. Later it became a commercial and religious centre. Athens, catching wind of its success, sought to claim it for herself. It's very centrally located and, in fact, Cyclades means 'islands around Delos'."

For someone who hadn't attended any of Fahim's parties, it was obvious Neills was well placed within the hierarchy. Maybe it was a working friendship, rather than just a friendship?

Let it go, Annabelle.

We walked on with Neills as he dropped morsels of history.

"The Athenians attempted to purify the peoples on the island, a tactic still used in parts of the world today, as I'm sure you're aware. Athenians brought in a decree that no-one could die or give birth on Delos and eventually the native population was banished to other islands. The Romans lorded over it too and declared it a free port, much like duty-free ports we have today."

"Like Gibraltar?" someone offered.

"Yes, I suppose so. In around the second century BC, as has happened so many times in history to so many places, its undefended wealth and treasures were gradually plundered. Passing seafarers looted the place. The island never recovered. When you look in any direction, you get a magnificent view of the Cyclades and you can understand why it was a strategic island to capture."

It was apparent that Neills loved history, with a natural talent for passing it on. By day's end we returned, exhausted, to the yacht. Slow walking and listening in the hot sun with little shade had frazzled us all.

I was glad of time for a brief nap before dinner. The night was repeated. We women dressed again in our gorgeous dresses and danced the night away. During the day trip, I became more familiar with the other passengers. All the young women spoke of having only met their men shortly before the trip. After chance meetings and having clicked with their men, they were invited as special guests aboard. The men knew Fahim, the women didn't.

An alert went off in my mind, but I told myself that I was a special case, in that I'd met Neills in London and my brother knew him before me.

So far, I had not noticed any switching couples. But how the hell would I know what went on from one cabin to another in the early hours of the morning? No one came knocking on my door.

On the day trip I became friendly with Eva from the Netherlands. She picked up that I wasn't relaxed. Her astuteness disturbed me. I'd noticed during my time in Europe that personal barriers came down easily amongst travellers. People shared their innermosts in a blink. Perhaps there was the thought that you'd never see the person again, so the offer of free therapy was too good to pass up?

"What's troubling you, Annabelle? I notice you're anxious when Neill is not around. Do you not trust him?"

"Oh, um ... am I? I didn't realise I was so transparent. Am I a blaring beacon of insecurity? How come you noticed?"

"Oooh ... wow, a lot of questions. It's a new relationship, am I right? More than just this short trip?"

"Um ... yes. I ... I really like him." I gave her a brief history of our meeting. "He's so elusive. It's like clutching at a cloud."

"Perhaps he doesn't feel the same?"

That shook me, to hear my fears spoken aloud. "Sometimes I think he does and other times, not."

"Mmm ... not all men can express their emotions, Annabelle. Some men are afraid of deeper emotions ... afraid of their own feelings. They fight them to stay safe. Settle back and enjoy what is."

"That's what I keep telling myself," I laughed. "Hearing that from someone else brings it home to me. And I have been told that before ... but it slips away." I had to ask. "Tell me, Eva, is there swapping going on? Is that what this party boat is about?"

"I don't know. It hasn't with us, but the thought crossed my mind. I'm not really into that stuff. I was told I'm Joel's guest."

"So was I. Well, I mean, Neills's guest."

Eva shrugged, I shrugged. Eva and I became friends. And I needed a friend.

A ritual developed. Neills collected me in the evening, I'd twirl, he'd tell me how great I looked, I took his arm and we walked to dinner.

Next port, Amorgós.

Forty-three

On the fourth night, Fahim spoke of our next visit to one of his favourite islands; a speech rather than a talk. Well-rehearsed and one I felt he'd given before.

He was dressed in his traditional attire, and by then I'd learnt the names of the clothing. A *thobe* covered his body, his head was covered by a white *ghutrah* and white corded *iqal,* and his *sirwal* were white pants. His sandals I don't believe had a name. Fitting as though moulded around his foot, they looked hand crafted.

"Amorgós lies far to the east of the Cycladic group and rises sharply out of the sea, long and oblong in shape. It's been likened to a gigantic snake ... lonely and quite eerie at times. In centuries gone by, sailors thought they had arrived at the edge of the world. The inhabitants, over hundreds of years, have withstood troubles of many kinds and survived. They pride themselves on being strong and stoical. Some of the oldest traces of human existence on the island date back to the fourth millennium BC. By the third millennium BC, Amorgós was the centre of Cycladic civilisation. There is a famous monastery called Hozoviotissa. It's battened to the cliffs and its whitewashed walls are striking against the rock.

"We can visit if anyone is interested, but women must have their shoulders covered and wear long skirts. If you don't have either, we have appropriate attire here on *Sea Falcon*. Is there anyone who would rather not go?"

Not a hand in sight.

"Again, strong walking shoes are a must. It's a rugged track to the monastery. A van is available to drive to a point where you will then walk. We will make this trip in the cool of the morning. If anyone wants to swim, there is a little beach, or you can use aft of the boat where we have a platform. You can dive, swim or just sunbathe and we can shuttle back and forth to the boat. We have bathing suits on board and caps too, if anyone is without. Later we will be dining ashore for afternoon tea at a small taverna. There you can taste traditional recipes made with local produce."

It was our first introduction to hearing Fahim speak at length. Not a cough to be heard. His slightly accented voice was deep and clear. I could see how his charisma worked to his advantage in business, for both men and women.

We walked a rocky path that zigzagged, taking us metre by metre into another world. By the time we reached the white, imposing monastery, the atmosphere at the door felt tangible. The vast Aegean Sea sprawled beneath and beyond as we rested above it.

With no other tourists around, this cliff-hanging monastery was especially breathtaking – both inside and looking out through the lopsided windows toward the beckoning sea. Its history was overwhelming. I expected religion, but it bumped up alongside mythology too. My own country is ancient and mythical, but not being of Aboriginal descent, I had little understanding of it. This was different. I felt the flavour of it. The timber floors creaked and whispered with each footstep. The walls sighed as if alive with the ancient inhabitants.

"Have you been here before?" I whispered to Neills.

"No. Fahim has often spoken of it ... Laars too ... but this is my first time. It's breathtaking."

When we emerged, the sunlight was blinding, brighter after the twilit world of silence. We maintained the silence as we climbed into the van, still spellbound. We stopped at a small, craggy beach. The heat had built and the water, blue and clear, invited us to cool off. To my surprise, it was freezing. We tiptoed wet and shivering across the stones to Peggy and another crew member, who held out big, thick colourful beach towels. These were followed by brightly coloured, striped beach robes.

After lunch, the yacht sailed close around Amorgós and anchored at the village of Mavri Myti. More stony paths led us from the shoreline to a tiny taverna. The coffee was sweet and strong and we were a spectacle for the local population. Children giggled and dared one another to get close and the braver ones to touch us. Especially popular was the English woman whose parents were from Trinidad. Her amazing cascade of dark curls fascinated all the locals. Dogs, cats and donkeys nonchalantly watched on. The food was indeed fresh and delicious.

Farewelling the little community with hugs and big smiles, tired and fulfilled, after walking back along the craggy path, we clambered aboard zodiacs and boarded the yacht. Drinks first, showers could wait.

"I could get very used to this," Eva said quietly to me.

"Get in the queue."

"Fahim ... he joins us but he's not exactly joining in, if you know what I mean."

"I know. I find it odd," I said. "What do you think he gets out of it?"

"Do you find him looking at you sometimes, as though he's studying you?" said Eva.

"Oh God, I do. I thought it was my imagination. Neills told me about his love of art and that he'd probably like to talk with me on the subject, but he hasn't. And yes, instead he studies me; well, obviously not just me."

I pressed Eva further. "I find it strange he has no personal friends on board. Neills talks a great deal about his friend, but I get the feeling they are colleagues rather than friends. Perhaps the friendship is Neills's interpretation. The other guys don't seem that close."

"I wondered the same. Is he a voyeur? Maybe he is sleeping with some of the women, but I don't get that impression."

"Me neither. Maybe if you're that wealthy, life gets boring if you can have everything you want," I said. "So you play spontaneously with whatever takes your fancy."

"He doesn't look like he's bored. To me, he looks like a man fulfilled." We both looked to Fahim, who was about to leave. "Anyway," Eva said, "how long are you on board?"

"I don't know." I laughed. "You know I forgot to ask. I was blown away by the invitation and I didn't ask questions like that. Now I don't want to, in case it's seen as being ungrateful. Neills knows I'm not in a hurry to go anywhere. What about you?"

"A few days, I was told."

"Can't kick the gift horse, can we?" I was quietly mulling over whether to ask Eva something. After a moment's thought, I plunged in.

"Eva, can I ask you a personal question? You don't have to answer."

"Sure. Shoot."

"Are you sleeping with Joel?"

She looked at me askance. "Of course. What? ... why?" She studied me. "You and Neills aren't sleeping together?"

"No."

"Wow ... that's weird. Is he homosexual?"

"That's what I'm beginning to think."

"Nothing wrong with that, but you'd think he'd say something. Have you asked him?"

"No. Should I?"

"If there's been some, let's say, preliminaries, I would say yes, ask him. Ask him anyway. Has there been foreplay ... flirting, kissing ... anything?"

"No kissing, just pecks on the forehead, a hug." I told Eva about my brother, London and the rest of the story.

"Not exactly foreplay, is it? Hold the asking, I'll ask Joel ... discreetly."

"Yeah, he might know, but I don't want it to get back to Neills. I don't want him to think I've been talking behind his back."

"I'll sound Joel out. He's not a tittle-tattle. Where is Neills now? He's not with the guys at the bar."

"This is what he does. Disappears. He's either with Fahim discussing the trip, on the bridge talking maps with the Captain, or God knows where else. He leaves and suddenly he's back talking like he's been there all the time. I don't want to seem like I'm keeping tabs on him. It's not like I'm not enjoying myself. Maybe it's my interpretation, but I thought I'd be with him. You know, sleeping with him. I like him a lot, but he keeps me at arm's length."

"I'll ask Joel. I'll be careful. I haven't known him very long, but he seems down to earth and if he does know, I trust him not to mention it. We got together while I was travelling; we clicked and then he asked me if I wanted to join him on this trip. I'll ask him how he knows Neills. I know they've met before, but I'm not sure if it's any more than that." She came closer to me. "They're coming back. I'll let you know."

The guys split from the bar. Neills was nowhere to be seen. Gradually the others returned to their cabins to shower, take a nap and, well whatever, to be fresh for dinner. I waited a while. Neills did not return. I went to my cabin, showered and lay down on the bed. My bed had become a sanctuary, a comfortable and comforting sanctuary. I dozed off into deep afternoon slumber grateful for Eva's support.

I was ready by seven. As usual, three knocks on the door and Neills waited in the passageway to escort me to dinner.

Lucile, ever present in the evenings; the only times I ever saw her. Fahim's ideas, Lucile's supervision. I thought of my mother, managing her own themed parties, her husband frowning in the corner.

Forty-four

The following day we sailed and did not go ashore. We anchored and swam aft, sunbathed and snoozed in the sun. After a leisurely lunch, I took a nanna nap in my cabin. When I woke, my gaze caught the Picasso. The familiar, formidable breeze came again. "Go away," I whispered. My heartbeat and panic rose. "What are you trying to tell me? What is it?" Silence answered my pleas.

A knock on the door sent me through the ceiling.

"Yes ... who is it?" My voice quavered.

"It's Peggy, Miss Lagoudakis."

"Oh ... just a minute." Wrapping the bathrobe and my wits around me, I opened the door.

"Hi Peggy ... what is it?"

"Mr Fahim would like your company in his quarters before dinner, if you would care to join him. I'll come for you at six."

"Oh, okay. I'll be ready."

Oh God. Is this it? Is this the swap meet? Slumping back down on the bed, panic hit me. I'd just left panic. Was the 'frozen moment' trying to warn me of this? Did this mean Neills would not be collecting me? I wondered if each female guest on board had received this call. One by one. Or perhaps we would all be there?

I put on one of the dresses supplied by Fahim, as I presumed I'd be going to dinner from Fahim's quarters, meeting Neills on the aft deck perhaps. My hand shook as I applied mascara.

Sharp on six o'clock, Peggy was at my door. I recognised it now: four knocks to Neills's three. Without a word, I followed her. She knocked on Fahim's door four times.

An answer, "Come in."

Peggy opened the door and indicated I pass through.

I gasped in wonder. Spacious luxury beyond measure. The room seemed so much bigger than the boundaries of the boat allowed. Paintings lined the walls and large sculptures were placed strategically around the room. Contemporary works, all made from found pieces.

"Please take a seat, Annabelle."

We exchanged pleasantries and he suggested we walk the room together. He spoke of his collection. Some copies, some originals. The sculptures were sourced from various countries through his art dealer in Rome and by his own research. Some he'd collected, sailing around the Mediterranean.

"I only have pieces on board that won't spoil with the salt air ... Neills has told me of your interest in art. Tell me your favourites."

"Very similar to yours, by the looks of things. Did you study art formally?"

"While I was in New York and London studying finance and subjects that would help me in the business world, I took an informal route. I spent hours at the wonderful galleries and museums in those cities. I took summer courses, much to my father's annoyance, as he wanted me home. But I wanted to learn how to create beautiful masterpieces. Sadly, I'm much better at business. My father was greatly relieved to know my talents did not lie in painting." He smiled.

"I did the next best thing and collected. My talents do lie there. Neills may have told you, I have a major collection at home. Now you, Annabelle, have you studied formally?"

"I wanted to, but my mother assured me I would meet a better type of husband if I studied law."

"And was she right?"

"I'm not married but when I return home, I expect I will be, to the better type of husband."

"As it should be. Please sit. I have a great favour to ask of you."

I sat, my heart racing. My thoughts straight to how to say no, for what he was about to ask me.

"You are a classical beauty, Annabelle, but I expect you know that. I've told you I am not a painter; however, I do dabble. I have a passion for Picasso, as you have no doubt noticed. I love the women Picasso chooses. I love especially the high-bridged nose he favours. I have noticed, Annabelle, you have such a profile. I hope that does not offend you?"

"No ... no it doesn't."

Where the hell was this leading. I was more nervous than ever. I hope I hid it.

"I don't think anyone has mentioned that before. As a teenager, I always wanted the ski-slope nose."

"Ski-slope?" He roared with laughter. "I've not heard that expression before, but I know exactly the nose you speak of. No, no, no, yours is a thousand times more interesting. You may think this an imposition, but I wondered if you would do me the honour of sitting for me. I'd like to draw you first, then paint, make a portrait of you."

"Me? I've never been painted before ... um ..."

A thousand guesses would not have led me to that.

"It's fine if you would rather not, but I would truly love to try."

"Um ... well of course ... I'd be honoured."

I wasn't sure I was, but I wasn't sure I wasn't either. After all, he'd given his guests – me – so much, how could I refuse?

"It would mean staying on board a few days longer. The other guests will be returning to Piraeus tomorrow. We have left notices in their cabins this afternoon advising time of disembarkation. We ... me and Neills that is ... would love it if you could stay on."

"Um ... what would I have to do?"

"You look worried, Annabelle. Please don't be. All that is required is sitting in a chair, while I do first quick sketches, then longer sketches. You will rest between sketches. I will both draw and paint. And we would love you to join us as we sail to Hydra, or Idhra as it is called in Greece. This is an island of many artists. Painters, poets, writers and musicians, among others. I think you would like it."

Gobsmacked could barely describe how I felt. "I'd be honoured to join ... um ... sit for you. And yes, I'd love to visit Idhra. I've heard about it ... ah ... um ... a portrait?"

Fahim laughed softly. "Of course, you're anxious, it will indeed be a portrait, head and possibly shoulders. You will be clothed."

He watched me as I tried not to let out a sigh of relief.

"Excellent. We will continue our discussion on this subject once the other guests have departed. I'll get Peggy to take you back to your cabin. I believe Neills collects you at seven."

Forty-five

Peggy must have been waiting outside the door. My feet did not touch the floor as I returned to my cabin. A confusion of apprehension and privilege filled me. And I'd get to visit Idhra. This island was on my list. Here it was, all laid out on a five-star platter and all I was obliged to do was sit for a painting.

That final evening for everyone else was a gala performance. More lights, more of everything. I'd never imagined there could be more, but Fahim's creative mind had found ways while Lucile's ability had produced them. We women were garlanded with flowers and each received a gift: a little box containing a shell from the islands, set in silver on a silver chain. Delicate and beautiful. What had we done to deserve all this? I, at least, had the opportunity to give something back.

Eva and I had grown closer. I told her I would be staying on board and what was presented to me. She was delighted, but there was hesitation in her eyes, which she tried to hide.

"What?" I said.

"Nothing, Annabelle. You know what you're doing. You are privileged. You have my blessing."

"Why do you need to give me your blessing?"

"Oh, it's just an expression. Don't read too much into it. I do hope you have a magnificent time. But tell me, are you still hoping you'll become closer to Neills?"

I looked at her and read immediately what she was hiding.

"Yes ... and I do believe this will give us the opportunity. He is staying on board too. Neills is delighted I've agreed and said we would have plenty of time together."

"Of course. There will be less distraction."

"Did you speak with Joel?"

"Yes. He doesn't know Neills that well, but doesn't think he's homosexual."

She said no more. The space at the end of her sentence was expansive and, to be honest, annoyed me.

That evening we danced and sang, and I forgot my annoyance, as Eva reminded me about enjoying every moment.

"Maybe I'm jealous," she said at one point.

By the following morning, everyone knew I was staying on board. As Neills was a close friend of Fahim's, the others saw nothing other than how lucky I was. Eva and I hugged and promised to stay in touch. I gave her my brother's phone number and where he worked, as she often visited London and expected to be there soon after she returned home.

I watched and waved as everyone disembarked. It seemed most of the waiters, some crew and Lucile, left the boat. I felt strangely bereft.

Sea Falcon sailed from Piraeus and once again I passed by the white breakwater. As I watched Piraeus disappear, I suddenly realised I'd never finished my letters to my parents or mailed my postcards. In truth I'd forgotten all about them. I could have given them to Eva to post.

Forty-six

Beyond Fahim's cabin, lay a smaller cabin. To me it was what an artist's studio should look like. Natural light through the many portholes gave the room an all-over even light. It held more copied Picassos. Fahim had chosen various series, but singularly, portraits of women.

My sitting started the day we left Piraeus. We had lunch and then I entered Fahim's studio. His record player was stacked with small forty-five rpm records, popular if you wanted a variety of music. Presumably, he didn't want to waste time changing them. A flute played softly.

As I sat in the chair, Fahim asked me to tilt my head. I noticed Picasso's 'Girl on a Pillow' completely covered the ceiling. I knew this painting. A clever copyist had painted directly onto the skylight. This painting had been picked for its round shape and fitted perfectly into the circular rim. Backlit, she glowed. I looked at her as she looked down on us, on me.

I had been instructed to wear whatever I liked. My choice was a simple pale blue t-shirt and skirt.

"I will make a few five-minute sketches to warm up, then I will ask you to change position. I'll be working on your profile for the moment."

After half an hour of these sketches, he suggested I take a break. I walked around the cabin. This space was so much smaller than the main room, but with the light there was a feeling of grandeur. Many paints and paintbrushes, pencils and sketchpads were strewn across a large table. His easel was set to the side. The fastidious tidiness of the rest of the yacht was in sharp contrast to this room. I doubted a cleaner would be allowed anywhere near Fahim's workspace. It was a room for his personal use only unless you were invited. At this point there was only me and Fahim.

Once the longer sketches began, I had time to reflect. It kept my mind busy, so my body didn't know it was aching and had to remain still. Fahim did not like movement of any kind while he was at work. I wasn't Annabelle any longer, but an object, like a vase.

My thoughts went to the dinner the night before, the first without the other guests. The change was huge from my point of view. At the table sat me, Fahim, Neills and the Captain, Eduart. The aft deck was now simply an aft deck, not a party space. A beautiful luxurious deck, now I could see it without the glitter. Conversation was sparse and mostly we ate quietly under the stars, listening to the lap of the waves. I had no idea where we were. Just somewhere floating on the Aegean. The food was excellent as usual. Simple Greek fare rather than an array of international selections.

Fahim and Neills were more relaxed than I'd seen them in the last few days. Fahim, I discovered, had a brilliant sense of humour, a British sense of the ridiculous he must have picked up from his studies there. Neills, although still tense, was much more the man I knew before we stepped aboard *Sea Falcon*. I'm not sure if it was my imagination, but there was a sense of accomplishment about him.

I was yet to know if it was because he now had time to spend with me, or whether he was impressing Fahim. Had Fahim thoroughly enjoyed himself with the guests? I only presumed so. Though maybe he was relieved it was all over, thus his relaxed attitude. If this were the case, throwing a party for strangers, why did he bother?

Fahim's voice broke my reverie. "You can take a break, Annabelle."

The trip to Idhra was delayed a day and by day two I was more acclimatised to the routine. A burning question right from the start needed to be asked.

During a break, I said, "Why me, Fahim?"

His voice softened. "Why you? I mentioned before about your high-bridged nose. I like your face. As I greatly admire Picasso's work, I take that back to Picasso's choice of models. He favours the profile, the high-bridged nose. Whether he falls for their profiles or the women who happen to have those profiles, I don't know. I haven't read any account of that."

Fahim would not let me see his drawings, saying he never made good grades in his art studies. "As we go along, if there is one I'm happy with, I'll show you."

Starting in pencil, he then switched to charcoal. Then quite unexpectedly, he said, "That will be all for now, Annabelle. More tomorrow. Ah no, we will be in Idhra tomorrow. Until next time ... thank you."

I walked myself back to my cabin. I knew the way, so no need for Peggy or Neills to lead me. I freshened up and changed.

Lunch was soon, so I picked up the book I was reading from Fahim's extensive library, went aft and settled into the soft wrap-around seating. I positioned myself so the warmth of the sun fell on my back.

Breakfast had been a brief affair, as Fahim said he'd be whisking me away, and he had apologised to Neills. So now I was relaxing with plenty of time. I didn't mind the solitude. I read a few pages, but my concentration drifted. I was sailing the ancient Aegean seas with history surrounding me. Time seemed infinite. The water lapped the hull. I dozed.

Something soft touched my face and I woke to see Neills gently stroking me with the corner of a napkin.

"Wakey wakey, sleepy head."

"Oh … hi … it's so beautiful out here. I was so relaxed I fell asleep. It sounds like the engines are running again. Are we on the move?"

"We are and lunch is ready."

We were three at lunch, the Captain back on the bridge.

"How is it going?" Neills asked Fahim.

"Annabelle is a wonderful model, Neills. Perfect. Exactly the profile I was after. Picasso can eat his heart out. Just as well I didn't invite him, he might sweep you off your feet, Annabelle. You're just his type."

"You know him?"

"We've met."

Of course they had.

"I think he might be too old for me," I said, laughing.

Fahim laughed softly. "Maybe for you but not for Picasso. His magnetism attracts all ages, including young women. Especially the young and besides, it's passion that counts."

We ate in silence for a while, then Fahim asked if I could sit again in the afternoon.

"Sure," I said. I was hoping to sunbathe on deck and watch the horizon across the sea, as we sailed into Idhra, but it was not to be.

"Are we still going to Idhra?"

"Yes ... we are ... in a couple of hours we will be moored. Then we go ashore for dinner and spend time walking around. Life continues on until the early hours. It's better if we are out of the heat of the day.

"Let your meal settle, Annabelle, then we will start again in half an hour. Neills will bring you down."

I briefly stayed on deck in the sunshine, until Neills suggested I change. Back at my cabin he waited outside, then walked me to Fahim's quarters.

"I'll be with you this afternoon. Watch how the master works."

Fahim used charcoal. Totally engrossed, he forgot to give me a break. Gently I reminded him.

"Of course," he said, but I learnt he didn't like to be interrupted.

Beginning to feel a little uncomfortable holding position after position, with longer drawing time and fewer breaks, my mind had time to analyse words which also took me away from the strain. And yes, I could have said 'no more', but then what? I was at his mercy. He had given me so much. I began to feel I was paying back not only for myself, but all the other guests.

We must be getting close to Idhra, I thought. I looked forward to the break.

What did Fahim mean, 'exactly the profile I was after'? It sounded like he'd put in an order. I must have it wrong. Neills met me in London. Did he know all this back then? He was friends with my brother first and hadn't met me, so no to that thought. Was he a scout for Fahim? The other women met their men only shortly before boarding. Are those men scouts, are they all scouts? Were those women chosen, like presenting a cake trolley and picking the one you like best? Not for sex but for portrait painting purposes. The thought was bizarre.

"Relax, Annabelle. You're tensing up. Just relax and I won't forget the breaks, I promise. We'll be finished soon to go ashore."

"I can see how this will work," said Neills looking over Fahim's shoulder.

So Neills was allowed to look, but not the sitter. Perhaps that is normal between artist and muse.

"It's the way Picasso fractures the women," Fahim replied. "He separates and repackages to form a different story. Fragments, disassembles and reassembles. Such a gift, though I think he stole the idea from other artists. He took the idea and pushed through barriers."

"All that aside, Fahim, it will work. You'll be using different paper, won't you?"

"Yes, of course. Not paper but board for the final painting."

Neills walked to the door and turned back.

"I'll collect you shortly if you'd like to go back to your cabin. Walking shoes again, there are cobbles throughout the town." He paused, "You're a wonderful model for Fahim."

With that, he left.

Was I? What were they talking about? I didn't know the processes of art, only end results, and what was this talk of types of paper and board? Fahim must be aiming for some final work of art.

Forty-seven

Ashore we walked as a small group: Fahim, Neills, Eduart and me, along with a man called Murat, who walked a short distance behind. I'd never met him or seen him the entire time I'd been on board. Where had he sprung from? I questioned Neills with a look. Fahim picked it up.

"This is Murat, my security guard, for want of a better word. He will be with us while we're ashore," Fahim said.

A little shocked, I reasoned that if a person is that wealthy, they must experience times of danger; kidnapping perhaps, as I'd heard of such things. Maybe that was why Fahim didn't go ashore before. It might not look good to have such a dour, threatening-looking person in amongst the partygoers. Murat was short in stature and built like a brick shithouse. Were we now safer as a party, or likely to attract aggressive attention?

The town radiated out and up from the curve of the small harbour. Shiny large cobbles made it difficult to walk and I was thankful for my walking shoes. I had experience of this from previous islands, so was prepared for the warning. Years of donkeys and horses' hooves across the stones had worn them slippery – beautiful in appearance, but treacherous to navigate.

The harbour was alive, the restaurants and cafés full. Laughter and chatter filled the air. Fahim was well known, with waves and acknowledgements from every eatery. A reserved sign was taken hastily from a table, so we sat by the water's edge. Murat sat at a small table quickly set up next to ours. What was this thing with Murat? Was this protocol for bodyguards – seen but not associated with? A shadow, a warning to those getting too close. I wondered if he carried a gun.

"Many artists live here, Annabelle," said Fahim. "We'll be visiting some of the small galleries tomorrow. They're hidden away, further back and up the hill, away from the harbour."

When we finished dinner, Eduart went back to *Sea Falcon* while Fahim, Neills and I, with Murat trailing, walked around the small harbour and along a path that took us away from the town and into the next bay. Another restaurant lay nestled into the cliff below.

"I think Leonard Cohen has a house up there somewhere," said Fahim pointing to the left. "Have you heard of him? Poet and singer? I like his music."

I'd been travelling now for a few months and wasn't up with all the latest music. The English party people had spoken of the latest happenings in London, of which I oblivious. And here too, so it seemed.

We looked across the sea to other islands, dark shapes in the twilight. The harbour was still bristling with activity until way past midnight.

"I think we'll turn in … well I will," said Fahim. "We'll be back ashore in the morning for breakfast. Happy with that, Annabelle?"

"Yes, definitely. I imagine it's quite different in the morning."

I'd had little to say since we stepped foot on the island, so mesmerised was I with the atmosphere and a little ill at ease with

Murat's presence. I had the feeling he watched me without watching me. All so different to the times spent with the Americans and the yachtie community. Sharing what we had with others on board our yacht or another yacht's offerings, evenings at cheap tavernas – it was vastly different to Fahim's life. A small boat was available to take us back to *Sea Falcon,* which was moored offshore.

Ashore at breakfast, we were five, with Eduart and Murat. Murat sat separately again and, although he ate, his eyes were constantly alert. Why he needed to keep me in his sights was beyond me. Where did he think I was going?

After breakfast, Fahim led us to a painter, then a potter. Eduart then sought out shops to look for presents for his wife and children. Fahim, Neills and I continued on. Fahim knew where the artists lived, their small houses doubling as studios. A maze of tiny pathways led us across and up the hill from the village. We found exquisite leatherware, paintings, pottery, weaving and everything in between, where artists and craftspeople sold directly from their premises. Fahim spoke Greek to them all. He sounded fluent, but as I didn't know the language beyond pleasantries, I couldn't be sure. The artists loved him. He bought something from all of them. They often pressed him with a small gift. The experience was a treasure for me. Left to my own devices, I would never have known these artists existed or found my way along the alleyways.

At one studio, Neills and I lingered outside, the space being so small we couldn't all fit. I took the opportunity to ask about Murat, who was out of earshot. I wasn't even sure if he spoke English.

"He travels everywhere with Fahim," Neills said.

"Why?"

"Fahim's father has a bodyguard, his uncles, his brothers … it's what the wealthy Saudis do. And not just Saudis, Annabelle."

I didn't know that, nor had I ever thought about it.

"I've never noticed him before. Was he around when the others were on board?"

"He was around. Murat is a professional. He's only seen when it is time for him to be seen."

"Does he speak English?"

"A little."

With Fahim occupied, I struck up further conversation. It was something I thought we'd be doing now with the others gone, but so far, we hadn't. Nor had we spent much time alone.

"How is your mother, Neills? Did she buy her house?"

"We're not sure it's the right one. Laars said he'd check in on her and the house."

"Your father, Neills, you seldom mention him. May I ask?"

"He left us when I was very little. He found another woman. Left my mother broken-hearted."

"Oh ... I'm so sorry. That must have been very hard for her. Have you seen him since?"

"No."

"Did she meet anyone else?"

"No. It was very difficult. She was still in love with him when it happened. Still is, I think. She never got him out of her system."

"Did he help raise you financially? Sorry, I probably shouldn't ask, but it's a beef of mine, when men get someone pregnant and then don't take any responsibility."

"Is it?"

"Yes, very much."

"What would you do if that happened to you?"

"Oh God, hopefully I'd never meet a man like that, never get involved in the first place."

"How would you know?"

That was a question I hadn't been confronted with or thought about.

"Hopefully I'd have the insight to pick a decent man. They say girls often pick their fathers to marry. Thankfully mine is a wonderful, decent man. Very honest and well meaning. He's very loyal to my mother and always had time for Peter and me. He's my role model."

"It's wonderful you feel confident in that way. And you say you've had a good example set for you. My mother was not so lucky. I don't know what example my mother's father gave her, maybe it was being charming like the man she fell for. This man, when she needed him and loved him the most, gave her a paltry sum and sent her out of his life. You say in English, pissed her off."

What could I say? He was still, after all this time, very angry, whether for his mother's sake or his own. I didn't want to question him further, dredge up old wounds. Neills had other ideas.

"We were blessed in other ways, as I've mentioned, with friends, especially Laars's family. My mother had no family left after the war." He was quiet, looked away. "You've had a blessed life, Annabelle."

Suddenly I felt privileged and guilty. "Yes, I guess I have been very lucky."

"It shows. Both you and your brother, Peter. No real crises in your life."

"Um ... no."

I scanned my life and could find nothing that matched Neills's. A tipped over toy boat that was still haunting me, ridiculous in comparison.

"No, I've been lucky. We have wonderful parents."

As if to close the conversation, Fahim stepped from the studio carrying a small bag.

"Come," said Fahim, "we haven't finished."

We found Eduart on the way and by then the hot sun was overhead with little shade. We walked to the harbour and took a table by the water. Time passed so quickly, it was already one-thirty.

Right by the water again, we ate simple food, succulent local produce: sheep's milk feta cheese, spring lamb and retsina from the mainland.

"We'll go back to the yacht, have a rest if you like Annabelle, then we can change and come back for dinner," said Fahim. "I think we should walk to the restaurant we saw last night, carved into the rock beneath the path. You remember? Would that suit, Annabelle?"

"Very much."

Fahim was certainly laying on the charm, unlike his time drawing me. I had a niggling thought that this was all to keep me happy, so I would continue to sit for him. I still didn't know how long I would be needed.

"After a rest we'll have a couple of hours to fit in a sitting if that will be convenient, Annabelle?"

Was I getting deeper into debt?

Forty-eight

What could I say to Fahim besides "Of course"? I could hardly show my gratitude by saying I didn't want to sit for him and would prefer to sit aft and enjoy the sun and the view.

Eva was heading home by now and, for a fleeting second, I wanted to be with her. To talk with her. She had invited me to join her and stay at her house. Neills and I had so far not become any closer. Did Fahim know there was something between us and that we might want time together? Fahim was not to know I slept alone. Then again, perhaps he did. I'm sure he knew everything that happened on board.

"Fahim's ready now," said Peggy, as I sat aft enjoying the warmth of the sun. I sighed. "Would you like me to walk you there, Miss Annabelle?"

"No, thank you."

The request was for me to wear one of the dresses provided, the colour was up to me. Without looking, I opened the cupboard and pulled the nearest off its hanger.

"Come in," said Fahim after I'd knocked. "Wonderful ... perhaps you can stand by the chair this afternoon. For the first sketch."

"Are these sketches for a painting? How many will you make?"

"I sense impatience in your voice, Annabelle. We are going to be stretching our legs shortly and enjoying a wonderful dinner. You will enjoy that, won't you?"

"Yes, of course, I'm looking forward to it."

After four, twenty-minute sketches, with five-minute breaks, Fahim finished.

"That will do," he said. "My hand is getting tired." He added quite absently, "Shortly we will go for dinner."

Walking back to my cabin, I felt quite shaken. Fahim's tone, more than his words, had been like a knife through my belly. I had no one to talk it through with.

Oh for Eva.

A knock on the door woke me. I didn't remember falling asleep. It was Peggy, rather than Neills.

Along with my troubling thoughts, I was drinking too much. Krug was poured without my asking. Krug was always available in Fahim's studio, even during morning sessions. I declined but soon felt it was something to do. I tried drinking less, but it seemed I was in fact now drinking more often. My inebriated condition became the norm. Dutch courage helped me through the loneliness, even when I wasn't alone.

So many questions were burning in my head; I didn't know where to begin. My mind felt like a basket, where I collected questions to ask at appropriate times, but could never spend them. The only person to ask was Neills. When I thought it would be appropriate, it turned out not to be. Why? How? What? All lay forlornly unanswered.

We spent another day at Idhra. Prior to going ashore the next evening, Neills and I sat quietly enjoying a glass of wine. A little tipsy, I found enough courage to fire my questions, but then the moment felt so blissful, I didn't want to spoil it. I said nothing. I looked at him in the romantic twilight. I wanted to kiss him very badly. In my tipsy state, he looked like the most gorgeous man on earth. And I was with him, at arm's reach, yet so far away.

Finally, I said, "I'm so attracted to you Neills, but I don't know if you feel the same."

No answer.

"Do you?"

"You are a beautiful woman, Annabelle. Any family would be proud to have you as a member."

His answer baffled me. Did he mean in marriage? Was he thinking of his mother? Was he wondering if she would approve of me? I left a space for him continue, but he didn't. A door was closing, but I stuck my foot in the gap to keep it open.

"Come, let's sit where it's comfortable," I said, taking the lead.

Grasping his hand, I walked him to the comfy seating. I snuggled in. He put his arm around me. I looked closely into his eyes and leant in to kiss him.

He whispered, "I think we should save this moment for a special time."

As if on cue, Fahim, Eduart and Murat appeared.

"Ready to go ashore?" said Fahim.

The evening was a repeat of the night before. Back on board, Neills walked me to my cabin and kissed me on the forehead.

"See you in the morning."

As I lay on the bed, tears rolled down the sides of my face. I was in the most beautiful place and situation on earth and I didn't ever remember feeling more alone.

Forty-nine

After breakfast the following morning, our routine resumed. During that morning's sitting, Neills did not join us. The sitting was broken by lunch. I felt suppressed. Things had changed so much. Lively people had populated the yacht and apart from my constant waiting for Neills, there were people to talk to, people to laugh with. Now I had become a mouse. Loneliness skulked in every corner.

My chance to interact at lunch was stifled. Not only could I not get a word in, I didn't know anything about the subjects discussed. I knew very little about navigation on the scale Fahim and Eduart spoke. Neills did not notice me. My mono-linguistic skills were a great shortfall when all three dropped into various languages, followed by laughter.

After dinner, I had the night off. Fahim went to his quarters, Eduart to his or the bridge, leaving Neills and I alone. The evening was glorious, warm with no wind. I decided to stay aft and didn't care if I was alone. The Krug waited for me. Surprisingly, Neills joined me.

He was eager to talk. I wondered if he was tipsy, as his manner was more open. While he talked, my mind panicked with uncompleted tasks.

"What's up?" said Neills. "You've drifted away. Have I been talking to myself?"

"I just realised my parents don't know where I am, or Peter. I meant to post letters while we were on Idhra."

"Oh, never mind, Annabelle. You can post them back in Piraeus. They will probably get home faster than posting them from an island."

"Are we going back to Piraeus soon?"

"That sounds like you want to, Annabelle. Have you had enough of being on board? You are sailing around the Aegean and seeing islands you may not have visited on your own. And it is your dream remember?"

As if I needed reminding.

"No, no ... don't get me wrong, I've had, I mean I'm having, a wonderful time and I'm so grateful to you for inviting me. It's been incredible. Of course, I want to stay," I said, suppressing my doubts and ever hopeful Neills would be responsive.

The subject changed and we talked about my life at home, my parents. We compared life in Australia to life in Denmark. How children played, their schooling and how idle time was spent. Neills repeated his thought that I'd had a fortunate life. I could only agree. His had been more of a struggle but, to balance that, he and his mother had received great kindness from close friends. This subject was thrashed to death now and I felt we could talk of other things.

During this time with Neills, Murat lingered far in the dark. I only saw him when he changed his position. A master of his craft.

"Is Murat with us to protect us? Are we under threat?"

"No, Annabelle. He's always been around. You've just never noticed him before."

"But we're here on board."

"Precautions."

"I don't understand." No answer. I moved on. "Where's he from?"

"I don't know. The Eastern bloc somewhere."

"Neills," I said, "this … this being here is so magical, isn't it? It fulfils all my expectations of what I imagined a Greek Islands trip to be."

Another glass or two of Krug had doubled the romanticism of my situation, colouring an already colourful experience.

He smiled. "And I am your Prince Charming?"

Neills put his arm around me, more friendly than romantic. "I feel I'm an experiment for you, Annabelle. Maybe a plaything, so that when you can return to your country, you can tell your friends about me."

His words astounded me. "Is that what you think? Is that what you've thought all along? Even back in London when I first met you?"

He shrugged. "I saw you talking with Eva. I know how girls talk. I don't want to be someone's trophy."

"Neills … that is so unfair. The reason I'm staying on board is because of you. The reason I'm sitting for Fahim, session after session, is because of you. I hoped, really hoped, we could form a firm and meaningful relationship. I'm still hopeful."

"You're so romantic, Annabelle. I'm flattered. I feel for your fiancé, though."

A second kick in the gut. "I'm not engaged, Neills. We took a break, I've told you that."

"And what? Waiting to see if you get a better offer? Yes, I know that expression."

"If you'd give me a chance." I couldn't find words through the haze of Krug. "I … I really like YOU, Neills."

Just then Fahim called out, "Don't stay up too late, Annabelle, I want you looking your usual gorgeous self in the morning."

I slumped. "How long am I going to be his model?"

"You're not happy with the trip?"

There was nothing to say. I collected my wrap and walked to my cabin.

Perhaps it was Murat who reported me.

Fifty

A loud thudding noise woke me. Peggy was at the door. "Wakey wakey, Miss Annabelle. Breakfast is ready. Wakey wakey."

Impatience in her voice suggested she'd been knocking for a while.

I rose and showered, powering through a hangover and a feeling of uselessness. Alone at breakfast. One place setting. It was a buffet and I helped myself. Peggy advised me that everyone else had eaten. She would take me to Fahim's studio when I was ready. I should change into the orange dress.

We were travelling and Idhra was far from view. Other islands lay in the distance. *Sea Falcon* was a fast boat so we could be any-where.

Peggy waited for me to finish breakfast and then stood outside my door while I changed. Did she think I'd run, disobey orders? Where would I go?

Fahim greeted me and we passed through his quarters, through the studio to another door. I heard a click as it opened. Fahim must have pressed something which I hadn't noticed.

We took a few stairs down and through a short, closed passageway. The room we entered was a triangular space. Were we deep in the bow? The room appeared to be the width of the hull.

The walls consisted of floor-to-ceiling Perspex backlit panels, which were arranged with one blank white-frosted panel, alternating with an enlarged fragment from a Picasso painting. I recognised them. One was 'Weeping Woman', another 'Portrait of Nusche Éluard'. Another from the 'Portraits of a Young Girl' series. I knew all these as I'd studied Picasso's works in galleries on my travels through Europe. 'Woman in a Striped Hat' was vibrant, with its stripes and exotic blues. The room was as light as daylight, although the area did not feature portholes or skylights. Finally, the ceiling glowed with the complete painting of 'Girl on a Pillow'.

I stood in awe.

"Annabelle," I heard Fahim say, how many times I'm not sure.

"This is amazing. You love this series of works," I said.

"Yes, I do. I love, as I've mentioned, the way Picasso fragments a face then puts it back together in a different order. The composition more complete than before fragmentation. But Annabelle, we need to get on. If you wouldn't mind sitting in the chair."

Soft flute and violin played. No other sound could be heard, just the vibration and hum of the engine. Now we were deeper in the yacht, the engine was louder. Soundproofing had clearly been unable to extract all noise. Fahim had certainly utilised all the space on board. I'd lost all my bearings so the room could have been at the stern end. Along with the Krug now I couldn't place where I was. I was disoriented.

Fahim was dressed in crisp new taupe trousers, a white Polo shirt and his usual leather sandals. He liked to stand while he worked. He'd explained previously, it allowed the creative energy to flow.

"This is the beginning of my new series, Annabelle. Thank you for making it possible. Neills will be here shortly. Although it's a little early, I thought we'd celebrate with a glass of champagne."

"A new series?"

What did he mean?

"Yes, after those preliminary drawings, I'm now ready to paint. Your profile with that wonderful high-bridged nose, is exactly what I've been after for a long time." He paused and looked at me. "You are perfect."

As he'd said many times before. How long was I expected to sit for him? What I'd just heard sent fearsome shivers down my spine. I had no obligations after this trip. No one was expecting me. Not my brother, not my parents, not even Eva. Not for a few months anyway. No letters had been sent. Neills knew, therefore Fahim must have known all this.

"Your face shows agitation, Annabelle. Please try and relax."

Just then Fahim put down his brush. He'd barely begun. He excused himself and said Neills must have arrived. What did he hear?

Neills entered the room carrying a tray with two glasses, an ice bucket and Krug. Wasn't that Peggy's job, to fetch and carry? Was no one else allowed to enter this room? Neills poured the liquid expertly into wide-rimmed, hollow-stemmed, champagne glasses.

"Step down for a minute, Annabelle." Fahim passed me a glass. "Here's to our new series. Neills, I've only briefly told our wonderful model about our new series."

Fahim did not drink, Neills took a sip and I took a gulp.

"Your new series, Fahim," I said, hailing my glass though I had no idea what I was toasting.

"Ours. We both had input. But okay, we plan to do a series of you, mostly your face in different poses using the concept Picasso uses. Deconstruct, fragment and reconstruct."

"I believe Fahim can do better than Picasso," Neills said.

"I wish that were true, but we shall see. We will be working hard. We have everything we need down here. Peggy can even arrange for us to eat here, although we'll still go back to our cabins to sleep."

"What do you mean? Are you needing me all the time?" I paused and looked at them both. They were a solid force. "Can't I get some sunshine?" A full tank of Krug had given me the courage to speak up.

"Of course you can if you crave it. We'll be able to take breaks," said Fahim.

"Do you paint too, Neills?" I said, partly to placate my outburst.

"I will have input into the concept, as we go along. Maybe."

"I don't understand. You make it sound like a long time. How long will this take?" Panic bubbled.

"It will take as long as it takes. How do you say, how long is a piece of string?" said Fahim. "Besides, do you have somewhere to be?"

I shook my head. "But please ... I don't understand."

"Come," said Fahim. He took me by the elbow. "Take your champagne. It's a little early in the morning, but champagne tastes good any time, doesn't it? Sip, dear Annabelle."

I did. I gulped. My body was shaking inside, and I hoped the champagne would calm me.

"Won't we even be eating up on deck?"

Neills looked at Fahim.

"We can tonight, I expect," said Fahim.

What did he mean? Tears and panic switched places behind my eyes and in my gut. Up down, gulp champagne and begin again.

"Please, Annabelle. Just relax and we will finish sooner. Please be still."

Fahim painted and Neills took photos. Sometimes using a polaroid camera, sometimes using a movie camera, other times an ordinary camera. He changed lenses from time to time. Neills sat on a wheeled chair and glided around me, as if propelled by a cloud.

Why was it suddenly necessary to record so much on camera?

"Wonderful," Neills whispered from time to time. Then to Fahim, "I'll get Peggy to bring down all her dresses. Each colour will reflect something different in the room, blending in with the panels."

"May I have another glass of champagne, please," I said. It was the only thing for me to do. "Do you plan to exhibit?"

"Maybe," said Fahim, "in a small, controlled way."

"In your house? Neills has told me you have a gallery in your house ... your compound, I think he called it?"

"Yes, more than likely. You can get up and walk about if you're getting stiff. Then return to the chair and be still."

"Don't you want me in other positions?" I said, as I walked about sipping on another champagne.

"We'll come to that." Fahim's words were final.

We stopped for lunch. Food and my change of clothes arrived. All facilities were in the large studio, including a bathroom and little kitchenette. I saw nobody other than the two men. Peggy obviously arrived, but left lunch and my clothes in Fahim's outer studio. Neills disappeared to retrieve them. I never heard a knock or any other forms of communication. By the end of the day, I was tired and drunk. We ate the evening meal on the aft deck. I gulped in the fresh warm air. I didn't bother to ask if it would be the same tomorrow, as I knew. Tomorrow I would insist time in the sunshine.

Fifty-one

I'd been dreaming when Peggy knocked the following morning. As soon as I woke, I lost the dream. Something pleasant, because for a moment I felt happy, free. I didn't know where I was. Then Peggy called my name and continued to knock.

"I'm coming."

Looking through my porthole, I saw the day sprinkling rain. Thick dark clouds hung heavy in the sky. A storm was brewing. My sunny wakefulness turned dark to match the day. There would be no sitting in the sunshine.

Breakfast again, on my own. The sensation of the sweet Greek coffee was strong in my mouth. It told me I was real. The rest of me felt numb.

Peggy escorted me.

The day repeated the same as yesterday. Now I began to think all the days were the same. First series, second series, it was all the same, now in a smaller room. Champagne arrived mid-morning. I didn't see whether Neills drank his. I asked for more. As time progressed, if my glass was nearing empty, Neills refilled it.

Fahim laughed. "Steady, Annabelle. We want you sitting upright."

Were they going to take away my only enjoyment? There was no point asking for deck time. I thought I heard thunder, but it could have been the music.

"It looked like a big storm coming," I said.

When I started to chatter, they suggested I remain quiet. I really didn't want to do this anymore, but as I was several glasses tight, I didn't have the energy to fight for my rights. Rights, my rights, my mind burrowed down a rabbit hole. Would anyone have rights on someone's yacht, who came from Saudi Arabia, as they sailed the Aegean Sea?

I'd come aboard for adventure, on a love pilgrimage and to fulfil my dream, before I settled down to a predictable and mundane life. Should I have included in that dream, being an artist's model with my love interest looking on and taking photos? Why didn't it translate into something wonderful?

"We'll stop for lunch," said Fahim. "You might like a rest after lunch, Annabelle. Apologies for no sun, so maybe your cabin will be best."

We ate on deck. Although the weather was bad, it felt exhilarating to be out in the air and as it was still warm, we sat aft. I hadn't eaten much for breakfast and was ravenous.

Now was a good time to ask.

"Can I ring my parents? I'd love to speak to them. Tell them where I am, what I'm doing. I never got to post my letters. You rang your mother, Neills, I'm sure you could ring Australia."

"We're out of range for Australia. I'm sorry Annabelle," Neills said.

"What about Pete? What about my brother? I could talk to him."

Just then Eduart joined us and the three men began talking about things I had little interest in, nor understood, even when they dipped into English. Neills patted my knee at one stage and apologised for the conversation. Boys' talk, he said. Neills had actually noticed me but didn't answer my question. I'd lost the energy to persist by then.

Escorted to my cabin by Peggy after lunch, I lay on my bed, my head cradled by the pillow. I instantly fell asleep.

❧

"Time to go, Miss Annabelle," Peggy said after nearly banging down the door.

I dressed. I still felt groggy from the Krug at lunchtime. I'd turn into an alcoholic at this rate. I'd probably reached that milestone.

Bad weather hung around and caused the mighty *Sea Falcon* to roll. I'd seen land in the distance from my porthole. Down in the dungeon, as I now privately called it, I asked if we were moored near an island. The engines were still.

"We're anchored not far from land," Neills said.

"An island?"

"I expect so."

"Which one?"

"I'll ask Eduart later."

End of conversation.

The only diversion was my change of pose. Sometimes I stood, but mostly I sat and tilted my head and shoulders, this way and that. With my head tilted upward, I was able to see the distorted face of 'Girl on a Pillow.' I hadn't noticed her pain before. Perhaps it was my pain, reflected back at me. There was tragedy in that face and I was glad when Fahim asked me to move. I began to see pain in all the backlit panels of Picasso's women. Surrounding the room, they all shared their pain and panic with me. There was a knowing in their look. A dread slithered into my being.

Fifty-two

Adream woke me before Peggy's customary knock. My parents stood clothed in 1930s style, coloured sepia. Daddy was dressed in a dark, fine-quality cloth, pinstriped suit with waistcoat. With both hands, he held a black top hat in front of him. Mummy stood straight by daddy's side, holding his arm declaring they were a union. Their faces were expressionless, staring straight ahead. Swirls of pale orange mist played around them. Floating slowly past in a bright white cloud was the *Sea Falcon*. Contrary to the boat's slowness, the waves hurled themselves onto the couple as it passed. My parents continued to stare straight ahead, unflinching as if they were behind glass. I was also in the dream, hovering above. I looked down on the scene and could see my limbs on the boat, moving about looking for my body. My limbs had ragged red edges, but no blood flowed. Although bright light shone on the scene, there were no shadows, giving the picture a one-dimensional appearance.

"Annabelle, what's the matter?" said Fahim.

His voice pierced through me. I looked at him, shaken, where was I?

"I remembered a dream. It woke me this morning."

"Have another sip of champagne and relax. You're doing really well."

Was I? What was I doing except sitting here? I'd seen nothing of the pictures.

Suddenly Neills left the studio. He returned and whispered to Fahim.

"Stay exactly where you are Annabelle," said Fahim. "The angle is perfect and I don't want to have to recreate it. We won't be long."

He won't be recreating it, I will be. Expecting them to return at any moment, I sat perfectly still. Time moved on. From somewhere I dragged up a little rebellious spirit, slid off the chair and walked unsteadily to the easel.

His attempts at fragmenting were pathetic. Amateur, clumsy. No wonder he took to collecting. Other pictures were lined along a wall, faced inwards. I moved stealthily across the floor and flipped a picture. Then another and another. All were poses of me, but all had spaces, missing parts of me. My profile missed an ear. My nose missing in another. One of me to the waist with my hand missing. And overall, the pictures were terrible.

Sensing they would be back any second, I returned to my chair and assumed my pose. Just in time. They both retuned with a look of concern on their faces. They said nothing.

"Everything all right?" I said.

"Yes, fine," said Neills.

It wasn't, I could tell. Neills poured me another Krug and Fahim asked me to hold the pose with my glass lifted close to my face, without tipping, as if I was about to drink, obviously not remembering my previous pose.

An urgency in his painting developed. He churned out work, returning to complete a detail. What the hell was he up to?

"When will I be able to see them?" I asked.

"Soon ... soon," Fahim said distractedly.

He wasn't concentrating, causing me to think his mind was on whatever had disturbed the session.

Fifty-three

The following morning while I ate breakfast alone, a coastguard vessel slid out of the sea mist and came alongside. In a flash Peggy was at my side.

"Annabelle dear, Fahim would like you in his studio."

"What, now? It's still early."

Peggy was always more than sweet when something untoward was happening.

"Yes please, dear."

I left my half-eaten breakfast, glancing at the coastguard. Three men silhouetted through the mist. I hoped they saw me but was unsure if they did. I had a quick thought of running over to them but imagined Murat would grab me back. Peggy walked me straight to Fahim's quarters.

"Shouldn't I change?" I said to her.

"Not this time."

As I was about to step into his quarters, I noticed Fahim looked straight past me, his eyes connecting with Peggy's. She must have mouthed something.

"Thank you for coming early, Annabelle." And to Peggy, "Thank you, Peggy."

He smiled sweetly and thanked me again. Too sweet, too polite. "Peggy will bring breakfast down for you."

Something was up, but I was still foggy. I must stop drinking. I thought I'd cut down, but my head suggested otherwise.

Food arrived and Fahim walked me to his inner studio.

"Finish your breakfast here, Annabelle. I'll go and get Neills."

Fahim was gone for some time. He didn't need me here, so why the rush? It must have something to do with the coastguard. Were they dealing in drugs, smuggling something? Painting me to keep me distracted while their real purpose was conducted? Fahim surely had riches to spare, with no need to smuggle. I didn't know anything about smuggling and the idea seemed ludicrous. People were smuggled, drugs smuggled, maybe weapons were the trade? That thought didn't make sense at all. Was I to be smuggled? Then why this facade of painting me? Was the coastguard around yesterday? Is that what sent them up on deck? Was that the cause of anguish on both their faces when they returned?

Then there was Murat. He was odd. His position was odd. A bodyguard who basically had nothing to do. Maybe Fahim had to keep him for the times he did need him.

Desperate now, I wanted to leave. How could I get away? It dawned on me then; I was never alone except in my cabin. Where once I walked to my cabin on my own, now I was escorted. I was escorted everywhere.

While I waited for their return, I tried the door of Fahim's inner secret studio. The dungeon. There was no handle. How did the door open? I couldn't leave even if I wanted to. Just then I heard the door click. I sped to where my food lay, half eaten.

In sensible moments, I drank less and only took small sips, then my glass was refilled. I noticed I was unsteady on my feet. The boat must be rocking. I felt woozy and figured I needed sunshine, or at least a decent amount of fresh air.

"Come," said Fahim. "We need to get on with the paintings."

Fahim walked in front of me and Neills was at my rear.

As soon as I sat, I was handed a glass of champagne. "No thank you. I'm drinking too much."

"We have it here especially because you like it. A little won't hurt."

I relented. Sipped. It would clear my head I told myself. I felt strange. Had I been drinking for so long now my blood had turned to alcohol?

"Neills ... can you prop her up."

I'd slumped.

"We'll have to sit her in a different chair. I think it might be time," said Neills.

"I hope so, Neills. I have a life to get on with."

"It's getting close." To me, Neills said, "Have some more champagne, Annabelle. You'll feel better."

I didn't want any more. They were saying strange things. Something wasn't right. I drank because it was now habit. I was back somewhere in my childhood, being a good girl. Drinking my medicine.

"I need an outcome, Neills," said Fahim.

"Yes, tomorrow. It should be tomorrow. I need to talk with her tonight. She needs to know."

"I can't believe you haven't had that talk yet."

"I will. Tonight, I promise."

Between two worlds, I heard their conversation mixed in with my mother talking. I had trouble deciphering which was which. Everything was surreal and I wasn't really there, or anyplace. They didn't seem to think I was there either.

"Okay ... tomorrow ... Eduart will need to take us to another location. We'll sail during the night."

Was that my mother talking? No. I think it was Fahim. Or maybe Neills?

"I'll ease up on the dose. I want her to be fully conscious," said Neills.

Fifty-four

I don't remember getting to my cabin but that's where I woke. I had no idea what time it was or what day it was. How long had I been asleep? I could hear the hum of engines, which meant *Sea Falcon* was on the move. Gradually I realised dinner was soon. That meant I would be collected.

I'd woken with a thirst like no other. I gulped the water by my bedside too quickly, causing me to feel nauseous. Easing myself from the bed, I took a cold shower. Each action helped me to full consciousness. I dried my hair and applied fresh makeup. I was back, almost. I chose to wear the dress I'd bought especially for my trip, back in London. That seemed a long time ago. The dress needed a tan, which I now lacked. My skin was sallow, I looked wan. Had it been that long since I'd seen the sunshine?

A comment made by Neills slid into my memory. He needed to talk to me. It must be something to do with smuggling. I did have a right to know, and it was clear they were running from the coastguard.

A knock. Peggy at my door.

"I'll be a minute or two."

She was waiting when I opened the door. It was pointless to say I knew the way. Why did she bother? Arriving on the aft deck, Neills greeted me.

"You look ravishing."

Why was he lying? All the same, any compliment was good. There were just the three of us at dinner. Eduart was up on the bridge taking us to a new destination. Peggy and Murat hovered. The mist had cleared. Murat kept his gaze out to sea.

"It might be a sunny day tomorrow," I said. "It would be wonderful to get some sunshine." My statement received no comment from either Fahim or Neills. Directly after dinner, Fahim excused himself.

"Come sit on the comfortable seat, Annabelle," Neills said.

I was forever hopeful, although by then I was doubtful. He changed from hot to cold so often, I never knew what to expect. He was in a warm stage, so it could go either way.

"Tell me about your father again."

"Why?"

"Just tell me. I like the way you talk about him."

Neills was like a kid, he wanted the same story over and over.

"Well," I said, "he's a wonderful father, as I've told you. He's my best mate."

"Even more than your fiancé?"

"Stop on that subject. You know about that."

"I know. You're leaving your options open."

I sighed in exasperation.

"So, your father. I want to hear it again. Are you his favourite? What about Peter?"

"I'm the girl, so I'm his favourite." I giggled. It was the first time I'd heard myself giggle in a while. "Of course, Peter is his favourite son. But I had my dad all to myself after Peter left."

"Peter is his favourite son," Neills repeated very softly, more to himself.

"Of course, as he's his only son."

"If I'd been a favourite son, what would I have had?"

"You are a favourite son."

"Yes, I am. But if I were to have a father."

Neills was being weird. "I don't know. You'd have to ask Peter. Daddy did everything with both of us. Took us sailing together. You know, we did stuff together."

"Football?"

"Daddy's not into football."

We were both quiet for ages. Me, I was remembering my father and felt desperately homesick. What I'd give to see my dear father right here on the boat.

"It's hard for me to imagine what it would be like to have a father. To know what I missed out on. What do you know about your father before he met your mother?"

"Not much ... but I imagine he was hugely popular, as he still is. I imagine the ladies loved him and that he was held in high esteem by men. That's probably why mummy fell for him. They're very close and daddy adores my mother."

I was drinking again when I said I wouldn't.

"Lots of girlfriends, eh? Anyone in particular?"

"I don't know." I chanced at humour. "I wasn't there." Dead landing.

"Did either of your parents mention anyone?"

"Er ... no. I'm not sure they would. I'm not their confessional."

"Yeah. He probably threw them by the wayside, like leftovers from the dinner table."

"That sounds awful. I'm sure he didn't treat women like that."

"How can you be so sure?"

"Because I know my father. He's honourable and honest and decent."

"With a mean survival side."

"Why do you say that?"

"Maybe he has other children. He is very charismatic, you say. Women couldn't resist him. Perhaps he enticed them, persuaded them to give of themselves, completely."

"I'm sure he sowed his wild oats. That's what men do. They're supposed to before marriage."

"Supposed to? What century are you living in? Hurting women, leaving them with a child and discarding them? That is what men are supposed to do?"

"Well, whatever he did, he's an honourable man."

Why was he talking like this? He knew nothing of my father. It wasn't my fault he didn't have one. I turned to look out to sea. I didn't want to go to bed, and I didn't want to be here getting the third degree about my parents.

"Out of curiosity, was your father born in Australia?" Neills said.

"No. A little island. A Greek island as it happens. He emigrated to Australia, like so many others, after the war. His father died long ago."

"Oh, a little island. You should have mentioned ... we might have been able to visit."

"I don't know it. He didn't tell me ... he said it was all in the past ... didn't matter."

"That's surprising. Most Greeks are very close to their heritage."

"I don't know." I was part pissed and part pissed off. Why was Neills being like this? "You're jealous. You're jealous of my life, of my home life, that I have two lovely parents. Well I'm sorry about that, Neills. But you're a big boy now ... grow up."

That last bit I must have yelled, as Murat was at my side in a flash. Neills waved him away.

Neills said he wanted to tell me something. I wasn't sure if that was it, but I'd had enough. To stay on deck was no longer possible.

"I'm going to bed."

I moved so quickly, Peggy didn't have a chance to escort me to my cabin.

Fifty-five

Peggy. Persistent Peggy.

"I don't want to go." I was awake but still in bed.

"Miss Annabelle, Fahim requires you to come. It should be the last sitting."

Fight or flight. I could try to overpower Peggy, but that was unlikely. My fitness and strength were long gone. My next obstacle would be Murat. Totally unlikely. Then the only way off the boat was to swim. I was a strong swimmer, or used to be, but with no idea where we were or how far I'd have to swim, that was also impossible. If I simply refused, I wondered about the consequences. Murat might be brought in. Adding up my options, I dressed.

With the intention of being as annoying as I could, I took forever to get ready. I'd had instructions to wear the blue dress, so I put it on and eventually opened the door. With the severity of an armed guard, Peggy again corralled me to the studio.

Fahim was more than cheerful. Spruced up in taupe trousers and a white shirt, he looked fresh. Dapper.

"How lovely you look this morning, Annabelle. We will finish today."

Neills was there. We nodded. Neills being in charge of the champagne, he opened the bottle and sat it in the ice bucket.

"I don't want any champagne."

Fahim turned on the charm. "Oh Annabelle. I believe you and Neills have had a little tiff. Let's sort this out and make a toast to our last day ... will that be okay Annabelle, dear? I'll even have a glass and so will Neills. Won't you, Neills?"

"It's too early," I said.

"Annabelle dear, when has that bothered you?" Fahim said. Neills passed him a glass. "Come now, Annabelle, let's toast to a wonderful girl who has been so patient."

I relented. I wanted that champagne. We clinked and I drank, my usual gulp.

"You didn't speak with Annabelle last night as you wanted, I believe, Neills?"

"No, our dear girl got into a huff, as it's called in English. She stormed off."

"Oh dear," said Fahim.

They were both watching me. Neills refilled my glass. I felt woozy after the first. I'd drunk it too quickly.

"I don't feel very well."

"You ate little breakfast, I believe, and then gulping your champagne, it's not surprising," said Neills.

My hold on reality was slipping. "I don't feel very well."

"What a shame," said Fahim. "And I was going to show you the paintings I've made of you. Though we know you had a good look the other day. You know I'm not talented like Picasso, but he is my favourite."

I was losing my grip on my body too now. I slithered down the chair. Neills grabbed me before I reached the floor.

"It's time," said Fahim. "Come on, Neills."

My hearing was functioning, but little else.

"Neills, speak with her now. She's conscious enough. We know she's seen the paintings; she needs to have an explanation."

"Can you sit in the chair for me, Annabelle?" said Neills.

One by one they held up the paintings. The ones I'd already seen.

"They're fractured, sort of," I said with slurred speech. "You've left out parts of me … on my face and my hands. Fractured, with bits missing."

"Yes, we've taken fracturing a step further than Picasso. He'd be envious if he knew. Isn't that right, Neills?"

My sozzled brain wasn't coping.

"If you have plans for those vacant areas, why do you need me? Can't I go?"

"It's your input that will make these paintings perfect, Annabelle," said Neills. "If we don't get an answer."

I clutched the arms of the chair and tried to stay sitting up, but my body wouldn't work properly.

"Let's finish this now, Neills. Speak with her … I'll go."

Fahim made for the door. He turned at the door as he seemed to notice something on Neills's face.

"Stop sulking, Neills, get on with it. She has a right to know. And I'm tired of this."

With that, he left.

Neills helped me out of the chair and took me to a bench. "You'll feel better if you lie down." He placed a cushion under my head.

"Tell me what?"

"I've contacted your father."

"What?" I struggled to sit but arrived back where I was.

"He is to pay up or we'll ... well, we'll commit a part of you to one of the pictures. More if need be."

"What?" My speech still slurred. "What the hell are you talking about?"

My brain snapped, as best it could, into action.

Neills smirked and walked around the bench.

"Yes, I've been in touch with him. He knows who I am."

"What do you mean? I want to talk to him."

"You can't. He doesn't know where you are. You don't think we're stupid enough to say where we are, do you?"

"You said you couldn't contact him, or my brother."

"Ah yes, well I wasn't exactly telling the truth there."

He continued to circle me.

"I have something to tell you." He came to a stop, face to face. "Perhaps it was a good thing you stormed off last night. It would have spoilt this moment for me. This is better."

I was looking into the face of a madman.

"I'm your half-brother, Annabelle. He's my father too. And if you don't mind my saying, he is an utter prick ... in that language of yours."

"What are you talking about?"

"Just that. My mother, my very pretty, wonderful mother, was already married to your father when he met your mother in Melbourne. They emigrated together to Australia. Plus, there was one extra who came with them. Me."

I looked at Neills. I had to be still intoxicated. Neills – my half-brother?

"They met during the war. When my mother was pregnant with me, they married. Or so my mother thought.

"Your father was an ambitious man and worked hard to get ahead. He pushed himself onto the right people. Through your grandfather, he met your mother. Very pretty too, I believe. Though not as pretty as my mother. He was instantly taken with her. He was also taken with the connections he could make through her, because of her grandfather. So important to your father. Your grandfather could offer introductions, turn our father into an honourable man, as you like to call him. Enhance business opportunities for him.

"So, my mother was ditched. He told my mother the marriage was not valid. During the war, everything was chaotic. He had arranged for a marriage certificate, along with passports. There was a simple ceremony with a few friends they'd both recently met, as by then they were living in the Netherlands.

"He didn't need to divorce my mother. My mother never met anyone associated with your mother or grandfather. In your father's eyes, she simply did not exist. He paid her fare back to Denmark and gave her a measly amount of money to set her up in life. She had no one to turn to. Her life was filled with your father and me. She adored him. I might add she had to beg for that money. He then told her not to ever contact him again. And so, both my mother and me were out of the picture. Your father was a free man."

Fifty-six

There was madness in the man. He circled and paced, eventually coming back to my side. He spoke close to my ear.

"We returned to Denmark, my mother and me. Her parents had died during the war and she was orphaned. She had the shame of returning with a son and no husband. She made up a lie that he had died and she had no other choice than to return to Denmark. The most humiliating part of the story is that my mother will still not speak unfavourably of him. Not that she brings him up, but occasionally I'll ask a question. She either evades the question, or remarks that people react in different ways. She excuses him."

He paused, circled me, came back to face me.

"Eventually she was able to establish herself. People stopped asking about the father. People accepted her as she was. Loved her. She found a job and was respected for her hard work. She still works at the same place."

He stood looking at me, staring. I looked back at him, but his eyes were so crazed, I had to look away.

"So, there we have it. I'm now waiting for your so-called

honourable father to get back to me, with the money I believe he owes my mother and me."

"You have the wrong man. That is not my father. You're a fool, Neills. You've got the wrong man and, by the sounds of it, the wrong half-sister too."

My words were purposeful, but I was still slurring.

"I don't think so. You only need to look at my facial profile, your brother's and yours. Besides, your father has acknowledged my existence by not denying it."

"Why would he believe a phone call? I don't believe he would."

"Ah, you see ... I picked out photos of those I took, and another one of a painting with the ear missing. I faxed them to him. Your ear and the painting will meet, if your father does not send the money I've asked for."

"That's ridiculous. I don't know what you mean; you faxed them. You can't send a photo that quickly."

I was so drowsy I barely understood what he was talking about, but knew such things were not possible.

"There hasn't been time to post any photos. Even your instant ones," I said.

"There you are wrong, Annabelle. Fahim has all the latest gadgetry on board. It's a wired facsimile transmission."

"Well, my father hasn't got whatever that is, so how can he receive it?"

"Fahim has connections. Your father received it."

"I don't believe you."

"We are in contact by phone now. I am waiting for him to ring me with details of where he has deposited the money."

"He'll never do that. And besides he would have demanded to speak to me."

"He did. But he doesn't know where you are. All he has to do is deposit money into an account and you will be free to go. We'll drop you somewhere."

Neills went to a cupboard. Pulled out rope.

"I'm going to tie you up now, Annabelle. I have to find Fahim and see if the phone call has come through. If the drug wears off, I don't want you trying to escape. Though in truth, there's nowhere for you to escape to."

I struggled as best I could while he tied, but I was no match for Neills's strength and, added to that, I couldn't move my body sufficiently to fend him off.

"Keep struggling like that and your hands and wrists will bleed."

He left me. I lay prone, my wrists and ankles tied. He was right, struggling only cut into my skin.

How the hell did a romantic trip to the Greek Islands end up with me tied to a plinth? And my father, he would never act in that way. Ditching a woman with his baby. But ... Peter, me and Neills did have similar profiles, very similar. I thought about how I felt the first time Neills and I went for lunch. He attracted me and I couldn't figure out what it was. There was a connection and I just thought it to be a romantic one. Oh God. The thought we may have made love. So there was some decency in this man. Keeping me at arms' length. If it was true at all.

My thoughts were a whirlpool.

I lay, tears streamed down both sides of my face.

Fifty-seven

My bladder filled. My legs came to life. My arms came to life. But what could I do with them? I raised my head and saw my wrists were raw from the ropes. The thought they might cut my ear off and attach it to a painting. Did Neills lack so much imagination he was using Van Gogh as inspiration? And Fahim, he was party to this. Why on earth did he need to be party to all this?

Perhaps I would wake and realise it was all a nightmare.

Disgust crept over me when I could no longer hold on. I weed. I had to stop thinking that I was lying in my urine. I cried then; deep, desperate sobs, sobs at my utter helplessness.

Several hours passed, or so it felt. Thirst overtook other senses. My mouth was dry and my body ached. I could arch my back to relieve some of the pressure. Tired, helpless, hopeless.

I could not believe my beloved father had spawned this man. I drifted into a place I'd never known before. A dark chasm of nothingness. Eventually I dozed off.

Somewhere off in the distance, I heard voices. Fahim and Neills stood in the doorway.

"Oh dear, she's messed herself," said Fahim.

"Your father is being very stubborn," Neills said. "If I didn't believe what you said about him caring for you, I'd think he didn't care at all."

"We're bringing a phone down here," said Fahim, "you tell her."

"You will only have a few seconds to tell him to pay up. We've warned him about contacting the police," said Neills. "We'll go ahead with your ear if we even suspect the police have been approached."

Fahim left, while Neills looked on.

"What a messy girl you are. You know Annabelle, I have been waiting half my life for this moment. Trying to find my father with no help from my mother. Then Peter fell into my lap. His profile was the first thing I noticed in the pub one day. I've been looking for profiles similar to mine all my life, and they had to be Australian."

Fahim returned with a phone and spoke into it, "Okay, go ahead," he then held the receiver to my mouth.

"Daddy, daddy, is that really you?"

"Bellie, my darling girl ..."

"Daddy, please pay them, they're mad, they're going ..."

"Bellie, tell me where you are."

"I'm on a boat call ..."

Fahim took the phone and clicked off. "You should get some action now," he said to Neills.

They both left. I cried, I wailed. To hear my father's voice and then he was gone. Beyond cruel.

Later Neills came back. "I'm going to untie you. You are to be given some food. You'll eat it here. You don't need the toilet, it would seem. Don't think you can escape; you can't."

Fahim came in with a food tray. What had happened to Peggy? She didn't know I was here. She didn't know this was happening to me. I was desperate for them to untie me, but they were messing around at a bench. I heard Fahim whisper to Neills.

"You're not really going to go ahead with this?"

Silence from Neills, unless I didn't hear an answer.

"Has he paid?" I asked, my heart hammering as they untied me.

"Not yet," said Neills.

A knock on the door. Fahim and Neills looked at one another. Someone they hadn't expected. Fahim opened the door to reveal Murat. He spoke in a language I didn't understand and was hustled in. Fahim and Neills rushed out. Had they heard from my father?

My food tray was on another bench, but I was terrified of Murat. I mimed that I wanted my food. He nodded for me to get it. My legs were unsteady as I took the few steps towards it. My appetite had left me but if I was going to think straight, I needed to keep up my strength. I sat on the bench and tried to eat. Murat stood by the door; hands clasped in front of him. He said not a word and didn't look at me. His stance, pure threat.

Fifty-eight

With my back to Murat, I picked at the food. I'd been so intent on my predicament and waiting for Fahim and Neills to return, I hadn't noticed there was a lethal-looking knife by swabs of cotton wool at the end of bench. The place Fahim and Neills had been fussing with. Were they really going ahead with this madness? My terror soared.

The food stuck in my throat. I stayed very still trying not to choke, as a chance swam around in my mind. I was sure Murat's eyes were boring into my back. I continued to peck at my food. Fahim and Neills might return any minute. Then what? Would they really let me go even if my father had paid? My predicament hit me all over again. There was no way out of this. Then the very slim possibility kicked in.

Easing back, as if stretching, I turned. Murat stood by the door exactly as before. Did the man ever get so bored he lost concentration? I doubted it. He was too well trained. Now I didn't want Fahim or Neills to return. It hadn't been that long since they left, had it? I couldn't be sure. Time passed very slowly, yet quickly.

If I managed to grab the knife, where would I conceal it? I was wearing a sodden dress, no pockets, no bag, nothing. Bunching up my dress and facing Murat, I inched over to where the knife lay.

"I need the toilet."

"You been."

He did know English.

I stumbled backwards, holding the back of my dress as well as the front.

"It's number two … it's urgent." He looked away for a moment as I clutched my privates, both rear and front. "Please, it's urgent. I have to go."

Murat squirmed. Crunching my skirt, I moved toward him. I stank, and at close quarters it must have been worse.

"Please, please."

While bunching my dress, I'd picked up the knife from the bench. I passed it to my right hand behind my back. Murat wasn't tall; we were probably the same height. I was close to him, very close. He scrunched his face and wrinkled his nose. I pleaded. He refused to speak and didn't move.

Quickly, even quicker than I thought I had it in me, my knee launched into his groin. I lost my balance at the same time as Murat went down.

The knife still in my hand I regained my balance. Although terrified, with an eye on Murat, I moved as fast as I could to open the door.

I couldn't get out.

Fifty-nine

Murat lay in a foetal position on the floor. He groaned and inched his way towards me. I kicked him around the kidney area. His body felt like steel. The kick stopped him, but I hurt my foot in the process. I had to act quickly. He might get up. He might have a gun. I had to use the knife, there was no other way.

I did not want to kill him. but I needed to disable him. I stabbed him in his buttock. The knife went deep and blood gushed out. He cried out. Having no experience with this behaviour, my terror caused me to shake and I wanted to vomit. He could go for me at any moment.

Desperately I tried to find the opening to the door. I pressed along the frame, down in the cornices, up over the top; nothing. Everything was flat. I stumbled over to the plinth I'd been laying on. I ran my hands underneath, pressing as I went.

Suddenly the door sprang open. Fahim and Neills stood there. I turned instantly. Could I run around them?

Neills rushed toward me. The knife was in my hand. He lunged for me and caught the knife in his ribs. He looked at me aghast. I didn't believe what had just happened. I pulled the knife back, still holding it towards him. Blood was pouring from his chest. He bent over in pain and dropped to the floor.

Fahim looked to Neills, then over to Murat, who still lay on the floor on his side. He said something to Murat that I didn't understand. Murat didn't respond, just lay, clutching his backside.

"Take it easy, Annabelle," Fahim said.

"Grab her, Fahim," said Neills, through gulps of pain.

"I don't think so, Neills."

"What? Grab her … stop her … she'll get away." Neills jabbered away in Danish. "Fahim … I'm bleeding, help me."

I was standing holding the knife, which by now was pointing at Fahim.

"Like what, Neills? You have that high-bridged profile too. Brother and sister portraits. Mmm … this could be good. Thank you, Annabelle."

With that, Fahim left the room. He pulled the door and it self-closed behind him.

"No," I said, as if to stop the door from closing. I still had hold of the knife.

"Fahim!" Neills yelled.

"The man has left, Neills," I said.

I pressed all along the rim of the bench again, but nothing happened. Maybe it wasn't me who opened the door before. It was a coincidence. Fahim and Neills had returned at that same moment.

"Where's the release mechanism?"

"I don't know," Neills groaned. "He keeps that to himself."

I looked to Murat, who was still on the floor. "You must have seen where he opens it." He looked at me. Ignored me.

Neills was still speaking, his breath coming in short gasps.

"I've only been in this room with Fahim. When we left, I didn't notice. It just sprang open."

"Why did you leave?"

"The ... I'm not saying."

Murat stayed curled on the floor. Either one could overpower me. If they joined forces, I was history.

"Has the money arrived?" I said.

"No."

"What about the coastguard? Are they back again?"

I was pressing every area in the room I could think of, looking for a switch of some kind.

"Ask Murat how to open the door. He doesn't want to answer me." I pointed the knife at Neills by way of encouragement.

"Murat, the door, how do we open it?"

Murat didn't answer. His reply was a sneer, or was that a sly smile? He lay seemingly helpless on the floor. Despite being stabbed in the buttocks and having had his balls kicked in, I was still sure he could get up and grab me. That he didn't, made me more fearful.

"Has the coastguard come alongside?" I said.

"It doesn't matter," Neills said.

"It does matter. And what about the money?"

Neills didn't answer.

"Answer me, you jerk."

My anger up, I put the knife against his neck. I didn't mean to cut him, but the knife was sharper than I realised and nicked his skin. Neills said something in Danish and grasped his neck. Blood appeared and trickled down onto his collar.

"Answer me."

"No ... not arrived."

"Sorry about the bloodstain on your beautiful shirt."

"Murat, do something," Neills said.

Murat made no effort to intervene and yet I was sure he was able to. Maybe he didn't like Neills.

"Your father doesn't give a damn about you," Neills said. "We can all see that … let me up so I can try to find the switch."

"Shut up." I'd had enough of him.

I walked to the plinth where I'd been lying. Hadn't I checked here already?

It was then I noticed little lights shining under the bench where my lunch sat and where I'd found the knife. I'd seen them before, but I hadn't made the connection. Power must come from somewhere. Maybe the door mechanism was powered as well as the lights?

I felt under the bench, close to the edge. I must have missed them before. Two switches. I pressed one. The lights went out. I pressed the other.

Bingo.

Sixty

The door sprang open. Outward.

"Sir, sir. You better come." It was Peggy. She fell silent when she saw me. She must have been about to knock on the dungeon's door. I let the door close behind me.

"Fahim's not here. Why do you need him?"

Peggy looked at me in horror, glancing at the knife. "What have you done to Fahim?"

"Nothing, Peggy, he left. They were going to cut me to pieces. Is the coastguard here?"

Peggy continued to stare at me.

"Tell me," I said.

She seemed to be stuck, immobile. Hating myself, I held the knife to Peggy.

"Yes," she said, in a coarse whisper, shock written all over her face.

"Sorry," I said in a whisper more to myself. "Slide that cabinet over to the door." She just looked at me. "Do it. Hurry."

She did. "Now come with me. Run."

We ran through to Fahim's reception room and came to the exit door. Now I knew about secret switches, I looked for a recess.

I found it in the glass panel on my right. A small bump. I pressed. The door clicked open.

"Stay there," I said to Peggy. I'd noticed the door could be locked from the outside.

Able to move more quickly, I kept going but was fearful who I'd meet. Fahim? Eduart?

I was thirsty and weak. I felt fuzzy, a little wobbly on my feet, I guessed from the drugs I heard them mention. No time to think about that now.

I met no one on the way. Fahim must be with Eduart on the bridge. Once I reached the dining area, I crept close to the wall. I heard nothing. I did notice bottles of water on a bench close to me. Laying down the knife, I drank. I tried to sip slowly; remembering my father's warnings from years ago, 'Sips only, Annabelle,' when I'd felt seasick on our yacht.

Where was Fahim? Something or someone had caused him to leave the studio. I worried who'd be after me. I was sure Murat could still function. Neills too. They could catch up to me any minute.

I picked up the knife again and crept along the inner deck area where we sometimes ate. I ducked past windows and came to the main door to the outer deck. I heard nothing. I looked around but could not see a soul. The yacht was motionless, the engine quietly idling. I moved to the other side of the boat, ducking below window level. I poked my head around the doorway and pulled back.

A boat was alongside. It was so close; I could only see a section of it. Fahim was talking. It was difficult to hear. Was the other boat friend or foe?

The breeze was blowing their conversation away. I made my way to the other end and listened with my head at the edge of the doorway. I looked to the vessel and saw its full length. It was the coastguard.

A voice from the boat spoke in English. "We believe you have a Neills Larssen on board. We'd like to talk to him."

"We had a Neills on board, but he went ashore at Idhra," said Fahim.

"You've been on our radar. We believe he was on board after you left Idhra."

"You must be mistaken, we had two Danish men on board, both named Neills. One with two l's and one with one. Neills Larssen is not on board."

"What about this other Neils?"

"He disembarked back in Piraeus, along with others."

"Associated with Neills Larssen is a Miss Annabelle Lagoudakis. Is she on board?"

My heart stopped. Risk it. I jumped out. "Help me … help … please. I'm Annabelle Lagoudakis." I clutched the balustrade. "Please."

Fahim stood between me and the men on the coastguard vessel.

Quick as lightening, Fahim lunged at me. I was not quick enough. He grabbed my hand, squeezed hard and the knife clattered to the deck. His strength surprised me. He looked fragile, gentle, especially with his flowing clothes. He grabbed my hair, bent down and picked up the knife. His grip on my hair was savage. The more I struggled, the tighter he grasped it. He had hold of me with the knife at my neck.

Two coastguards came on board. Fahim was flashing the knife at them, then back at me.

"Stay away. Touch me and the girl gets the knife."

His grip remained tight on my hair. He was manoeuvring me closer into him. Even though it hurt like hell, I fought to keep a distance. I guessed he was trying to put his arm around my neck. Still bent forward I couldn't see what was going on.

Suddenly I felt his grip on my hair release and the knife hit the deck again.

One of the coastguards had grabbed Fahim's arm. The other coastguard was at his side in an instant. They had Fahim in an arm lock from behind. They struggled with Fahim moving him to the edge of *Sea Falcon's* gangway area. The coastguard must have opened it. Fahim fought furiously and it took the two of them to keep him and themselves from falling overboard.

One more coastguard was still aboard their boat. He called to me.

"Can you jump aboard? I'll grab you."

With little space at the gangway, and like lightning had shot through me, I leapt aboard. The coastguard grabbed both my hands. He quickly seated me inside and wrapped a blanket around me. Wasting no time, he rushed forward to help his colleagues.

The two coastguards on *Sea Falcon* were struggling with Fahim. He was kicking and yelling in Arabic. He thrashed about like a wild cat.

They finally got him aboard and were about to tie him down. He kept up the yelling, now in a deep, commanding voice, he spat in English.

"You have no right to do this. I am a resident of Saudi Arabia. You have no jurisdiction over me or my boat."

One man let go of Fahim to fetch something to tie him and in that instant Fahim, with only one man pinning back his arms, lashed out violently and freed himself. Intending to get back to *Sea Falcon*, he wasn't quick enough. Both men lunged for him, caught him by the shirt and dragged him back from the edge.

The Captain of the coastguard had joined the struggle. It took three men to knobble Fahim. Pushing him to the floor, they tied his arms to his kicking legs. Fahim's arms and feet were then tied with rope to railings on the deck of the boat. He kept up his yelling in Arabic and English. An oily cloth was pushed into Fahim's mouth, another tied it in place at the back of his head. He grimaced, as the stinking rag sunk into his open mouth.

Not so commanding now.

"Where is this Neills Larsson?" one of the coastguards asked me.

"He's down in a hold, injured, with a bodyguard called Murat. Be careful, they might ..."

The coastguard jumped on board *Sea Falcon* just as Murat appeared.

Murat grabbed the coastguard and held a gun to his head.

I looked to where I'd stabbed him, but he must have put something over it, under his jeans. I could see a bulge and a dark patch which travelled down his leg. He must be in pain but didn't show it. It was a sight. Murat holding a gun to the coastguard's head.

In Murat's grip, with one arm around his neck and the other holding the gun to his head, the man still managed to yell to his colleagues. The language went back and forth, urgent and staccato, all in Greek.

"He's a trained killer," I warned.

Sixty-one

I shivered under my blanket, more from fear than cold. No one was listening as I muttered "He'll use that gun." I was sure he would. His loyalty to Fahim was paramount.

Just then, Neills staggered onto the deck, blood oozing from under a cloth tied around his chest, with Peggy close behind him.

Neills called out, "Fahim, why didn't you ..."

Before Neills could finish his sentence, *Sea Falcon* sprang like a bullet. She was off. Eduart must have been watching the whole thing. With a coastguard on board, he must have realised they had leverage to get Fahim back.

Froth and foam were all that was left of *Sea Falcon*.

The coastguard revved the boat's engines, thrust forward, and chased in hot pursuit, but it was clear the smaller vessel was no match for *Sea Falcon*. I heard radio communication, but of course, all in Greek, then we slowed and changed direction.

With Fahim trussed to the boat's railing, one of the coastguards came and sat with me.

"What's happening?" I said.

"We are returning to Piraeus. We have the owner of *Sea Falcon*.

We will not hand him over until our colleague is returned."

"Do you know where *Sea Falcon* is heading?"

"We're tracking the yacht, but we think out of our jurisdiction. As long as we hold Fahim, they will stay in contact. I want to know what happened on board."

I told him the story from when I stepped on board. As I spoke, I could see Fahim through the window trying to shelter his face from the wind. He'd held us all in such awe. His ego must be taking a beating.

He also knew I'd stabbed both Murat and Neills. I doubted Murat would want anyone mentioning that a mere woman had got the better of him. And Neills had been more accident than intention. He'd walked towards me but, in truth, I'd plunged the knife. I wasn't sure how seriously injured he was. His moans hinted it was bad.

All this I left out of my explanation to the coastguard. I told him I'd struggled and managed to free myself shortly after Fahim left. Now I just had to hope Fahim didn't mention the incident. I seemed to be in his debt again. Although what they'd threatened me with was far worse.

"Did you come looking for me or for Neills?" I said.

"We had a call from your brother in London. He's on his way to Greece. He may have already arrived."

My dear brother. I could barely wait to see him.

The coastguard who'd spoken with me brought me a hot drink. I've no idea what it was, perhaps tea. It was hot and sweet. To this day, it was the best hot drink I've ever had.

They didn't speak to me again until we arrived in Piraeus.

Sixty-two

On the way back to Piraeus, I had time to think. It became clear to me I'd been drugged. I wondered for how long. It hadn't been just the alcohol that made me so woozy. I shuddered.

My profile, with my high-bridged nose, was all that interested Fahim, so he said. He'd asked me to sit for him, which I did, so why go to all that trouble? He'd told Neills to get on with it, he had a life to live. Then when I'd injured Neills, Fahim had no interest in him. It was Fahim who didn't care about Neills. Not my father about me. How misguided Neills must be feeling when his treasured Fahim didn't give a toss about him.

Would Fahim have really been party to hurting me? Would Neills have really gone through with what he threatened? I shuddered again. I couldn't believe what had happened to me and how lucky I was to escape.

I wondered how far back Neills's plan went. Did he know about Fahim wanting to paint someone with my profile back in England? Or did his quest to find his father coincide with the muse idea? So many questions.

Then there was this story about daddy being Neills's father.

Maybe it was all just invented to get money? I hoped and prayed Peter had arrived in Piraeus by the time we docked.

Just before we moored, the coastguard apologised that they couldn't let me go straight away.

"We need to file a full report and you will need to be present."

"I'm happy to help. If my brother is there, will he be able to sit with me?"

"Of course."

As we pulled into Piraeus, I saw the white breakwater. Right then I hoped I'd never see it again. Gently and kindly the coastguards took me ashore. Fahim remained tied on deck. People arrived to meet the vessel, but I didn't see Peter. I was escorted to the coastguard's offices.

"Your brother is waiting for you."

Tears fell when I saw him. My brother, my beloved brother. He stood at the top of some stairs. He ran down as I stumbled up. We hugged and both of us cried. It was hours of talking with the police and authorities before I could talk to Peter privately.

The coastguards and the police insisted I be checked out by a doctor. I assured them I felt fine, as I was desperate to be with Peter, but they would not release me until I was declared medically fit. When I was finally free to leave, I was asked to give details of where I'd be staying, in case they needed to speak to me further.

I'd not told the whole story. Would they believe Fahim if he told them I'd stabbed his bodyguard and also his friend? It was burning me up. Rather than relieved the whole thing was over, I now felt uncertain, scared.

It was evening by the time Peter and I left.

"Do you want to go back to the hotel. Or find somewhere to eat?"

"I'm starving," I said. "I just want to do something normal. Can we eat somewhere quiet?"

I was very hungry. Apart from tea on board the coastguard boat and coffee with Greek biscuits during the questioning, I'd eaten nothing for hours.

We walked down by the water, and along the wharf where ferries docked, neither of us saying a word. I was safe, I was with my brother. That walk, without words, filled me with so much love, I felt fit to burst. As with many siblings, we'd taken each other for granted, but a bond was forged, stronger than any time before or since.

Sixty-three

We found a restaurant that suited us both. Once we were settled and had placed our orders, we told our stories.

"You know, sis, you didn't have to go to these lengths to get me to join you on a holiday."

I looked at him. Loved him. "Well, I couldn't get you to shift your arse out of London any other way."

"Ooh ... well put. You go first," Peter said.

"No, you ... okay ... I wrote you a letter while I was on board *Sea Falcon*, but Neills told me to hold the mail until we returned to Piraeus. Mail from the islands takes ages, he said, which is true. But before I go on, I want to know how on earth you found me? Back to the beginning."

"Dad got in touch ... he phoned me. I'd just finished my shift and was going out. He said it was urgent. He told me to sit down, as he had a story to tell me first. It didn't seem like dad ... too much drama."

"Before I met your mother," he said, "I was in a relationship with a Danish woman. I've not been a good man, son. I'm sorry."

"I would have been surprised if you hadn't been in a relationship," Pete had replied.

"Don't interrupt. This is hard for me."

"Zipped."

"One day, out of the blue, I met this beautiful, vivacious woman. Your mother. I fell head over heels in love and knew she was the woman I wanted to spend the rest of my life with.

"I had a son with the Danish woman. We'd met during the chaos towards the end of the war.

"I fought my feelings. Men were circling your mother. I knew she felt the same about me but if I didn't act, she would walk. She didn't know about the other woman. I never told her. She thought I was playing the field and couldn't make up my mind."

Dad had paused then. Pete said he had to give him a minute before he continued.

"It was the Danish woman's choice to return to Denmark, as she knew by then I'd met someone else. I gave her all the money I had, which was quite a lot back then, booked her and the boy a passage and have had no contact since.

"Then I proposed to your mother. She still doesn't know about the boy or his mother. I hoped Lucy would never have to know. I'm sorry, son. This is not a situation I'm proud of."

"You have another son?" Pete had said. "Wow ... I'll have to digest that later. I can't say how I feel. Is that why you're ringing? You're coming clean?"

"No ... it's not. That son is named Neills and I believe you've met him."

"Um ... have I?"

"He says he's met you."

"I do know a Neills from Denmark. He pops over to London every now and again. We hang out. Or rather he hangs out with us. He met Annabelle. Took a shine to her. I think they were meeting up in Greece. I haven't heard from her for a while, though."

"That's the one. He did take a shine to Bellie. For the wrong reasons. He's her half-brother. Your half-brother."

Pete was silent, gobsmacked.

"Are you there, son?"

"Yes … yes. I'm here. I … can't believe it. I feel a bit sick. It's … it's so sneaky. Neills used me. Why would he not just shock-me-to-shit and come out with it?"

"That wasn't his aim. He's been blackmailing me. Did you give him my work address? Not an accusation son … I just want to know. He only started this once Bellie left England. I ignored his letters. I thought that would be the best thing."

"I don't remember, dad. I may have mentioned the name of your business. Thinking on it, he asked a lot of questions. He said he'd like to take a trip to Australia, and I just took it as an interest in a country he wanted to visit. What a fucker … using me like a dumb-arsed Aussie … and I fell for it."

"That explains it. Why would you expect this, son? Don't beat yourself up. Anyway, letters have been coming to work. He threatens to tell your mother."

"Do you think he has? Told mum? Has she been acting any different?"

"No. The only thing she's been concerned about, is that we haven't received a letter from Bellie for a bit. I told her not to worry."

"Go on."

"The first letter from Neills let me know who he was. The second asked for money. If he didn't receive the money, he'd tell Lucy. Since then, he's been demanding money. A lot. Then he started phoning me from a yacht, said Annabelle was on board. If I didn't pay up, he couldn't be responsible for what may happen to her. He'd sent a picture to me of a painting of Annabelle with the ear deliberately missing."

"What," Pete had said. "You mean ... what, that he's going to cut Annabelle's ear off? And put it on the painting? Do I have that wrong? It sounds absolutely ridiculous."

"It does, but judging from the tone of the letters, I'm really worried. I was able to speak to her, very briefly."

"Jesus."

"This is the reason for my call. I'm flying over, I need you to go to Greece and find her.'

"Dad," Pete said, "did you pay him?"

"No. Once you answer to blackmail, it will never stop."

"I know where she is. She's on a boat called *Sea Falcon*, owned by a Saudi man."

Pete went on to tell dad that Eva had come to see him in London. She'd been worried because she hadn't heard from me, and she didn't like Neills; didn't trust him. She told Pete that the party on the boat was over, but I'd stayed on with Neills and Fahim. Pete said he hadn't thought much of it, he thought I could take care of myself.

Dad had burst out, "She's on a boat with unsavoury types. How the hell can she look after herself? Dive overboard in the middle of the Aegean?"

"Dad, I didn't know all this stuff. Give me a break. I'll go straight away."

"Good son, thank you. I'm flying over, but can you get back to me and keep me up to date? I'm not sure how long it will take me to get there. I'll see you in Athens. Send a telegram to your mother as I may be on my way by then. Let her know where you're staying. And the phone number."

"Dad ... what will you tell mum?"

Dad was quiet for ages. Pete asked if he was still on the line. Then he heard a deep sigh.

"I'll have to tell her. Think of a way. God ... that's going to be terrible. After all these years, will she forgive me? I gotta go, Pete. I feel sick. Call me back, reverse the charges if you want. I'll let Lucy know you may ring in case I've left. She wouldn't mind hearing from you, in any case."

Sixty-four

"I've never heard dad so defeated," Pete said. "I got in touch with Eva. I didn't mention the half-brother bit. I told her I was going to Piraeus. She offered to help any way she could. She's a good friend, Bellie."

"Yes. She was my ally on board. Eva said she may be visiting London. I'm so glad she sought you out."

"When I arrived in Piraeus, the coastguard told me they'd found the *Sea Falcon* with you on board. Dad had been in touch and told them what I told him."

It was my turn to speak, and I told Pete everything. He'd heard most of it when he'd sat with me while I gave my statement, but I told it again from my personal experience, saying how I'd felt about Neills, the emotional side. And how Neills's story about his mother didn't quite match what dad had told Pete. Neills was all for effect.

"I was starting to get anxious about the situation, but as it turned out I was anxious about the wrong thing. I thought my heart was in danger, not my life. Then anxiousness turned to fear."

"You could never have guessed what they were up to, Bellie." Pete said. "It's all so bizarre. This thing about the paintings. To go to so much trouble for a high-bridged nose."

"God, those awful paintings … and yet Fahim thought he'd come up with a way of extending Picasso's brilliance. He thought if Picasso got wind of his idea, replacing the missing parts with real parts, Picasso would steal it. It wasn't even Fahim's idea, it was Neills's."

I stopped talking for a moment. I needed to catch my breath, thinking what a close call I'd had.

"I still haven't figured out why they drugged me. Whether it was all Neills's call and Fahim was just playing along."

"Perhaps you might have tried to escape, though I can't think where to, or refused to sit for Fahim anymore? Perhaps drugged you were easier to manipulate."

I cried then. We had to leave the restaurant. Once outside, I sobbed and sobbed on Peter's shoulder. I clung to him, scared he'd disappear.

My crying exhausted, I said, "Pete, I hate Krug and I'll never drink it again."

"I'll remember that next time we're celebrating something. Hell, Bellie, you're a regular James Bond-ess. Escaping like that."

Trying to cheer myself up, I said, "Yeah, well, someone's gotta do it."

I had to tell Pete the whole story. I couldn't keep it in any longer.

"Pete, I didn't tell the police everything. Or you. I'm scared."

Pete looked at me. "There's more?"

"Um … yeah. I stabbed them, both of them. Murat and Neills."

"What?"

"I kicked Murat in the balls, like I said, but as he lay on the floor, I stabbed him in the bum. I didn't want to kill him, just wound him somewhere that would stop him coming after me. I'm still sure he could have."

"Bloody hell, sis. And you stabbed Neills too? Although I feel you were justified in doing that."

"Stop it. I'm not a violent person. How the hell did I find myself doing that? Neills came towards me with his hand outstretched, asking for the knife and I just … sort of … stabbed him in the chest. I'm worried Fahim will tell the police and they'll pick me up for being violent, or whatever the technical term is. I realised later that there was blood on that knife. The coastguards didn't pick that up. I think it was left where they'd forced Fahim to drop it."

I told Pete about Fahim not seeming to care about Neills and what he'd said about Neills also having the high-bridged nose and how he could use that.

"Shit sis … you really are a James Bond-ess. If the knife was never picked up then they can't prove you did it. Except, I suppose, eyewitnesses."

"I'm really scared. I could be in heaps of trouble. The police could have me for not telling the whole truth and stabbing."

"I don't know anything about Greek law, but I think they're more concerned with getting the coastguard back. And I bet Fahim buys himself out of keeping a young woman hostage. He could so easily twist the whole thing saying you'd enjoyed his hospitality and agreed to sit for him. It just might be dad who wants to take it further."

"Pete … don't tell dad about the stabbings. Okay?"

Sixty-five

While we waited for our father, we checked in at the coast-guard every morning to see if they were still holding Fahim and if their man was off the *Sea Falcon*. So far, the yacht had disap-peared, along with their fellow coastguard. The Greek authorities would on no account let Fahim go until they had their colleague back. For two mornings it was the same answer. For three, four.

As I was in there, the coastguard continued to ask me questions and if I'd remembered other partygoers. The only one I knew well was Eva. I had no contact details for any others. Peter offered to ring Eva and said perhaps it would be better if they spoke to her in person. Would they pay her fare? Not particularly happy, they did. Eva was more than happy to comply.

A few days later, I couldn't thank Eva enough for getting in touch with my brother. She stayed on after she'd spoken with the coastguard. Pete and I had found a cheap pensione in Piraeus, but we moved to a bigger place to house not only Eva but our father, when he arrived. There was no phone for our use, so Pete gave our father the coastguard's number. Messages were being passed to and fro.

Daddy finally arrived and the sight of him, tall and strong, made me weep all over again. I clung to him and wouldn't let him out of my sight for the first day. Our mother didn't come as he had left in a rush, and it was not intended to be a holiday. Plus, the trip was expensive.

I had to shelve what I thought about my father abandoning a woman with his child. It seemed impossible that this child was Neills. He was such an awful person, even if it were only half true, I could absolve my father of anything. The fact that daddy had admitted it to Pete was something I didn't want to think about either. There had to be more to the explanation.

After visiting the coastguard and police, daddy wanted to speak with Fahim. He wanted Peter along, but not me. He said I'd had enough to deal with. I should enjoy Eva's company. He gave us some money to go shopping and have a slap-up lunch. There had been so much catching up to do with my brother, then Eva and finally my father, it wasn't until Eva and I went to lunch that we talked about life on *Sea Falcon*.

"I thought a lot about you on my trip back home, Annabelle. It worried me, how obsessed you were with Neills. He was throwing you lines and reeling you in, but you couldn't see it."

"Did everyone notice?"

"Probably not. Everyone was wrapped up in their own lives and what they could get out of their good fortune. It's not every day that you get to sail on a fabulous yacht for nothing. It was extraordinary, after all. You probably know he uses those guys to recruit women."

When I heard those words from Eva, it felt as if I'd been kicked in the guts. I'd suspected it while I was on board, but had put the thought out of my mind.

"Something nagged at me," I said, "but I didn't want to see it, Eva. I refused to see it. I was obsessed with Neills, as you say. Naïve, I guess. I'd never come across that sort of thing before."

"According to Joel ..."

"Joel?"

"Yes," Eva laughed. "You've forgotten already. I doubt his name was Joel but that's what he called himself. Joel gets paid to bring pretty women on board."

"Have you stayed in touch?"

"Heavens, no. I'm as bad as everyone else. I was in it for the experience, for the fun, being on a rich man's boat."

"Well, tell me Eva, how did he recruit you?"

"He has a good chat up line. He said he had a friend, a rich man from Saudi, who was sailing for a few days around the Aegean in one of the most fabulous yachts I was ever likely to see. Did I want to come?"

Eva smirked and shrugged her shoulders.

"I was on holiday on my own, a couple weeks off work ... he was good-looking ... I was putty in his hands. Joel was upfront with me and asked if I'd sleep with a good-looking Saudi if I was asked. Sure, why not. I'm on the pill."

"And did you? Sleep with Fahim?"

"No, he never asked. I'm not sure he slept with any of the girls. But as it turned out, the trip was for another reason, wasn't it? Fahim has everything he desires in the world, more young women than he can handle if he wants, I'm sure, but he was looking for you. He wanted a muse. One with the right profile."

"Do you think Fahim has parties where he does sleep with the pretty girls?"

"I'm sure of it. But not that time."

"Eva ... was I really naive not to see it coming?"

"Not at all. How could anyone possibly guess that story?"

"And do you think Neills works for Fahim, like the other guys?"

"I imagine so. Maybe he's in charge of them. Maybe he recruits the men first."

"Neills told me and Pete, when I was in London, that he's a human rights lawyer. I mentioned it to his friend's father, Ute, when I was sailing with the Americans. He said, 'Well if that's what he says, I'm not one for names.' I thought it was perhaps an English language thing at the time, but now I doubt if that story is true. The only thing real about that man is, he's a creep."

"And you mentioned the half-brother thing. How does that make you feel?"

"Very icky. I don't want to believe it. I thought at one stage that Neills was just pressing my father for money because it was a convenient lie. A man he'd happened on. A man he could milk, who couldn't disprove his story. But Neills did have a point. We look alike. Our profiles are alike, just like our father's. And now daddy has admitted it to Peter. And now my father is talking to Fahim."

It must have been the look on my face, Eva asked what was wrong.

"Something's troubling you. Can you tell me?"

I told her the remainder of the story. She now knew every last detail.

Sixty-six

Peter and daddy arrived back late in the afternoon from that first meeting with Fahim. I didn't get to speak to either of them until the following morning. Neither my father nor Peter revealed anything.

Waiting for my father to tell the story was harrowing, partly because shame and worry hung heavy around my shoulders. My grand year of freedom had dissolved into a complicated and expensive mess. Not just for me – it now involved my father and Peter, not to mention Eva. I was so very glad my mother hadn't come. Her gloating presence would mix my shame with anger. Not that she would say much but written on her face would be 'I told you so'.

As we laid the table with the provisions Eva and I had bought the day before, Eva said, "Mr Lagoudakis, would you like me to leave while you discuss this situation?"

"Of course not, Eva. You are the one who saved my daughter. I would be honoured if you'd stay. You're family now. And please call me George."

Daddy settled in his chair and helped himself to food, while I poured a Greek coffee. I wondered how he felt sitting in his homeland, his cultural home, eating his cultural food.

"Your mother could not have coped with this trip, kids. I'm exhausted, she would have been doubly so."

I waited for the visit to unfold. I glanced at Peter who gave nothing away. Silence continued. My father never liked to be pushed into a subject until he'd adequately collected his thoughts.

"Coffee's lovely, Bellie."

We waited.

"I thought you'd be curious about what went on yesterday, Bellie. Aren't you?"

"I'm busting here."

"Well, why didn't you say so?"

For heaven's sake.

"Go," I said.

"The coastguard who was abducted has been returned. Fahim is still in the coastguards' custody."

"But I thought it was to be a swap?" I said.

"Fahim told his Captain to let the coastguard go ... don't interrupt, Bellie."

Back like a shot into my naughty corner. I waited.

"That was what the coastguards originally intended. Between you and me, I think they wanted a little fun with Fahim. They were happy to wait for me to get there before they let Fahim go. A father still counts for something."

"Is he okay?"

"Who?"

"The coastguard who was captured."

Daddy sighed and glowered. "Yes. He is. If you'll let me tell the story without interruption."

Out of the corner of my eye, I saw Eva suppress a snigger. Well, it wasn't funny – my father was being annoying.

"They dropped the coastguard off in Istanbul, where he contacted Greece's coastguard headquarters in Piraeus and his colleagues were able to pick him up. They feared he may have been hurt, but apparently, he's fine. He was tied up by a ferocious-looking bloke who never spoke a word to him. But he wasn't hurt. He was given food by a woman called Peggy. She was the only person who spoke to him. Very briefly, she said that once Fahim gave the word, he would be released."

"Did he see the room, Fahim's studio?" To hell with my naughty daughter corner.

"He didn't mention that. I think he was kept in a cabin. He did say the yacht was incredibly luxurious, the part he saw. Well chosen, Bellie."

I glared at my father. "For heaven's sake, daddy. What about Neills? Did he see Neills?"

My father's voice quietened. "The coastguard didn't mention him either."

"What happens now ... to Fahim?"

"Fahim is allowed to sail the Greek Islands provided he contributes an annual donation to the coastguard's Christmas fund."

"Dad contributed too," said Peter.

"They have a Christmas fund here?" I said.

"They do now," Pete said.

"I can't believe this. I was held captive, drugged, threatened and now he's being treated like a wealthy benefactor?"

Daddy continued. "If you'll let me finish. I rang the coastguard while I was en route and asked them to hold Fahim until I got here. I had to have my chance to talk to him. He's an arsehole, a rich one, but still an arsehole. So yesterday I confronted him about holding my daughter. He told me all he wanted was to paint you. Nothing more. It was Neills's idea to threaten you with atrocities."

Daddy was quiet. He put his coffee down and looked at me. Then he burst out laughing.

"You stabbed Neills I believe. Well done, Bellie."

I sat opened mouthed at my father. I opened my mouth to speak but daddy quickly held up his hand to stop.

"He was patched up by a doctor in Istanbul and returned to the yacht. I believe you stabbed his bodyguard too. Though both Murat and Fahim are embarrassed by that. Very much so for a tough bodyguard."

"It was not amusing or brave or anything like that." Glaring at my father, "I was terrified. I still don't know if they would have gone ahead with cutting my ear off."

The whole episode was about my father's supposed son. He seemed to be forgetting that. Instead of my life feeling calm and safe now, it had a chaotic quality. My father didn't seem to get it. With him present, I flipped between thinking it was my fault and remembering I was the prey.

"I seem to have made such a mess of everything," I finally said.

"Darling, remember how back at home when this was just a dream, I said everyone should have a trip of a lifetime before they settle down?"

I nodded.

"So you did. You've dodged a bad bullet but one that's given you life lessons. You don't do anything by half measures, do you, darling? Trip of a lifetime, it's been."

"I'm not sure I needed life lessons quite so extreme."

My father's view of the world wasn't really helping me.

"Daddy, don't you think Fahim just said it was all Neills's idea to save his own skin?"

"Yep, I thought of that. He said the thought of making his paintings three-dimensional intrigued him. He was guilty of not stopping it earlier, but he would never have gone through with it. It was Neills's baby. Neills convinced him I'd pay up. Neills asked Fahim to go along with the idea in payment for getting him the muse he was after."

"Those paintings. There were spaces where bits of me were to be placed. They were messing about with a *knife*."

"You might be being a bit dramatic, Bellie. Besides, it came in handy for you," said my father. Then he roared with laughter again.

I was beginning to get angry with him. It felt like my beloved father was suddenly not on my side. He carried on before I could say so.

"Peter asked Fahim about the knife. Fahim said he was having a bit of fun with Neills. He found his obsession amusing. Fahim was curious to see how far Neills would go but he would never have allowed it to happen. Too messy."

My father thought that was funny too.

"I'm glad you find it so amusing, daddy. I was being drugged. Fahim was party to the whole thing. He wanted someone with my profile, he'd been looking for ages for the right model. Who had the obsession?"

"He's a very wealthy man. He can indulge himself with any whim he chooses. I really don't believe intentionally cutting off someone's ear is one of them."

"Did you ... pay up?" I said.

"No. And don't think badly of me. I doubted he would have gone through with it. As I said to Peter, paying blackmail is a bad game."

"So Fahim gets off scot-free, except for annual donations to a Christmas fund. That is nothing to him."

"It's satisfied the coastguard. Fahim is very charismatic, very professional, I have to admit, Bellie … Eva," turning to Eva to include her. "I can see how he charms the pants off people, literally or metaphorically. With all that money and natural charisma, that guy will squeeze through many tight places during his life. Collecting girls for a party on board would be simply playtime for him. A mere interlude in his life. Something to amuse him briefly. And in this instance, he was after something else to amuse himself."

I was incredulous. What had I thought my father would do? Something heroic? Playing along with a Christmas fund wasn't it.

"What happened to Neills?" I said.

"Back on board, I think," my father said.

"So what happens now?" Eva said. She'd remained politely quiet until then.

"As I've finished with Fahim, the coastguard and the police will release him."

"On your say so?" I said.

He nodded. "Yep."

Something wasn't right. My father didn't hold that much power, in Australia or anywhere else. Something was amiss but I couldn't find the right question to get the right answer. I decided to ask my brother later what had really gone on.

Sixty-seven

To calm things down after all that had happened, the four of us spent time doing some undemanding sightseeing. I couldn't get Peter alone until a day or two later. Eva and daddy struck up a friendship as we strolled around the Plaka, so I took that opportunity.

"What really went on, Pete? I can't believe they would release Fahim on daddy's say so."

"DAD," Peter said.

"Oh, for heaven's sake. Leave me be."

"Dad asked me to leave the room at one point. He said he wanted to talk to Fahim alone and that Fahim would likely open up more if they could talk one-to-one. I didn't think too much of it. You know dad. He's a deal maker. It didn't seem unreasonable, so I went outside and chatted with the coastguards. Some spoke English. Great bunch of blokes. They told me lots of stories about tourists, how they get lost, aren't prepared for the volatile Aegean, think they know everything about sailing. Not to mention the parties on board and what they get up to."

"And ..."

"Fahim did say that Neills was not his friend. Just someone who worked for him. It seemed like Neills was a convenience. Good at pulling girls and organising others to do the same, to cater for his parties on board. Fahim said he found the man unsavoury."

"That could be true. After I injured Neills, Fahim just left, as if he wasn't bothered at all. Neills couldn't believe it." Pete and I walked a while. "I can't believe I've got mixed up with people like that."

"Yeah, it's a struggle for me too. My demure little sister mixing with professional crims. I got sucked in too, don't forget."

"I feel stupid about the whole thing, but way back in England, when I liked him, I can't help wondering if Neills found out where our father lived and decided to recruit me when he met me. Or maybe Fahim's request came later."

"Hard to know. He hung around me a lot. He'd turn up at The Swindlers Alms, or the Ferret and Fox, and invite me for a drink. I believed him when he said he wanted to visit Australia. He said he was curious about the place. In retrospect, his questions were probing, especially when it came to my life and family. I had the vague feeling he wanted to ask if he could stay with mum and dad in Sydney."

"So, what happens to Neills now? Was that mentioned?"

"Nothing I heard."

"He might continue harassing dad, or me or you. Plus, I injured him, which has probably left him very pissed off. Has Neills left *Sea Falcon* yet?"

"I don't know, sis ... ask dad."

"The stabbings I was so worried about dad knowing, seem inconsequential to him. I sure hope mummy never finds out."

Pete gave me that look.

"Okay Pete ... mum. For heavens sake."

When we caught up with dad and Eva, I did ask him again what had happened to Neills. His answer was much the same. That I should not worry any more about that man.

"He won't be trying anything like that again. I think he's learnt his lesson."

This left me none the wiser, with still more questions. At dinner, I asked dad how he was enjoying being back in Greece after all these years.

"It was too long ago, Bellie. I was only a little nipper when my father left Greece."

"You never did tell me which island you came from."

"To be honest Bellie, I'm not absolutely sure. We moved to mainland Greece. Then the war came, and my father was killed. It was just my mother and me. I think it was a broken heart she died of a short time later."

"So, you don't actually know where you were born? Which island your father came from? The islanders seem so close-knit, I would have thought he'd mention it."

"He didn't."

My father's life was all very vague. I was certainly not going to get any more out of him. That was the first time that I could remember he'd mentioned his parents. Now I was an adult, I had come to understand that parents are not just parents but have their own lives. Had their own lives. I realised for the first time how self-centred children are.

I needed to speak with Peter again, but dad and Pete stayed up drinking and chatting until late. Their two-year separation needed more massaging. More father-son bonding time. Meanwhile my questions festered.

Sixty-eight

My father must have made an impression on Fahim, as he wanted to take the four of us out to dinner.

"What?" I burst out when he suggested it.

"Come on, Bellie, let him make it up to you," dad said. "He remembers you too, Eva."

"Dad ... I don't think you realise just how frightened I was ... you don't seem to have taken in what I went through!"

"Take it easy, Bellie. Okay, I'll tell him we have plans. What about you Eva ... do you say no, too?"

"I do."

How could my father be so heartless and unfeeling? I'd always had the image of myself as daddy's coddled little girl. He would protect me from my mother's expectations of who I should be. Daddy never put pressure on me. I suddenly realised he had no expectations of me. I was his daughter and not his son. My year away was broadening my understanding of my world, left, right and centre.

Eva planned to leave the following day, so she and I spent a day together, leaving Peter and dad to continue their bonding.

Eva turned out to be a very amusing person, something I'd not had time to appreciate before. She'd broken up with a man shortly before I met her. They'd been together since high school and she felt, when they split, she'd lost an arm. Against her parents' wishes, she took the trip to Greece alone. This was her time, like mine, to get to know herself. She jumped into situations without a thought.

"My spontaneity was out of control. 'No' didn't enter my dialogue. That's why I hooked up with Joel. I'm glad I did. But I've moved on from that craziness now. I've levelled out. I've met someone else, but it's very early days. This time I will take it slowly. What do you plan to do now, Annabelle?"

"After here I'm going back to London with dad and Pete. I'm not ready to go back to Australia. I still have some of my year left."

"When you do go back, will you get back with Clive?"

"Oh God. What a thought. I can't imagine that life, the life I was expected to live. Dad said Clive comes around quite a bit and was worried when he hadn't heard from me. I haven't spoken to dad about my life back in Australia. We haven't had time. It was my mother who was keen for me to marry and do the right thing. The world has moved on. I don't think it's like that anymore. Certainly not here in Europe."

"Expectations of women are changing slowly in my country. They don't just want to be doing the washing up and changing nappies. I certainly don't. Exciting times, Annabelle."

That evening the four of us had a farewell dinner. Eva left the next morning promising to keep in touch. The Lagoudakis family planned to head back to London. On the way, I would break away and stay with Eva in Holland for a spell.

I had one thing to do before we left Greece.

Sixty-nine

I wanted to see Fahim and worried he may have left already. My father didn't understand why I wanted to see him, as I'd already declined Fahim's offer of dinner.

"I have questions I want answers to," I told him.

"Well, he's probably left."

"I'm going over in case he hasn't. You and Pete can have more time together."

"How about we come with you?" said my father.

"No, that's not necessary. Why are you bothered?"

"I'm not. I think you're wasting a journey. And what do you want to speak to him about? You could have done that at dinner."

"I need to speak to him one-on-one, not at some jolly dinner. I want to know what happened to Neills for a start. Most importantly, I want to know why. Why Fahim was prepared to treat me like that. Would he have gone ahead with it? Did he really want a painting with bits of me on it? Did he really want to one-up Picasso? He just doesn't seem the sort to care that much. He's up there, he doesn't need to prove himself."

"We've been through all that, Bellie."

"You have. I haven't."

"Maybe he was bored with painting in the ordinary style."

"God knows, he's not an artist. A long-held passion to paint in the Picasso style? Mmm ... maybe. But those are the sort of questions I want to ask him. You seem to be exonerating him."

"I'm not. And I told Fahim as much. But I can assure you, Neills won't be bothering our family anymore. You used a knife on him, which I hope he remembers."

"It was nothing I intended. He rushed at me, and I stabbed him to stop him coming after me. He may have tied me up again. And, in case you've forgotten, that knife was meant to slice my ear off."

"Take it easy, darling. You were incredibly brave." Dad came over and gave me a hug. "My darling daughter, I am proud of you. I didn't know you had it in you."

"You talk like it was a great thing I went through. It was awful. I was afraid for my life."

"You put two of them out of action." said Peter.

I glared at Pete.

"I think Murat was playing possum. I'm sure he could have got up. I had the feeling he didn't like Neills and was enjoying seeing Neills suffer, and then be rejected by Fahim. You're both glorifying the whole thing."

"Were there more crew on board?" Peter said. "Murat, Peggy and the Captain seems a small number for such a lavish boat."

"I didn't see anyone else, but I don't know for sure. Many left the boat along with the other guests. I didn't see Murat until the others had left, and he'd been there all the time."

I was explaining myself all over again. There was no need for me to keep repeating my ordeal. My questions were for Fahim's ears only.

"How come you're so friendly with Fahim anyway?" I said to my father.

He sighed and shrugged his shoulders, the conversation dismissed.

"Well, I'm going. You two enjoy yourselves."

As I walked to the coastguard I rehearsed my questions. Was Neills still on board? Was he all right? Although I had reason to dislike Neills intensely, I felt sorry for him. If it was true my father had dumped both him and his mother, that would have left an indelible mark. With some distance, and in the cold light of day, I figured all he'd ever wanted was to be recognised by his father. Strange way to get it, but judging from my father's reaction, it hadn't worked. This, of course, was if the story was true.

Seventy

Fahim had not left the coastguard's headquarters. When I arrived, he was in the midst of a party. Coffee and a selection of pastries lay on the table. Off-duty coastguards must have come in for the day, along with administration staff. There were far more people than I'd seen before.

Here was a man who, only a few days ago, had been manhandled and tied down on the coastguard vessel, and was now best of mates with the lot of them.

A hush fell across the room when I walked in. The coastguards who had saved me came over and invited me to join them. The man who'd been taken hostage on the *Sea Falcon* was with them and seemed in good spirits. Away from Fahim I asked if he'd been treated fairly, if he was well? Had Murat injured him in any way?

"Murat was put in the same cabin, to guard me. He massaged his backside from time to time but other than that, he just sat with me. Peggy brought in coffee and pastries, then left. Murat smiled when he heard the click. He didn't answer when I spoke in both English and Greek."

"He probably speaks both, but he doesn't talk much. He was a mercenary among other things. Maybe that was part of his training. Not to talk unless absolutely necessary," I said.

"Eventually Peggy came back and said something in a language I didn't understand. Murat mimed an apology, then tied me up and left the room.

"We arrived in Istanbul and Murat walked me to the gangplank, inclined his head and waved his hand for me to go. I had no passport or papers. I contacted the coastguard in Istanbul and here I am. Now Fahim apologises to us all with money deposited into a Christmas fund your father set up, and with this farewell party."

"What? My father set it up?"

"Yes. Then Fahim contributed a large sum. It's all sorted," the coastguard said and winked.

"Fahim's a charmer, that's for sure," I said.

"And don't worry. Fahim won't be taking any action against you either." He smiled reassuringly.

My jaw dropped. I couldn't find words. Take action against me? Was he being serious?

"What?"

I was ignored.

"Are you here to speak with Fahim?"

"Yes I am."

"Well good luck. Look, one of my colleagues has left the table, there is a seat for you, next to him."

I made my way over to the seat and Fahim turned to me with his fabulous smile.

"It's lovely to see you, Annabelle, and looking well rested. You declined my offer of dinner and now you are here."

"I'd like to speak with you privately, if I may."

"Very formal, dear Annabelle. Of course. I'll ask if they have space somewhere."

We were ushered into an empty office. Everyone was in the main area enjoying Fahim's hospitality. Most of the other offices seemed to be empty.

"I have a lot of questions," I said, "but first I want to know what happened to Neills. Where is he?"

"You want to see him again after all that's happened?"

"No, I don't want to see him. I just want to know what happened to him. My father tells me Neills won't be bothering us anymore, but he won't tell me why."

"Why do you think I know?"

"He was on your boat, Fahim. Of course you know."

"Your father and I came to an agreement, but if your father chooses not to tell you the details, there is no way I would come between a father and his daughter."

"I accidentally stabbed him. Is he all right?"

"Is that what you call it? You did more than that, Annabelle. You injured Murat. Something I'm sure he is most embarrassed about. And threatened Peggy with a knife."

"Have you spoken with Murat?"

"I've only spoken with the Captain."

Now facing Fahim, my resolve weakened.

"Are your questions over?" he said.

"No. I was a guest on your yacht, then a prisoner. I have a right to some answers."

"That's not quite true. You were my muse and you happily agreed to sit for me."

"Drugged and not allowed up on deck, except to eat."

"You came willingly on board, you were given excellent food and drink and tours of the islands and waited on hand and foot. You think everything is free? If you play with fire, Annabelle, you are likely to get burnt."

I had no experience of this world, where people's views of right and wrong were so different to mine. Yet it seemed my father navigated this with ease. Fahim sat looking at me, waiting for me to respond.

"Neills … is he alive?"

"Yes."

"Where is he?"

"On board *Sea Falcon*."

"Willingly?"

"Why wouldn't he be?"

"I don't know. Where … when is he getting off *Sea Falcon*?"

"You want to see him?"

"Of course not."

"Oh, you are using tactics here, Annabelle. Well done. We shall travel down this road together."

He was playing with me, like I was a little kitten, and he was using a piece of screwed up newspaper attached to string to taunt me.

"Where and when is he getting off your boat?"

"He is coming home with me. All the way to Saudi Arabia. He will get a chance to see my gallery and my horses and meet my wife and two boys."

"So, you are rewarding him? You didn't seem like a friend when he was injured. But now you are buddies again?"

"I didn't say that."

"I'd imagine he is honoured to be going home with you and meeting your wife and children."

"He doesn't know yet."

"So, he stays with you and then goes home to his mother, I presume?"

"I didn't say that."

"Okay, I'll try and unravel the riddles you're weaving. Where does he go after he stays with you?"

"He's not staying with me, Annabelle. He will come to my place and see what I have told you. Then he goes on a trip to an oasis."

"Is that a place he wants to visit?"

"I don't know, Annabelle. Maybe. He likes to travel."

"Then what?"

"I don't know. I will not be joining him. What he does from then on is up to him. He has free will."

"Free will. How is he getting there?"

"Murat will be escorting him."

"You're dumping him in the middle of nowhere?"

"Not me personally, but let's not split hairs. And besides, it's not in the middle of nowhere to the people who live there."

"Does he know how to navigate his way out of an oasis?"

"Annabelle, if you wish, you could join him."

"We call people like you 'smart arses.'"

"Oh, I like that. I'll use it one day."

"Are there roads from this oasis?"

"There are tracks."

"He'll be able to get to a town after he's done his penance, I presume?"

"Presume all you want Annabelle."

"Does my father know this?"

"He suggested it, after we negotiated other options. There, you've made me say it."

Neills was being dumped in a desert with no assistance. He'd have only his wits to help him return to Denmark. I thought of how Neills had manipulated me. But I was brought up to believe two wrongs don't make a right. I needed to get away from Fahim. He was insidious. I got up and made for the door.

"The interview is over, is it, Annabelle? I thought you had more questions?"

With the door partly open, I briefly looked back at Fahim's smirking face. I turned and walked through to the main office area, where by now, the coastguard personnel had thinned. I walked down the stairs and out to breathe in cleansing, salty sea air.

My feet took me to the water's edge. I needed the sight of the sea to clear my head. How could my father be a party to this? His own son. Neills had done my father wrong by blackmailing him. My father definitely did not like being taken for a mug. Fair enough. I'd heard him described as a hard businessman. 'You can't put one over on old George, unless you're up for the challenge.' Among his mates, these comments were common, but always said in a joking spirit. Did my mother know he had this streak?

This treatment of Neills was too sinister and didn't fit the image I had of my father. Neills's behaviour had been appalling, but there must be other ways of dealing with him.

I looked back at the coastguard office and wondered if I should go back and finish my questions. No. Fahim had played with me. If I went back in, he'd just play me again. I'd lost ground by walking out. The rest of my questions would have to remain unanswered.

Seventy-one

Eva's presence would have been so welcome right then. I needed someone who would listen. I wanted to talk through the feelings I had always cherished for my father.

As I walked in the door, my father said, "Ah, here she is. We're going exploring. See where our noses take us. We've been waiting for you."

I looked at him with a new awareness.

"What's up, Bellie?" he said.

Was he curious or just concerned for my reaction towards him?

"I spoke with Fahim."

"Good girl. That's out of your system, then. I'm surprised he's still around."

"He was throwing a party for the coastguard. He told me of the plans for Neills."

"Okay, good ... let's get going then."

"No, dad. *The* plans ... your plans for Neills."

"Oh ... and what would they be?"

"You darn well know. Leaving him to die in the desert?"

"What?" said Pete.

"Don't believe everything that man says, Bellie. He's a born liar."

"Fahim is carrying out your wishes in repayment for you not laying any charges against him with the Greek authorities."

"Why are you so concerned? Think of what he was about to do to you."

"So, you are admitting it. Neills is your son, daddy."

My father did not reply.

"Fahim was not interested in hurting me. He was just playing along with Neills."

This was one of my questions that remained unanswered, but I was going for it.

"It sounds to me like you're believing that man over me, your own father."

"Well, you explain, then. Why would Fahim go to all that trouble to be rid of Neills?"

"I'm disappointed in you, Bellie. I thought you would have more loyalty than that, considering I have come halfway around the world, at great expense, to save you. I suggest we do not discuss this again and we enjoy our trip back to England together. First, we'll finish seeing Athens."

The ground beneath me felt like quicksand. He was twisting my words and thoughts as Fahim had done. He still had a hold over me. A hold I hadn't realised was so tight.

My father rang our mother before we left Athens. I'd spoken with her when the coastguard first brought me back to Piraeus. She'd wept with relief. This time she was bubbly and cheery. She said George was trying to persuade her to make the long trip to London, but she was having a grand old time with all her girl-friends. She sounded different. Carefree. I feared my father would not get the pampering he was used to when he returned. I was surprised she didn't question me about my return to Australia and my betrothal to Clive. All she said on that matter was that Clive would like a phone call too. I didn't get around to ringing him. The time wasn't right for me.

We completed our sightseeing of Athens and, by order of my father, nothing more was said of my experience. Peter obeyed that order too. From Athens we took trains, staying two or three days in the big cities, en route. Travelling and sightseeing with my brother and the warmth of being almost a complete family unit, helped me pack away my ordeal into a cupboard and close the door. I hadn't known, but my brother and father loved the buzz of cities. The bigger the better. Me? I didn't mind and was happy enough to give over to their enjoyment. Although I'd visited some of the cities travelling in the Kombi, many places I had not visited. It had been too expensive to stay in cities with few, if any, camping sites, so we had stayed in smaller towns.

Once we arrived in Paris and I'd seen the sights with Pete and dad, I took the right-hand turn to Eva's in Holland.

We were both excited to see each other. It was time together, to have fun, laugh and explore. She showed me all her favourite haunts in Holland and, by the time we finished, there was no time to travel further afield. Eva had a job to get back to, and I had to return to London. My father said he'd stay in London until I arrived. He would then decide whether to stay on before returning to Australia. He intended to again ask Lucy to join him, now that my troubles, as he called them, were over.

My father met me at the train station in London. I'd sent a telegram to Pete's work, letting him know of my arrival. Dad had moved out of Pete's tiny bedsit and was staying locally in a small hotel. He said the accommodation was big enough for both of us.

Something in my gut told me the games had just begun.

Seventy-two

During the time I'd been with Eva, dad had become the local character at Pete's drinking hole, The Swindlers Alms. Peter had always been popular, but now there was a double act. The proprietors of the pub where Pete worked, the Ferret and Fox, complained they were losing business to Swindlers. Where was the lad's loyalty?

My father had by now learnt Pete was not working as some high-flyer in London's square mile, but as a simple barman. Dad shrugged and said a lad has to do what a lad has to do. He didn't tell my mother, all the same. Perhaps it was better my mother didn't make the trip.

My father managed to drag himself away from the pub long enough for the two of us to experience London, with Pete joining when he could. There was a lot I hadn't seen. It was all happening at that time. Music, clothes, attitude; a brand-new culture. Dad enjoyed it as much as I did, and I feared he might delay his return.

As had become our routine, the three of us walked to the Swindlers for lunch, before Pete started his afternoon shift.

"How come you drink at The Swindlers Alms, Pete?" I asked, having meant to ask months ago. "You frequent one and work at another up the road. What's the story?"

"Nothing special. When I arrived, I thought the easiest way into the city was through the pub. If I became a local, I'd find work. The Ferret and Fox took me on. By then I'd been chatting to a few blokes at the Swindlers, locals mostly and some out of towners. I'd made friends, so I kept it as my local. I wanted to be in London, mixing with Londoners. I didn't want to just swim on the surface and sightsee.

"It's not a posh pub, as you know, but I think it has atmosphere. And it's very old, as so many are. I meet all sorts, from top business-men and creative types, to ordinary mums and dads, and low life. They're always interesting. I never did find that other job. But I never really looked. I like drinking here and I like working at the pub up the road ... easy. I get invitations to stay in England and all over Europe."

Dad nudged me. "This son of mine might never come home. Not that I blame him. Though when you meet the love of your life, Peter my boy, you might change your mind."

By then we'd reached the Swindlers.

The usual routine was to go to the bar first, order drinks and food, catch up on the latest from the bar person, then move to a table and wait for lunch.

"Someone's been waiting for you," the barman said.

He nodded his head to the left. We turned.

"Nice to see you again." A hand was offered.

The three of us stood, mouths agape, too stunned to move.

"Well, if you won't shake my hand, let me buy you all a drink." Neills nodded to the barman, "I'll get this round and make mine a lime and soda."

We watched the barman pour the drinks so intensely, he said, "Everything okay?"

"I've booked a table, over in the corner there. Private, can't be overheard," Neills said. "You all seem shocked. Were you expecting never to see me again? The end of a chapter?"

We continued to stare at him. "An answer would be good." He waited. "Okay, grab your drinks and I'll fill you in."

We crossed the room like robots, taking our seats like they were red hot coals.

"You ... got out of the desert?" I said.

"Fahim never had any intention of dumping me in the desert. In fact, he was shocked at your cruel suggestion, George. Fahim said he could never do that to one of *his* sons. He did ask me to pass on his thanks for not bringing charges, though. And of course, he thanked you, Annabelle, for the same. He gave me a handsome commission for getting you on board. He has plenty of photographs and movies to paint from."

My father finally found his voice. "What do you want from me, Neills?"

"Recognition that I'm your son." Without waiting for my father's answer, he said, "Hold that recognition for the moment. That will come. I've upped the price. But first."

I couldn't believe this was happening. Our expectant silence darkened.

"I want another form of recognition." Neills raised his hand and waved someone over.

A tall, striking, slender woman glided across the room. She smiled. The room lit up. Although older, she was beautiful.

Seventy-three

"You remember my mother, George? … Kirsten," Neills said. He nodded to Pete and me, "my mother." He turned to his mother. "Mor … this is my half-sister Annabelle and my half-brother Peter."

"Pleased to meet you," I said.

Still so stunning, I wondered what she had been like back then. My mother was also beautiful, but there was a calmness about Kirsten. Maybe my father preferred my mother's more scatty, excitable and energetic ways. I looked at my father. He looked engulfed in awkwardness and anger.

"George, it's been such a long time," said Kirsten. "I'm glad you agreed to see me."

Agreed? Underneath the calmness, she was no fool.

"What do you both want?" my father said.

I sat mesmerised by this woman and my father's reaction, after more than a quarter of a century. I found it hard to imagine what that must feel like. He must have thought about her and his son. The energy around my father felt ready to explode.

To break the impasse, Pete stood, reached across and offered his hand to Kirsten. "I'm very pleased to meet you."

Was my brother deliberately trying to annoy our father, or was he being diplomatic? A brief chat ensued as Pete enquired after their trip to London.

Instead of relaxing the situation, my father galloped towards breaking point.

"You've tried to belittle me, but it hasn't worked," my father said, venom in his tone.

There was a sharp group intake of breath at his outburst.

"You think you've cornered me, but I have news for you. Especially now. You will get nothing from me. Not only because of this affront to me, but because you tortured my daughter. Yes Kirsten, you may not know, but he terrified my daughter to extort money out of me. She was in fear for her life. You have raised an evil son."

He glared at both Kirsten and Neills. There was no reaction from either.

"Come, kids," he said to us, "we're going."

"Sit."

Neills's tone was equally strong. I didn't know he had it in him. We stayed seated.

"You owe my mother, you owe me. As you won't give us recognition any other way, I'm giving you twenty-four hours. Twenty thousand pounds sterling. Not a lot for you, George. It will go to my mother. Something to set up her retirement. A small amount of what you should have paid towards child support. Twenty-four hours ... come mor."

To us, all Neills said, "Back here same time tomorrow."

"Sit." My father's turn. "Or what? You really think I'm threatened by your demands?"

"Have you forgotten your past George? The one you ran from all those years ago. Many haven't."

"Rubbish. What past? Something you've made up in that evil mind of yours," said my father.

"You probably wish that were true. Maybe you even have regrets? Somehow, I doubt it. Your actions never show any remorse … Kristos Aristos Pagonis."

My father's tan drained to white. Pete and I looked at him.

"What?" we said in unison.

"Ah … I can see you do remember and have not mentioned it to your children."

"What is he talking about, daddy?" I said.

"A good question Annabelle," Neills said. "George was your father's best friend. During the Second World War, as George lay seriously injured in a ditch, your father, Kristos, swapped his identity with George. Who knows if he died of the Germans' gunshots or if his death was hurried along by Kristos. Your father was wounded too. I bet you still have those scars on your back, eh Kristos?"

Oh my God. I had seen those scars. Dad told me he got them when he first arrived in Australia. He'd been injured working on a building site. When I was little and we were at the beach, I'd trace them with my tiny hands.

"You thought you could just walk away, didn't you, Kristos? You didn't realise the Germans, who had aimed to kill you, watched with amazement. They then captured you. Admittedly you were probably tortured, just enough for you to agree to spy for them. How wonderful to find someone with no moral compass to do some dirty work for them. They allowed you to keep your new identity. Your family and the real George's family thought you were both dead, though they never did find your body. Eh, Kristos? The other body so mutilated, it could have been anyone.

"You were sent deep into Europe to spy. What a prize for those nondescript German soldiers outposted on a Greek Island. When the war ended, your superiors fled, leaving you to your own devices. You'd supposedly married my mother by then and I'd been born. You, my mother and baby me joined the queues and hiked it to Australia, before truths of the war started to surface.

"And here's another important fact, Kristos. The marriage you told my mother was fake, in fact was legitimate. I've checked the Dutch records. Even though the war years were chaotic, the Dutch were good record-keepers. And my birth in the Netherlands was also recorded. Marriages took place quickly in those times. Who knew how long anyone had to live? You loved that fact, didn't you Kristos?"

Pete and I looked at one another. At least Neills was born legitimately, which must have important in those days. I wondered when daddy got divorced.

Neills wasn't finished.

"All that aside, something else puzzles me, George ... why you needed to get a new identity at all? What had you done before the war? Or even at the beginning of it? Maybe if I continue to dig, I'll find out."

I looked across to Kirsten. She obviously knew the story and sat patiently awaiting its outcome.

My father gazed at Neills as though not seeing him. He sat very still. Not even a flicker crossed his face. Ghost white. The air from his body already discharged. He'd visibly shrunk. With a sudden gasp, his reflexes took in air. No one spoke. All eyes were on my father, though after a minute I had to look away. It was too dreadful, too painful, to see his unspoken admission.

"Okay, George. We're leaving now," said Neills. "As I said, same time tomorrow with twenty thousand pounds in cash. It's possible, so don't tell me otherwise. And to the … *or what*. The *News of the World* licks its lips for a story like this. It would go across the world, of course. To Australia, to all your business colleagues, your social circle, not to mention your wife. And your daughter? What of her chances for a good marriage? So important to her mother and probably, deep down, to her too."

Neills looked to me and smiled.

Patronising shit.

"Then there's Peter's reputation here in London. He's well liked, as you know. He mixes well with people, from the very rich to the very poor. The upstanding and the dodgy. He also has a good heart. You've probably observed that. Not sure where he got that, perhaps his mother? He's started making his way here in London. He has an excellent reputation, which of course would be ruined if the newspaper got hold of this. The world loves nothing better than a scandalous war story. Fairly common in Europe and England, but perhaps rarer in Australia. They're going to love it over there."

Seventy-four

My father recovered his composure. His chest involuntarily filled with air. His spine uncurled. The body programmed to survive.

"You have no proof of anything," he said to Neills.

Neills and Kirsten were standing, ready to leave. Neills turned.

"Oh ... but I do."

Our food arrived.

"I've been to the island, your island," Neills said. "I spoke with the parents of Kristos Aristos Pagonis. Only your very old mother and your brother live on the island. Your father died some years ago, in case you didn't know, Kristos. He died of a broken heart, they say. Your brother takes care of your mother. His wife has passed, and his children have left the island.

"The family of Kristos received their son's broken and mutilated body. All these years they felt that body wasn't their son. George's family lived in hope that one day their son would return. He never did, did he?

"The war was just ending. The Germans were still stationed on Amorgos and one of them gave away the truth. This German was a chatty type of fellow and liked to be friendly with the locals. He made a special effort to hand over the real George Lagoudakis's personal items, few as they were, to his family. The son believed to be missing but not killed. The locals felt this was strange. Had he run away? Had he defected to the Germans? They could never believe he would do that.

"The Germans then made a hasty retreat, to the Fatherland.

"Your poor friend, George Theodore Lagoudakis. What of his family? A question always hung. In time, young people have their own lives to live and most of them have left."

"We went there," I said.

The words tumbled out before I could control them.

"We went to Amorgos. Is that where you're from, daddy?"

Neills jumped in. "No. We were so near to your father's island. But Amorgos is not it. Though that's where the capture and killing took place."

I opened my mouth, about to express my shock. I was there. I was on that island of Amorgos. The island I found so beautiful. The island that held such a grisly secret. And Neills had been with me, knowing all the time about my father's duplicity. My father must have seen me about to speak.

"Don't," my father said, before I could say another word.

Neills hadn't finished.

"It was many years before anyone could go near that now dilapidated hut, where the Germans spent unofficial days off duty, so I believe. I did my own searches, too, in Germany. Records from outlying Greek Islands and other outposts have been meticulously kept. I might not have finished my degree in Human Rights law, but I know people who have. Imagine how I felt, knowing who my father is? My mother felt sick. She's here to support me, by the way, not to see you, George. Although she is curious."

I thought of the times I'd asked my father over and over, about his island.

Straight-backed but cornered, my father said to Neills, "I thought you were going."

"Yes, we'll go now. It's quite amazing how one man can ruin so many lives. Tomorrow then," said Neills.

"And the friends I mentioned who are lawyers? I gained copies of all the documents related to the Germans stationed on Amorgos and surrounding islands. The documents of the repatriation of bodies to their families. If anything happens to me, George, my lawyer friends will know why."

Neills, ready to leave with his hand on his mother's back.

"Oh my goodness, I so nearly forgot. Further to your marriage to my mother. This is important too, George. You told my mother, when you dumped her in Australia, that the marriage was a fake. The ceremony in Holland was just a sham, not a legal one. The marriage document was fake. In fact, you said, the pair of you were never married. But you lied.

"How easy it was for you, George. You said you didn't need a divorce and my mother, who was young and naïve, believed you. She was so broken, she had no fight in her. She took your miserable token of money and travelled back to Holland. You made that bit easy for her. You booked the passage by boat to England and gave her the money to get her back to her hometown. With a babe in arms, all on her own."

§

My upstanding father. The man I held up as a paragon to all men. The revelations were piling up and I didn't think I could listen to anymore.

"Yes," said Neills, "your father is a bigamist."

"What?" Peter and I said together.

I felt sick. What was this going to do to my mother?

I barely heard Kirsten. Her soft voice and lilting accent.

"I'm sorry."

Pete and I looked at one another, at Kirsten. She'd been so quiet. She was sorry. In how many ways, must she be sorry?

How sorry were we?

Seventy-five

We picked at our food. Neither Pete nor I said a word to each other, or to our father. What could possibly be said?

My father's lunch lay untouched. His body sagged again. His appearance, marble-like, looked cold to the touch. He occasionally made a move to stand, then sat back down.

My mind slowly began to work again. What would my father do? As if answering my thoughts, he said,

"Peter, you have friends. We need to talk. Outside. Not you, Annabelle."

Was I still his little girl, who couldn't hear bad things? I hoped what he had to say to Pete was the truth. It would be cut down to size, I expected. He would tell part of the story, but certainly not all of it. How much of Neills's story was true?

While they were outside, I thought through my father's reaction. I hoped to find something that would confirm Neills was a shyster, an opportunist, or was wrong. I wondered what my mother had faced in her time with him. What would she think of this? I could hear her now: "Don't be ridiculous, dear".

But me. Here and now. This was grown up stuff. This had come from a world of such darkness; I didn't have the experience to fathom it.

Pete and my father returned. I searched Pete's face. He caught my eye and, with minimal movement, shook his head. Don't ask.

"We're going, Annabelle. Pete has work to go to."

I grabbed my bag and trotted after my father. He gruffness stopped me asking where we were going. We walked to the first cluster of shops. It contained a travel agent. We walked in.

A smiling lady looked up and asked us to please sit. That smile seemed so out of place right then.

"Two tickets to Sydney via the United States. First stop New York. San Francisco. Hawaii and on to Sydney."

"Yes, sir."

Delight written all over her. A fat commission coming up.

"And when would you like to travel?"

"The first flight out."

I looked at my father. "What? No daddy. I'm not ready to go home yet. It's not been a year."

"You've had more experiences than you need already. I want to see you safe at home."

"Then why are we making travelling home a holiday?"

"To give you a break. We can enjoy some time together."

To give me a break? He was delaying facing his wife.

"No, daddy. No. I'm not going."

The agent's smile faded. No doubt she'd seen family squabbles before in her line of business. Her fat commission was vanishing fast.

"Annabelle. This is not a discussion. Return another time. Perhaps with Clive, on a honeymoon."

I could not believe what he had just said. This was not my father talking, this was my mother.

"No."

He still held sway over me. He'd found his strength. The marble exterior had cracked and shattered, leaving a raging bull, free to charge.

"You are, Annabelle. We return home and in a year you can come back. I'll pay for it."

The travel agent's eyes lit up again. "We can organise all that from here."

"The flights to the destinations I've mentioned, then to Sydney. That's all thank you."

"But ... but ..." I said.

"Stop it, Annabelle. I don't believe it's safe for you to stay."

"What about Pete? What about his safety?"

"He has work to do."

We had our last night with a takeaway meal in Pete's cramped flat. I could see why my father had organised us to be at the flat. I couldn't find an excuse to get Pete outside, so there was no chance for us to talk. Clever move, daddy.

Seventy-six

We flew out of London's Heathrow airport. Our goodbyes to Peter the night before were subdued. My reluctant tears fell for so many reasons.

Again, my father took Peter aside in the street outside his flat, just as we were leaving. I was not to hear this conversation either. It should have been me talking to Pete. But the opportunity was long gone.

"What's going on, daddy? Why can't you talk to me too?" I said as we walked back to our hotel.

"Don't go worrying your pretty head. I want to get you as far away as possible from Neills. I thought I saw you softening towards him. You're still young and impressionable. You still need protecting."

"What about Pete? He's not even two years older than me."

"He's a man, darling. It's different. Men understand things differently."

I expect my father had always spoken to me like that, but I'd never heard it so acutely as that night. Was it just his age, or did all men think like this? Did Pete?

As much as I wanted to rebel, I travelled with my father.

I'd succumbed to being his daughter, his little girl. I didn't have the strength to fight him. It was as though he had me on a leash, and I was trotting along behind him.

He was my father, but maybe deep down *he* wanted *my* support. He didn't want to be alone. On that level, I felt needed and useful.

We checked into an expensive hotel in New York and took a quick walk in Central Park, utilising the limited time left of the day. Dinner was sent up to our suite and, with the time differences and all that had happened, we were both exhausted. I slept like a log.

The following morning, we were breakfasting out when my father announced he was going to the library.

"I'm coming, too."

"You don't need to, Bellie. Go and look at some shops." He handed over some cash. "Buy something nice, something for your mother, too."

"It's okay … I'll come along. It's a place of interest, one of the buildings to see."

I walked beside him. He walked briskly, possibly hoping to lose me. Inside the library he headed straight for the local and world newspapers. They were displayed like an art exhibit. Although the papers were a day or two old, depending on the country, you could read anything about anywhere in the world. My father's first choice were the English newspapers.

"Too early," he muttered.

"Of course, it is. Are you expecting it to hit the papers so soon?"

He'd forgotten I was there.

"Just keeping up with the news. You know how I like to do that. Come on, let's go shake up New York."

Two days followed with the same routine. We saw a lot of New York and for a while I was able to forget all about my father's ugly past and Neills's threat. By the third day, my father was annoyed after reading the papers.

"Well ..." he muttered to himself, "it might not make the papers. I need to ring Pete. What's the time over there?"

He looked at his watch and sat for a minute.

"It's good. I'll go back to the hotel and make the call."

He turned to me, a little surprised to see me still sitting there.

"You can stay here, darling, browse at your leisure."

"I want to know what's going on daddy. I have a right to know."

"Don't worry your pretty head, Bellie. It's men's business."

"No ... I'm coming with you. I'd like to speak with Pete too."

Fast walking again; he had no choice and wasn't happy.

"Bellie's here," daddy said, as soon as Pete answered.

I smiled then and realised it was code, my father was going to have to speak briefly.

In a casual, happy tone, belying his angst of moments ago, daddy said to Pete, "How's it going? ... ah huh ... okay ... ah huh ... so when?" A long pause while Pete spoke. "That's not good enough, son. You know all sorts, you've admitted it."

I grabbed the receiver. "Hi Pete ... me ... what's going on?

"Nothing sis."

"What do you mean, nothing? Did you meet at the appointed hour? I mean with Neills, the next day?"

"No, I didn't show."

"God, he must have been furious. What did he do, turn up at work? At the pub?"

"Yes, he did. I said it was nothing to do with me. Then he asked where dad was."

"God, what did you tell him?"

"The truth, Bellie. I told him you and dad had left the country.

He cursed and said what a coward his father was. That made me feel weird. His father."

Pete was quiet for a moment.

"What happened then?" I said.

"He hung at the bar for a bit. I suppose he was thinking what to do. He didn't say any more, just left."

"Have you seen or heard from him since?"

"Nothing. Eerily quiet. Like I'm expecting an explosion. Waiting for big headlines to hit the papers."

"I guess it still could. Or maybe his mother talked him out of it."

"Could be either. Hopefully the latter."

I wanted to say; supposing it's all true? But with my father right next to me, I couldn't.

Pete and I talked gossipy stuff, who was doing what. How my father and I had walked the streets of New York, what we'd seen. Daddy got sick of listening to me and took back the receiver.

"Keep me informed," my father said and hung up.

He sat in silence, in a cloud of darkness.

"Well, that's all good, daddy. Neills is nowhere to be seen. Maybe his mother has talked him out of going to the papers."

"Yeah, maybe Neills has come to his senses and he and Kirsten have gone back to Denmark."

His tone was superficially cheerful. I wasn't sure if it was for my benefit or his. He returned to his darkness and said no more. I had the feeling something else was going on. I hadn't been game to talk more deeply with Pete, with my father sitting next to me.

"Daddy, I want to know ..."

"Come Bellie, let's go out. See some more of New York."

With that he was holding open the door.

We spent two more days in New York, with my father reading

the papers first thing and ringing Pete both days. I said 'hi' each time, but no further comment was made to me, other than the latest pub gossip.

My attempts to ask my father if what Neills had said was true were always cut short. I could barely keep up with his level of energy. He was acting as if he was constantly trying to catch a train.

We flew to San Francisco. Our routine in New York was repeated there. Neills's threats and lies, so far, had amounted to nothing. San Francisco's atmosphere was more relaxed, and this seemed to seep into both of us. Daddy's step was definitely lighter, but he still checked the newspapers first thing in the morning.

"So, daddy," I said over breakfast one morning, "you've not said a word about the story. I'll not wait any longer. We are not rushing out the door. You will sit here and tell me the truth."

"Truth about what, Bellie?"

"Don't be silly, daddy. You know darn well what. I'm not stupid. Speak to me ... about the war. Was it true?" He didn't answer.

"I need to know," I said with such force, it startled him. And me.

He looked up from his plate, full in my face. "What if it is?"

I stared at him in disbelief. I expected side stepping, or a change of subject. Or, at the very least, denial.

"All of it?" I said.

"Yes."

I gulped.

"You're not George Lagoudakis but Kristos Pagonis?"

"Yes."

Seventy-seven

Even though we were in the relaxed atmosphere of San Francisco, my father went from bad to worse and on to defeated.

"It was the war, Bellie. You've no idea what life was like. You can't possibly imagine. Everyone hung on to life. Anyone could die at any moment. There was no tomorrow. There was no yesterday. Survival is all you have. You don't even know how to survive; you just do what you have to. There's no time to plan beyond perhaps, at the most, the next day. You just act.

"That's what I did. I acted. George was almost dead. The Germans did torture us. I did spy for them. I lived. I saved Kirsten who had lost everyone. We had to leave any way we could, to anywhere we could. It happened to be Australia."

"You were married when you met mummy?"

"Yes. The marriage to Kirsten could have been fake. Marriages were happening quickly. Kirsten was pregnant with my child. What was I to do?"

"You say, *could* have been fake? But it wasn't. You just dumped your wife and child. It's just something I could never believe you would do. Had nobody, at that time, met Kirsten or Neills?"

"No."

We sat in silence for an age in our hotel room. Not speaking, just sitting, staring at nothing. I couldn't digest it. Listening to it all over again, it hit me with double horror. And no, I couldn't imagine the horrors of war. But the war was over by the time my father reached Australia. I'm sure it was in his head, but he knew where he was, what he was doing.

And to learn my father was a bigamist. I didn't know where a child stood with a father who was a bigamist. Did that mean I was illegitimate? And Neills must be the only legitimate child but of a fake person? What a jumble.

God, it was all too awful. I could not go home. I could not travel any further with my father. I could not be there to witness my father tell my mother. Or deny it. It would be as though I was party to his lies.

My father broke into my thoughts as if reading them.

"Please don't leave me, Bellie. I need you. I need Peter. And I desperately need Lucy. I can't go on if I don't have you all."

"Continue your trip, daddy. Fly home. Talk to my mother. I really don't know how she will take it."

"She doesn't need to find out."

He looked at me then, like a lost puppy. My strong father – wilted and defeated.

"We know, daddy … dig deep, dig into that strength that has carried you this far."

We left the hotel room and walked around San Francisco in a sort of dream. Nightmare, to be precise.

I could not go on with this farce. When we got back to the hotel, I told my father I would be travelling back to London.

He begged and begged me to stay.

"Find your power again, daddy, stand straight and drill this down. You have to. You're not the type to be defeated. Hold your head high and explain to my mother what your world was like."

By the next day, he'd picked up a little. He was brighter. When I asked if he was beginning to feel stronger, he told me he was. A little. He said he knew what he had to face. He knew what he had to do.

I was relieved he was gaining strength. He had purpose once again. He said he'd prefer it if I stayed. Couldn't I do that? I told him it was not my fight. I never wanted to be returning to Australia in the first place. I was relieved he seemed brighter. Although I did not want to be with him when he told my mother. I felt he was gaining the strength to face the actions of his past.

We both agreed, if he was prepared to come clean, there would be nothing for the newspapers. Neills could go whistle.

My thoughts went to Neills.

"Perhaps you could embrace Neills as your son too, daddy ... and give Neills the money."

Seventy-eight

Pete saw me as soon as I stepped in the door. He bounded around the bar, came over and hugged me.

"Sis, I thought you'd be home."

"I couldn't go, Pete. I left daddy in San Francisco."

"Come, let's see if I can get the rest of the day off."

We walked back to Pete's place and dropped off my suitcase. A little park was close by, and the sun was shining. A cheerful place to talk.

"Tell me, Bellie ... what happened?"

"The whole time in the States we'd not talked about Neills, or the story. In San Francisco, I couldn't stand it any longer. I confronted him ... asked him straight out if it was true. Hoping like hell it wasn't. He admitted to the whole thing. You probably know that already."

Pete would of course know. All those secret conversations they'd had that I wasn't allowed to be party to.

"He said that, before I judged him, I should understand war is a totally different world. He said the mind warps. He said his friend could not have lived. He was mutilated. Dad said I should have anger towards the Germans, not him.

"I reminded dad what Neills had threatened. He said he was sorting that out with you but wouldn't say what. Finally, I couldn't face the farce of going home. I said he needed to tell our mother. That he needed to find his inner power, the power that had carried him through the war. After a couple of days, he'd picked up.

"What were we going to do when we got home, Pete, play happy families as though nothing had happened?"

I paused a moment to let my mind rest, let the sunshine warm me. Pete waited for me to continue.

"I desperately wanted to talk to you privately, before we left and on the phone, but daddy, dad, was always next to me."

"I figured as much," Pete said. "That's why I couldn't tell you everything. Sis ...," Pete paused. "He wanted me to take out a contract on Neills. Worse still, on Neills's mother too. Do you know what I mean by that?"

"Of course I do. He wanted you to organise for them to be killed?"

"George was terrified the story would hit the papers."

George – Pete had called him. No longer dad. Pete had distanced himself from our father already.

"Neills's mother as well?"

Our father was more gruesome than I could have imagined. I went to my thoughts I'd had in San Francisco. The war was over but not for him. Not just in his mind, he was still there. I must have blanched.

"Are you okay?"

"Not really, no. Is this our father showing his true colours, Pete? It's hard to believe he would ask his own son to carry that out. How come we never saw any of this at home?"

"I dunno, sis. We were children. He was highly regarded by our community. I guess he lived as if he'd eradicated the past. He must have been successful at it. We all believed he was such a great guy.

He was desperate to appear to be that community-minded man, keep up all the hard work he'd put into it. He'd turned over a new leaf. But it seems he hasn't."

We sat, not talking for a while.

"So, what did you do?"

"He gave me money to pay for the contract. A lot of money. I couldn't do it, of course, but I feel sick that I initially thought about it. He must have done those kinds of things before. He seemed to know how it all worked. I figured, finally, the money was his admission of guilt."

Pete paused. "I'm not my father. I don't live in those desperate times. George laid all kinds of guilt on me about loyalty to a father, and how I don't understand what those years were like. I said nothing. I did nothing. When my head was clear and I was out of our father's power, there was no way I would even contemplate what he'd asked me to do. I've been having trouble living with myself, that I didn't protest to his face. What sort of coward am I?"

"He holds a lot of influence over us both, even though we're adults. And you are not a coward. You're brave. Brave, do you hear me? Brave to defy our father and to realise you're a different man. It's been days now ... where is Neills?"

"I don't know. He seems to have disappeared. I suspect he has gone to the papers. Maybe it takes a while to get a story checked out and written up. I've been waiting. It's been an awful time. I wake every morning thinking this is the day the shit will hit the fan. Then what would I do?"

"Presumably dad knows now ... that you're not going ahead with ... what he asked you to do?"

"I've been waiting for his daily call, but as you're here, maybe he's just gone straight home."

Seventy-nine

Two days after I arrived back in London, a police car drew up outside Pete's flat. I happened to be by the window. Pete and two burly policemen stepped out of the police car. My heart sank. My thoughts went to Neills. He's done something.

"Sis ... these policemen want to talk to both of us." Pete turned to the police. "Come in."

Full to overflowing, with three men and me, the flat was so cramped its space shrank to claustrophobia. They asked us to find a seat.

"We've received word from the San Francisco police," the policeman said. "I'm so very sorry, but your father has committed suicide. He hanged himself. A cleaner found him. We are so terribly sorry."

In that claustrophobic space, the walls closed in. Pete and I were speechless. I felt I couldn't breathe and hung my head out of the window. Of all the things I imagined my father would do, that was not one of them.

"In San Francisco?" Pete said.

"Yes, sir."

When I could speak, I said, "How long had he ... I mean, when did he do it?"

"We think two days ago."

"That's about when I left. Oh my God, Pete ... he wouldn't have done that if I'd stayed. He was so much brighter, said he felt ready to face what he had to do. I thought he was talking about going home. Oh God. He wasn't. That's what he meant all along."

"No ... stop that right there, sis. It's not your doing. If the story had come out, who's to say, he might have done it then." Pete hugged me. "It was his decision. Everything was his decision."

One of the policemen said "Can you go there ... to San Francisco? Ring the police there first. They need you to identify him. You can ring from the station if you like. They also need to know what to do with your father's body."

"Christ," Pete said. "I can't believe this. You're sure it's our father?"

"Hotel staff have identified him from his passport. But they need a family member to confirm that he's ... George Theodore Lagoudakis?"

Pete and I looked at each other.

Eighty

Pete and I flew home escorting our father's body. Our mother met us at the airport. After the required checks, the body was transported to the funeral parlour. Within a few days the funeral took place. Hundreds attended. The funeral notice in the paper advised he'd died of a heart attack. We no longer feared a scandal reaching our shores, or anywhere else.

Before we left London, Pete rang Neills's mother in Denmark. Pete had not seen nor heard from Neills, even though, as we learnt from Kirsten, he was still in London. She thought he must be giving George's story to the newspapers, as George had not shown up at that appointed time. She was dismayed to hear that George had committed suicide.

Pete contacted Neills and asked him to meet with us.

We briefly talked in the little park near Pete's place. As chance would have it, the sun was shining again. Then my brother gave Neills the contract money. Neills was a subdued man, not the angry one we'd met before. Although not expecting it, he was not surprised to see the money.

"He rang me," Neills said.

"What?"

My words to my father had penetrated. He had listened. And still he could no longer live with himself.

"He simply said, 'you are my son'. Nothing more, then hung up. I was ... well words in English fail me, but I stopped breathing. And then to hear from my mother he had ended his life. I wept. I never meant for him to die," Neills said.

But you were going to hurt me, I thought.

As if reading my mind, he then looked to me.

"I'm so very sorry Annabelle. It was an abominable thing I did. And could I go through with it? No, I'm sure I couldn't. No ... no I couldn't have." Neills buried his head in his hands. Lifting it, he said, "It's no excuse, but I was desperate, for my mother as much as for myself.

"I'm not sure about taking this money," Neills said, looking to both of us with questioning eyes.

"Look upon it as your inheritance," Pete said. "For your mother's retirement, as you intended. You're our half-brother, Neills. We want to let bygones be bygones, if that's okay with you."

Pete wasn't there and I wasn't sure I agreed with him. Neills had said his piece, but I wasn't sure I could just dismiss what he'd threatened me with. But I was happy for Neills to get the money. He was my half-brother and nothing could change that.

Neills had started the ball rolling with the newspaper story, but immediately put a stop to it. Fortunately, he hadn't given them the full story. Neills said he would return to Greece. He hoped the families who had been so hurt by our father's actions, could find peace and let bygones be bygones too. As they were poor, he would donate some of the money to them.

❧

On the plane home, Pete and I talked about what we'd tell our mother. We felt there had been enough lies in the family and the truth needed to come out. At least, where our mother was concerned. We'd be there to collect the pieces.

I was surprised to find our mother had changed since I'd been away. She was distraught, of course, but had more resilience than I ever imagined. The discovery of her independence while our father had been away had given her a sense of her own uniqueness. Qualities she never knew she had or could enjoy.

As it turned out, way back, she suspected my father had a shady past, but she chose to ignore it. Surely, he'd made amends, she'd thought. He'd proven to be such an upstanding member of society.

Outside our immediate family, we let the heart attack story and public view of our father, prevail.

Our mother listened as Pete and I told her everything. Rather than interrupt and feign a headache, she took it on the chin. It might have been just for our benefit, but she appeared stoic. There was an intelligent understanding in her eyes.

Who was this woman?

I'd found a mother who gave me a whole new reason to love and cherish her.

My mother surprised me again. No longer rampaging about marrying the right man and living up to her expectations, she simply said I should see Clive. She realised, before we even discussed the subject, that the engagement would not go ahead. She'd noticed how I'd grown into a fine young woman. Someone she could be proud to call her daughter. Bless her.

I had not had time to see Clive before the funeral, so we arranged to meet the next day. We sat in a park and talked and talked. While I was away, he'd hung on to the hope we would get engaged and then married, but in his heart of hearts, felt we would not last. He'd realised it the moment I'd said I was going away, though he didn't want to admit it to himself. I was the same young woman who left Australia, he said, but also changed. I'd grown. This was music to my ears. Sitting in the park with the sun shining, everything looking so fresh after the recent rainfall, it became so clear Clive and I had no connection. I doubt we ever had. We amicably parted ways.

Although my year away had been cut short, discovery of myself had been fast tracked. I did feel changed and, by then, very hopeful. With our mother secure in her circle of close friends, Pete and I flew back to London. Both our futures looked bright. Even the 'frozen moments' I no longer feared. They'd done their job. My misgiving was I had not taken notice or understood their meaning.

Now, sitting in the plane, I realised I'd learnt an important lesson. The superficial things that surround us shouting, me, me, me, are not what counts. It's our soul we must listen to. Not always easy, with all the noise everything else makes.

Acknowledgements

Thank you to my editor, Victoria Steele. Clear, concise, with excellent suggestions in progressing the story. Always helpful, always delivers.

A big thank you to Stuart Clark, who shared his sailing anecdotes, listened and good-naturedly gave me answers to my nautical questions.

A note here to an experience I had in the Aegean Sea. Many years ago, trusting those who knew, but didn't, we sailed from Piraeus to Kea. We were becalmed, ran out of fuel and very nearly ended up on rocks.

Thank you to David Robinson, who has supported me and even given me the title for a future book.

And thank you to Ann-Louise Crotty, who read my very first draft. What amazing patience. Along with Alan Betts, equally patient. I appreciate both your time and support.

Born in England, Pamiela moved with her parents to New Zealand, aged seven. After school years, including an unorthodox remote boarding school, Pamiela started her own travels, aged nineteen. Four years passed before returning to New Zealand and a few months later she moved to Sydney, where she now lives. A chance glamping holiday on a small, remote island in the Great Barrier Reef started the writing of her first novel. Now living near the beach, she loves to swim and snorkel. The sea inspires her writing.